The
WINDS Of
Darkness

The
WINDS Of
Darkness

Gary McConville

THE WINDS OF DARKNESS
Copyright © 2024 by Gary McConville
All rights reserved, including reproduction of this book or portions thereof in any form.

The Winds Series by Lagomorph Publishing LLC
Suite 420-328
855 Woodstock Road
Roswell, GA 30075

ISBN: 978-1-6653-0923-3 - Paperback
eISBN: 978-1-6653-0924-0 - eBook

Library of Congress Control Number: 2024912004

∞ This paper meets the requirements of ANSI/NISO Z39.48-1992 (Permanence of Paper)

Guidance /Editor /Proofreader:
   Valerie Mathews of The Exit 271 Studio, Athens, GA

Rough critiquing:
   An array of creative writers: The Lawrenceville Sci-Fi Writers Critique Group.

Storyline edits:
   Nancy Ford McConville

Final Grammarian edits:
   Heidi Nichols of Durango, CO

Final storyline edits:
   Misty Parker of Dallas, GA

Cover art and interior graphics:
   Kaj Johnson of runrabbitgraphics.com

070124

This novel is dedicated to Gertrude Steiner McConville, deserving mother and always a generous provider. Also, to one of my dearest friends, Frossula Statheros. With a wonderful Greek outlook on life, you had everyone smiling. Taken away too soon, you are both missed terribly. Likewise concerning my first cousin, Deborah Van Rooyen of whom there was never enough time to get to know each other better.

CONTENTS

PART 3: MINGLINGS

PART 4: A GLIMPSE

PART 5: TITAN OUTPOST

PART 1
PANIC

CHAPTER 1
The Captain's Bridge

Day 10 - Titan Outpost rendezvous: 761 days

The door swooshes open. Andorf enters the *Atlantis'* bridge to see Thom Mallory sitting in the plush, over-padded captain's chair. "Oh, I have mighty bad feelings about today," the captain groans.

Andorf takes a deep breath before approaching the captain. "You are not alone in such feelings, Captain. Even my companion bunny, Binky, is acting strangely."

"Binky! Binky! Enough about your so-called telepathic rabbit. If I was to believe everything you say about the rascal, I'd expect him to be maintaining his own ship log. We would see him roaming freely about the *Atlantis*, hopping about anywhere he pleases. Hell, for all we know, this Binky of yours could be running the damn place."

In silence, Andorf raises a brow.

Rising to his feet, the captain confronts the fleet's most-famed passenger. "No one was prepared for any of this, Andorf. The rattles ... the ever-present humming floor ... the crushing weight of pitch-blackness outside ... these are enough to drive anyone nuts. During the four-year stints servicing relay satellites, our only sanity was counting down the days until returning to Earth. But there'll be no returning to the mother planet this time. Life aboard this tin can for us first gens, as we call ourselves, is totally different. It's all we'll ever have."

Thom begins to pace about the bridge, stroking a greying beard while struggling to verbally name a single crew-member or passenger with an inkling of space mileage under their belt. He gazes past the wall full of shiny knobs and buttons to spy on Pol as the communications specialist fiddles with radios while scratching his head. Though the radioman appears confused, he carries a reputation of being able to pull voices out of seemingly random noise. Still, Thom wonders aloud about the prime pick of comm-specs.

The captain pauses to gaze at the variety of measuring sticks dangling on hooks above the navigation screen. His head tips to one side as if wondering how such archaic tools could become the death of him. He mumbles about it not so quietly.

"And Peter over there, being a skilled navigator, appears to be a good fit. The guy would not have been my first choice but he's got old-school knowledge, a rare commodity nowadays."

"Now as for my first mate, I'm not quite so sure."

The captain turns his head. Murray appears lost, staring wide-eyed at the array of green console lights and the oxygen indicators before him. Lacking compassion for space travel, the guy displays low self-confidence and few leadership skills. However, one thing is certain about Murray; he despises the Canine Empire more that anyone aboard our three-starship fleet. The burned-off digit on one of his hands proves as much.

Thom peers back at Andorf. "It appears I've bitten off more can than I can chew this time. No one aboard the Atlantis, including myself, has one bloody idea of what can happen out there. Hell, I've never ventured beyond the Titan moon base. Danger lurks around every corner. Everyone must keep on their toes."

Pausing to peer out the twin front portals, the captain catches himself about to slam a fist against the front viewing portals. Instead, he runs a nervous finger along the edges, examining the rubber seals encasing them inside their frame housings. As if scratching an itch that never subsides, he gazes back at his cushy captain's chair. Appearing fixated on the emergency suit stuffed beneath and more importantly, the twin molly bolts securing the chair to the floor, a bead of sweat drips on the bridge floor. "With something so important, why are there never more than two?"

Andorf turns away from the captain and rookie crew to peer out one of the frontal portals. He gazes beyond the tiny spider-cracks spanning the length of the glass pane. "I too have mighty bad feelings about this voyage."

*

Binky's log – 10-124215:

Passengers should be proud of surviving that rough takeoff in the hijacked starship ten days ago. Most appear to have settled into their mundane daily tasks, accepting many sacrifices exchanged for new-found freedoms. Still, I detect subtle signs of anxiety everywhere I look.

CHAPTER 2

The Mila

Day 21: 0530 -
Titan Outpost rendezvous: 750 days

Andorf arrives in the G-deck cafeteria well ahead of the early morning crowd. At more than one gypsy chef's disapproving glare, he fills his and then a second takeout box for his beloved. He stands alone at the food nozzle, grimacing at liquids solidifying in the four segmented compartments. Poking a finger in what should be dessert, he squinches as a firm finger all of a sudden pressed dead-center of his back.

He spins about, expecting another lecture from an irate chef. Instead, he finds a gypsy, a good foot superior in height, face looming inches from his own. Except for Brutus, he has never met a real live gypsy in the flesh. Andorf steps back, allowing the towering man to look him over from head to toe.

"I take it you're the one sharing a wife with Brother Brutus Bittner?" the gypsy says, grinning somewhat.

At Andorf's reluctant nod, the gypsy tilts his head as if directing him to the nearest table. The man's bottom covers two seats, leaving Andorf a chair across the table, facing the vacant food-dispensing area. He eyes the stranger even more suspiciously than those food substitutes in the open takeout boxes on the

6

table before him. Feeling the stranger scrutinizing him, Andorf's eyes drift away, scanning for the nearest exit. Taking a seat, he grins back at the gypsy.

"What gave away my identity? Was it my Ben Franklin glasses, my long brown—?"

"No. No. No," the burly man says, chuckling much too loudly for Andorf's comfort. "It's your clothes. They're covered in fluffy, white fur. I take it Binky is a heavy shedder."

Andorf brushes a white wisp of fur off his pants only to watch it casually float through the air. The fur fluff lofts high above his and the stranger's heads only to return to the exact same spot on his pants. Andorf's eyes narrow upon the stranger.

"How do you know my rabbit's name?"

"Huh?"

"Binky, how did you know about Binky?"

The gypsy casts a sheepish grin. "You see, it was months ago. Brother Brutus spoke of a white rabbit possessing strange, telepathic powers. I didn't believe him at first. Then he told me stories involving the rabbit. He implied the same may be true of you. So, I'm hoping you being Brutus' good friend, could possibly help me with my terrible dilemma."

"Oh, Brutus did, did he?"

The large stranger nods. "As with your rabbit's fur, the problem is nothing one can simply brush away."

Sizing up the situation, Andorf wets his lips. He focuses on the stranger's face.

The stranger raises a brow. "You're Andorf—Andorf Johnson, are you not?"

Andorf leans forward. "For the moment, let's assume you are correct. What can I do for you mister ...?"

The gypsy pushes his tray aside. Leaning closer with elbows resting on the table, he blows warm air into his cupped hands. "I hope you take no offense to my rash manner. I have depleted my options. I would not bother you but I have nowhere else to turn. Please, Mr. Andorf. I am begging for your help."

Again, Andorf's eyes drift toward the well-lit exit sign just beyond the food-dispensing area. This time he spots a young girl in the otherwise vacant serving area. He watches the young girl hold a canvas bag beneath the filler nozzles. After looking about, she rolls the bag into an oversized coat and then hastens out the exit. Andorf turns back to the stranger. "What about that little girl? I've seen her before in the serving line."

The stranger covers his tray with his beastly hands as he glances behind. He then shrugs his shoulders at the easily distracted man. "It's only your imagination," he grumbles, removing hands off his tray. The gypsy moves the tray closer and lifts the spork, which appears puny in his giant hand.

"I'm not kidding you. I saw the child, alone at the dispensing nozzles. She appeared to be scruffy and was scavenging food."

Trying to speak while choking down his food, the gypsy snarls. "Aren't you even the least bit familiar with gypsy mythology? Haven't you heard of the ancient beast?"

"Are you implying the girl is some kind of pookah?"

The stranger grins. "This one is called Mila. It's been known to take many forms. She's sometimes a bear … a raccoon … or in your case a young vagrant child. Milas appear around food … always in the presence of a gypsy."

"And always behind a gypsy's back," Andorf mumbles, scratching at the week's growth on his stubby chin.

"What's that?"

"Months ago, I was dining here with Brutus and Serin. I saw that very same vagrant girl. Like you, they didn't believe me."

The large man curls the carbene spork, bending it between his thumb and index finger. Instead of snapping like a plastic fork, the spork unfurls into a perfectly-shaped spork the moment it is released. The gypsy snarls. "This Mila is merely an aberration … a figment of your imagination. If it's true what Brother Brutus says, I would have expected you of all people to have known half as much."

Taking his life in his hands, Andorf reaches out. He grabs hold of the gypsy's hefty arm just as the gypsy raises a loaded sporkful to within inches of his gaping mouth. "You must believe me, mister. I saw a young girl in human form as clear as I am seeing you now."

At the large man's narrowing eyes, Andorf lowers his hand to point.

"Her scruffy face was right over there … at the dispensing nozzles, I swear. I saw her tiny hands filling a canvas bag with food—" Andorf winces at the remains of the gypsy's near empty food box. "—or whatever this stuff is. Mila or no Mila, no child should live like that."

"Utterly impossible. Trays must be in exact position. Else the nozzles won't squirt a single drop."

"But—"

The stranger's voice loudens. "Now, forget your damn Mila. I've got real issues here. Ones you need to address. Right here, right now!"

Andorf braves a second peek inside his takeout boxes before sealing both and sliding them aside. Peering into the crazed man's eyes, he clears his throat. "All right, but I must warn you, mister, I am by no means an expert in gypsy psychology."

"Fair enough."

"Now with that out of the way, if you describe what bothers you so terribly, I shall give it my best shot."

The gypsy chokes down the rest of the morning grub. He drops his spork to present open palms to Andorf. "I'm at wit's end, I tell ya'. My wife of twelve years has left me, as have every last one of my friends. Take a good look at me, Mr. Andorf. Is there something I am ... something I've become ... something in the way I speak ... something about the way I smell that offends you? Go ahead. I can take it. Be brutally honest with me."

Tipping his head to one side, Andorf stares at the giant-sized man, suspecting a catch. He takes a long moment to scan the stranger's very normal features for anything other than him being a beastly-large man. Andorf grabs one of the man's huge shoulders and gazes deep into his teary eyes. He peels away layers of the stranger's outer thoughts, probes for traces of anything terrible enough to have driven the man's wife and friends away.

The gypsy begins to twitch. Eyes rolling around in their sockets, his face breaks in a heavy sweat. His head jerks violently as horizontal lines consume his large face. With the man appearing on the edge of convulsing, Andorf releases his hand and mental grip. Scooting back to a safer distance, he waits to speak until the burly man's shaking subsides.

"I can tell your soul has vanished. Even *you* have abandoned your being to die. Every gram of hope within you has evaporated. Your thoughts are so drained that I ... I cannot begin to tell you where everything has gone or why your soul has suddenly vanished."

Appearing confused, the gypsy shrugs his bulky shoulders.

"What you are experiencing, my friend is being dried up on the inside. You long for companionship but you lack an inner self. You have been left feeling nothing but emptiness inside. Am I correct?"

The ends of the gypsy's mouth pull tight. Leaning closer, his sad eyes confirm Andorf's suspicions about his sincerity. "I have lived with this pain far too long. Short of taking my own life, I see no end to the madness. What can I do? Please, Mr. Andorf. I'm begging you. You must help me. You're my only—"

"Hope?" Andorf says, relaxing at sight of the beastly-large man leaning against the backs of his chairs. He half-smiles at the troubled gypsy. "I suggest acquiring a companion. A furry friend may be just the thing to restore your humanity."

"A pet?"

Andorf winces. "I was thinking more on the lines of a companion. You will become one with the furry guy and most important, with yourself. Friends will soon appear, if not for you, but to baby your new soulmate." He taps the gypsy's bulky arm and chuckles. "Fur on clothes would be a good look on you. If nothing else, it displays a trustworthy character."

The gypsy's stiff mouth morphs into a genuine smile. For the first time in many months, a glimmer of hope appears in his eyes, excitement in his voice. "I cannot believe how simple you've made this, Mr. Andorf. You're a genius … a true Goshi if there ever was one."

"Goshi?" Andorf mumbles, sighing in relief.

The gypsy's eyes widen. He spins about in his chairs and turns back to Andorf. "I hate to tell you this but your Mila child has returned."

"What? You actually see her? The Mila girl is not just in my head?"

"You'd better run after her," the gypsy says. "Hurry, while the beast has human form."

Andorf peers around the bulky man, verifies the young girl has indeed returned. He sees the Mila at the filling nozzles gathering seconds and readying her bag about to leave. The girl lifts her head. For a brief moment, she and Andorf lock eyes, staring at one another. Then Andorf blinks and the Mila is gone. He wonders if what the gypsy tells him is true, that his Mila is merely a mirage.

"Go!" the gypsy yells. "Run after her."

The chair squeals as Andorf pushes off the table. He grabs his food boxes and then dashes after the girl, listening to the gypsy's jolly words.

"You'll never catch the Mila. Gypsy folklore says the beast can run through walls."

Outside the dining room, Andorf looks to his left, then right. Dismissing the gypsy's mocking laughter, he focuses on the Mila's thoughts. He envisions the vagrant girl with a heavy knapsack pulling on her back. He hears her labored breath, sees her running scared, sprinting down the long, crowded G-deck hallway.

Andorf sprints after her. Rounding corners, he catches brief snippets of the girl's trailing shadows as he races past the floating steps toward the main stairwell in the rear of the starship. Following the winding hallway, he slows through crowds of people. The girl darts beneath people's feet but twenty-eight-year-old Andorf must bend around people. He soon tires, but sighting the stairwell door at the end of the hallway, he presses on. He flings the stairwell door open and chasing the girl's faint, echoing foot-taps, jogs down six flights of steps to the lowest deck of the starship. On the M-deck, he swings the exit door open only to collapse in the hallway, drained, out of breath, and finally admitting he is no match for the Mila's youthful vibrancy.

He scans for the Mila's thoughts, but with loud machinery noises pouring out of the adjacent mechanical room, finds it an impossible task. Instead, he sits on the cold floor, cursing himself for losing the Mila, somewhere in the hot, greasy bowels of the *Atlantis*.

*

Binky's log – 21-054515:

It appears Andorf's introduction to the old gypsy folklore has left at a dead end. I only hope he gets used to his new nickname.

CHAPTER 3

Binky's Quest

Day 21: 0547

Binky scampers about his people's cabin. What to do? What to do? My human counterpart has gone to fetch breakfast and left me with his nine-month-pregnant mate. I hear her moaning in the next room. She doesn't sound at all well. Why did you leave an eight-pound rabbit in charge? How could you do this, Andorf? How could you?

Leaping onto Andorf's desktop, Binky hops back and forth, sending important papers floating into the air.

As noted in my recent telepathic log entries, Serin has been acting sickly. I see her stumbling about the bedroom, with her huge belly. Oh no! Now she's fallen. She's curled up on the floor, lips barely moving.

"Get help, Binky," Serin calls out in a series of strung-out, faint, hollowed breaths.

Binky leaps onto the floor, charges on a tear across Andorf's papers into the bedroom. After sniffing Serin, he trots back into the front room. He peers at the emergency door release button high above. Binky recoils his hind legs. He leaps high in the air. Inches shy of the release button, he rappels off the wall. He tries again with more fervor but still falls short. As a last resort, Binky scratches fiercely on the cabin door, hoping some human … any human on the other side will hear. After a few minutes, he tires.

These blasted paws! What I need is human hands … ones that can open this door. If only I had biped legs or a human voice, but instead I'm trapped inside this furry body. In short time, nothing will be the same, not for Andorf … not for Serin … not for anyone aboard this stolen starship called the Atlantis. *Major hell is about to break loose and now I am left here dealing with Andorf's sickly wife.*

Cocking his head to one side, Binky pauses to contemplate the dire situation. "Perhaps, I'm exaggerating things. After all, life is quite different when you have four legs which are measured in inches. How bad can things really—?"

Serin wails out from the back bedroom. Binky tears off, hopping at full speed. At the sight of Serin sprawled across the floor, he turns to run in tight circles as if chasing his own tail. He thumps to a sudden stop.

What the hell am I doing? I'm not a dog. I'm wasting precious time. I must hop onto that desk … contact Andorf … inform him of the trouble at home. Andorf will hurry right back … fix whatever's wrong with Serin and then go on to save the starship from self-destructing. I know he will. Human Andorf is able to do those things. With a bit of my furry inspiration, he'll fix things better than before. But how do I alert him? He is not hearing my telepathic thoughts else he would have already returned. There must be another way.

Binky hops across the papers strewn across the floor and leaps onto Andorf's desk. Nudging the transcriber with his nose, he focuses intense thoughts on the device. After what seems like forever, the transcriber couples with his inner thoughts. The starship's voice awakens. Siros beeps.

"Siros, patch me into *Atlantis'* paging system as Andorf Johnson."

Siros: User ID, please.

He stares at the lanyard mounted ID badge dangling from a mirror frame. "Andorf Johnson, first generation, ATL0003."

Siros: Security code, please.

"Are you kidding me, Siros? We've got a level one emergency here."

Siros: State the nature of the level one emergency.

"Dammit, Siros! Can't you hear Serin Gray? She is dying in the next room. Patch me into the public address as Andorf Johnson, first generation, ATL0003."

Siros: Security code, please.

Binky shakes his head side to side. He begins to wail out but pauses to think long and hard. *What would human Andorf use as a passcode?*

"Serin … Serin Gray … no wait!"

Siros: Beep! Incorrect code. Your account will lock after two more invalid entries.

"November 23rd … no wait!"

Siros: Beep! Incorrect code. One entry remains before your account locks for fifteen minutes.

Binky thinks long and hard as the transcriber counts down its timeout.

Siros: Transcriber disconnect in twenty seconds … nineteen … eighteen …

Binky's heart races. Eyes swelling, he begins to pant. He hops back and forth across the length of the desk, clearing off the last of Andorf's important papers.

Siros: Ten … nine … eight …

Large white fluffs float about the room as Binky's paw scratches at his temple. *All life aboard the* Atlantis *is on the verge of extinction and here I am arguing with a stupid machine. Now what the hell is that damn passcode?*

Siros: Five … four … three …

"Wait! I need more time, another …"

Siros: Beep! The transcriber has been rebooted.

Binky growls at the transcriber's flashing red light. Baring incisors, he wants nothing more than to gnaw through the cord, rip the device right off the wall.

"You cheated, Siros. I still have one more guess."

Silence.

"Binky! The pass code is Binky. B-I-N-K-Y!"

Silence.

The rabbit's eyes cross. "Dammit, Siros, you heard me. The passcode is Binky."

Siros: Your account will unlock in fourteen minutes and fifty-two seconds.

Binky leaps off the desk and then races for the cabin door. He scratches madly, giving it his all as though his and everyone else's fate relies on him.

*

Binky's log – 21-060423:

So, the starship's conscience thinks it has the best of me. Siros has obviously never dealt with a master Goshi.

CHAPTER 4

Replicator Number Six

Day 21: 0608

Six 3-D replicating printers located in a far corner of the mechanical room are purposed to replenish depleting parts inventories. But one troubling machine lives in a constant state of disrepair with Brutus fighting a never-ending battle of protecting number six from techs daring to cannibalize her parts to keep the other five replicators operating. Between training a handful of incompetent technicians and maintaining three starships, it is a miracle the chief engineer maintains any semblance of sanity.

Head buried deep inside the problematic replicator and with sweat dripping down his grease-laden face, Brutus begins to hyperventilate. He pauses to extract a fiber bag from a rear pocket. His greasy hand places it over his mouth. Taking a series of shallow breaths, he waits impatiently for a 38-millimeter header extractor tool from a new hire. With an outstretched hand protruding from the replicator's inner workings, he wages a losing battle with claustrophobia.

"How in the blazes of Argon do they expect me to keep three starships running with limited resources?" Brutus growls, as he turns an eye to see his clueless trainee fumbling with an assortment of screw drivers. Climbing out of the replicator, the chief engineer slices an arm on the cabinet's sharp edges. He mindlessly wipes blood onto the clinging remnants of his shredded shirt. His filthy hands pluck wax plugs from his ears and place them atop the off-balanced machine. He tucks the crumpled fiber bag inside a rear pocket before sliding the helpless tech out of the way. Brutus then grabs the extractor from another roll-around cart drawer before wedging himself back inside replicator number six.

The trainee yells at him above the sequenced milling noises. "You're killing yourself, big guy! You care more about that damn number six than you do about yourself. For goodness sake, shut 'er down while you're working inside."

Brutus slithers out from behind the replicator. Stuttering and staring cross-eyed, he shouts back at the clueless tech. "A replicator shutdown? Why it'd take ten minutes to run through shutdown sequences, another fifteen powering her back up. That's thirty-five Wymore rhiners … eighty Calico fasteners ... one hundred and twenty Harlequin hangers."

"When will you ever trust us, big guy? We're not half as useless as you think. Go ask Silas over there." The tech gazes at the replicator and then back at Brutus. "Say, can I borrow the distributor arm from number six while it's—?"

Brutus grumbles as he brushes the parts thief away with a swing of the unwieldy extractor tool. He then reenters the problematic replicator. "I could trust you more if—"

A familiar face suddenly appears around the backside of the spasmodic sounding replicator. "If what, Brutus?"

The chief engineer extracts himself out of the tight cavity to get a better look and gains a new head-gash in the process. He wipes the blood off with a greasy hand while peering at the visitor's clean clothes. Brutus casts greasy palms toward his old friend. "Andorf? What the hell are you doing down here? No one visits the mechanical room to socialize."

Andorf cringes at sight of the burly man's collection of bruises and blood spanning his arms, legs, and face. He quickly steps away from Brutus' greasy paws. "Remember that little vagrant girl from the cafeteria? Well, she reappeared. Only *this* time, she stared right at me. I chased her footsteps down six flights of steps to the M-deck until losing her in all this damn machinery noise."

Brutus dismisses his friend's euphoria with hardy gypsy laughter. "As I told you months ago, the child is but a mirage. Your vision is to the likings of Mila from ancient gypsy folklore."

"Would you believe one of your gypsy friends actually pointed her out to me? He told me to chase after her while she retained human form."

"What? A gypsy actually saw this, Mila? Ha. Like that'd ever happen."

Andorf swipes a marginally-clean rag off a tool dolly and wipes fresh blood trailing down Brutus' forehead. "Take it easy with those gashes. You cannot be killing yourself down here. We need you to keep our starship fleet running."

Brutus looks around at the technicians standing idle before shaking his head at his old friend. "You must find me good help, Andorf," he yells above the ratcheting sounds escaping replicator number six's open rear door. "Can't you see what I'm working with here?"

The replicator's clattering intensifies, as if competing for the chief engineer's attention. "Leave him alone," it seems to sound out in milling noises.

Andorf steps back from the harmonizing machine. "I doubt I will find anyone. Everyone able to work has already been tasked. And besides, Brutus, you appear to have a handle on ..." Andorf takes a moment to look around the busy room. "Whatever it is you do down here."

"Are you kidding me, Andorf? Training ties up two of my replicators. Sickbay's insatiable demand for customized parts for their lab instruments tie up another pair. Number six here is on her last legs. With one remaining replicator, I can't churn parts out fast enough to supply our starships. Take a look around. Part inventories are dwindling. This place is literally falling apart. I don't know how much longer I can keep everything together."

"Whoa there, Brutus. Things cannot possibly be so bad."

"Check out the flaky gravity generators across the room. Keeping them running on three starships 24x7 takes ten people. I've got five."

His and Andorf's eyes follow one of the techs drifting by in a daze.

Brutus winces. "Better make that four and a half. Then there's the *Phoenix* and the *Mayflower*. Anytime either of *those* ships has problems it yanks me off the *Atlantis*. If a stray meteor or even space dust damages any of our starships we'll be in a world of hurt. And to make matters worse, every time I turn my back, another tech is robbing yet another piece off number six." He turns away. Face dripping in sweat, he grabs at his back pocket and then breathes heavily into a fiber bag, worn too thin to own wrinkles. "It's all or nothing out here in space."

Andorf cringes at the pair of wax earplugs crawling down the replicator's cabinet like inchworms. "Still dealing with claustrophobia I see."

Head again stuffed in the fiber bag, Brutus nods.

"Well, I cannot do anything about your machinery. But I will certainly do my best to find more help, even if it means shaking down the *Phoenix* and the *Mayflower* for able bodies."

Brutus pulls the bag off his face, folds it up, and then stuffs it into a rear pants pocket. He looks his trainees over. "Don't go picking just anyone off a food line and be expecting them to have mechanical skills. I need a dozen … maybe two dozen qualified techs. Ones who are actually good with their—"

A tech approaches holding a grease-stained drawing in one hand and a controller arm dangling from the other. "I see where this goes, boss, but I can't make it fit. I've tried for close to an hour with a crowbar."

Brutus snarls. He pockets a handful of small wrenches and with Andorf and tech in tow, jogs down a half-level of corrugated metal steps. They pause at the sound of replicator number six behind them changing her chugging rhythm to that of a whimper. Again, she churns out concerns in milling noises.

'Don't leave me alone.'

As if consoling lonely number six, the other five replicators sympathetically seem to sound off one by one. The trio exchange glares before shaking off crazed thoughts.

The tech leads Brutus to a halted idle air purifier unit with one of its side panels removed. Brutus grabs the stained print from the rattled tech's greasy hand, flips it over, and hands it back to him. He then holds the replacement arm up against the open cabinet. "The arm attaches beneath the chain on the wet sprocket like this, you toad."

Brutus turns away, leaving the head-scratching tech to split views between the print and the replacement part. Jogging up the half-level of corrugated steps with Andorf trailing behind, Brutus glances back at his old friend. "See what I'm dealing with, Andorf? I can't teach these clowns common sense. And to make things worse, parts are wearing out faster than I can churn out replacements. As you can see, most of my shelves are empty."

Andorf jogs to catch up. He taps Brutus' bulk arm and then retracts his hand to inspect it for grease. "I hate to inform you, Brutus, but sickbay requires your fifth replicator, two … three months tops."

Brutus slams a fist against the sidewall of the nearest gravity generator. Trash wedged in the casing cracks fall out as the machine loses its clunking rhythm before sputtering back up to speed to suck the trash back into the cracks. During the brief lull, Brutus hears the techs laughing and spots them standing around idle. "Get back to work!" he yells, but once again, machine noise becomes too loud for anyone more than a few feet away to hear.

Andorf touches one of the machines in passing and then wipes grease off his hand. "Relax, Brutus. Serin's having our baby any day now. We still have a crack at having the first space baby."

Brutus throws his hands up. "Even with all this going on around me, the thought of Serin having our baby in that disaster of a sickbay is what terrifies me most. It keeps me awake at night. Why, I haven't slept in forty nights."

Andorf grins. "No worries. Assemblers have reverse-engineered medical devices from files found on the pica chip Serin smuggled out of the Empire. You should see all the lights and wires running everywhere."

Brutus gulps. Holding a hand on his chin, he stares at the high ceiling. "Lights and wires are running everywhere? Hmm. Something sounds fishy. Do the assemblers have any idea what they're doing?"

Andorf shrugs his shoulders. He retrieves his boxed breakfasts and then bolts for the exit.

Brutus yells above the busy machinery. "That's it, Poo! Run back upstairs … check on our wife. And you'd better hurry, before I shove a wrench into those pasty little hands."

"Be glad your wife has two husbands, boss," one tech shouts above the machinery noise. "Or else it'd be you on her short choker chain instead of Andorf."

Brutus extracts the worn-out fiber bag from his rear pants pocket and takes short breaths. He then turns back to the lumbering tech. "Ha Ha. You've had your fun, everyone," he yells. "Now get back to work."

The tech jokingly blows kisses at the chief engineer. "Does your wife know about you and Nosix?"

Replicator number six whimpers at the touch of Brutus wiping off the grease staining her rear cabinet door. "Never call her that," Brutus yells. "Her name is number six … replicator number six. Everyone will call her that from now on… if they know what's good for them."

*

Binky's log – 21-061522:

It appears the chief engineer has a second love interest. Poor Andorf, his heart belongs to only one.

CHAPTER 5
Baby Wants Out

Day 21: 0616

Andorf trudges up the stairwell, spitting foul, oily reside from his mouth. He wipes his mouth on his shirt but it also reeks of nasty machine lubricant. The main stairwell door slams shut, leaving machinery noise behind. Exiting into the crowded L-deck hallway, he creeps through the crowded hallway to claim a place in line at the floating steps. At the base of the lower atrium, he leans back and peers up the seemingly endless set of floating steps, extending eleven flights up to the A-deck.

Feeling a bit dizzy, Andorf feels friendly hands bracing his back to prevent his fall and spill of his and Serin's breakfast. Thanking everyone, Andorf advances with the line. About to step onto the first floating step, he senses a commotion. He spins around to catch sight of the vagrant girl weighed down by a large knapsack running past.

"Mila," Andorf mumbles, grinning at the raggedy stuffed bunny tucked under the young girl's arm. Without thought, he leaves the line to give chase. Hugging corners of the L-deck, he follows pointing fingers through the twisting corridors until the pointing fingers and corridor abruptly end.

Knowing the girl has nowhere else to go but inside the storage hold, he pauses to examine the heavy metal door dangling from its last hinge and a single screw. Entering the musty-smelling room, Andorf senses rapid breathing. He scans shelves, footlockers, and packing blankets, imagining the many places a rat, or in this case, a Mila could hide.

She could hole up in here indefinitely … sneak out to eat and returning between work shifts without much notice. I would not know where to begin.

Andorf begins to leave but freezes at sight of a raggedy stuffed bunny wedged between dusty packing blankets. Pulling on the toy, he feels resistance. He pulls a tad harder as does whatever is on the other end. Bending down to squint, he sees the sparkle of the young eyes, buried well-within packing blankets. He releases the stuffed rabbit and watches it disappear.

"You know I have a real live bunny back in my cabin," Andorf calls out, raising his voice an octave. "Yep, a fluffy white one named Binky who loves pets on his cheeks and the bridge of his nose."

Silence.

He grins at the tiny eyes blinking from deep within the blanket, beyond arms reach. "If you come with me, little one, you can play with a real live bunny. So, what do you say? I'm sure Binky won't—"

An overhead speaker awakens. Andorf winces at the raspy voice he has heard in his thoughts many times before. "There's trouble at home, human Andorf. You must hurry home."

"Binky?" Andorf says, eyes widening as he stands up and looks around. "I must go, my little Mila. My wife is about to deliver our baby … perhaps the first child to be born out here in space."

Andorf darts into the crowded L-deck hallway, past the door hanging by a lone hinge and single screw. With no time to lose and Binky's message repeating, he dares not look behind. "I can fly up the eleven flights of floating steps to the A-deck in record time," he utters, weaving left and right around lingering people. Around the last bend, he slows for the line forming at the floating steps. But something magic happens. As he approaches, everyone steps aside to grant him free access. Andorf steps onto the landing about to take the first of the floating steps when a tiny voice calls out from behind.

"Wait! Take me with you."

Goosebumps run the length of his arms. The sound of the child's innocent voice and sight of the girl's filthy face melts his heart. Seeing her carrying her stuffed toy in one hand and a packing blanket in the other, he freezes. He barely catches the glimpse of the girl before she flies into his open arms. The Mila wraps both arms around his neck and buries her head in his chest.

Not a moment to lose, Andorf jogs up the floating steps, defying not only the safety handles, but every one of his own safety protocols. He feels the young vagrant squirming in his arms, seemingly terrified by the rising motion than by his rapid pace. Between juggling the foam meal boxes in one hand, the child's death-grip on his neck and Binky's warning echoing from the ship's speakers, eleven flights of floating steps seem to never end. He finally leaps onto the A-deck landing, out of breath and flailing his arms at everyone to get out of the way. Arriving at his cabin, he reaches for the doorknob but finds the door opening on its own. Greeting him with tilted head, Binky leads him into the bedroom before quickly hopping away.

At sight of a real live rabbit cowering under the bed, the girl drops her stuffed bunny and blanket. She wiggles out of Andorf's arms and crawls beneath the bed alongside Binky. Stroking his fur, she and Binky observe the adults from a safe place.

Andorf is near-panic. There in front of him is Serin sprawled across the floor dressed in but a bloodied robe. Serin struggles to look up. In a series of jerky movements, she gasps in labored breath. "Something's terribly wrong, Andorf. My water broke and … I—I can't stand up."

Andorf wraps the child's blanket around his beloved. He gathers Serin gently in his arms and pauses at the exit to examine deep scratches in the wall leading up to the shoulder-height emergency-release button. He gazes back to see Binky in the bedroom licking dirt off the vagrant girl's face.

"Take care of our little Mila." With Serin in his arms, he turns and again pauses at the door.

The girl's eyes dart between Andorf and Binky as if somehow following Andorf and Binky's telepathic exchange.

"That's right, Binky." Andorf nods. "Yes, Mila … like the girl in ancient gypsy folklore. Am I the only one unfamiliar with … Ayla, that's right. I have not forgotten—huh? What about twins?"

"Not now," Serin moans, eyes half-open and torso twisting in Andorf's arms.

Shifting Serin's weight in his arms, Andorf jogs out into the hallway. He dashes for Brutus' cabin next door, takes the private elevator, and then runs through the G-deck screaming for everyone to get out of his way. With Serin withering at every bounce, he runs as fast as his legs can carry him toward the delivery room at the far end of the hallway.

Serin clutches his neck so tightly he can hardly breathe. She squeezes tighter with each contraction. "Hurry, Andorf" she squeals. "This baby wants out."

*

Binky's log – 21-063110:

For once in my life, I'm terribly scared. If anything bad happens to Serin, Andorf will never be the same.

CHAPTER 6
Revisiting An Old Crack

Day 21: 0632

Thom Mallory feels a tug on his arm. Before the captain knows it, he is plopped down in the communications specialist's buddy seat, staring wide eyed at an array of knobs and shiny buttons. He flinches at Pol's cold hands slipping a pair of headphones over his head. His ears throb in pain as loud rushing noise funnels directly into his brain.

Pol leans close and yells above the noise. "Hear that, Captain? Can you hear that angry man's voice?"

Knowing the comm-spec's uncanny knack for pulling weak voices out of the ether, hearing things others merely pass off as noise, Thom listens hard to the weak voices riding barely above the noise blasting at his throbbing eardrums. No longer able to withstand the pain, he yanks the phones off and flashes Pol a 'so what' shrug. "I hear the same rhetoric the Canine Empire has been spewing since we escaped in their prized starships. 'Return our starships ... all charges will be dropped' ... blah blah blah."

"No, Captain. Listen carefully ... beyond the Empire's idle threats. There's something there in the background, really faint."

Thom stares past his comm-spec. Not knowing the young man well, he ponders the likely notion of the radioman pulling a fast one. Thom slips the headphones back over his ears. Apprehensively watching Pol twist knobs, he presses the cuffs firmly against both ears. For fifteen minutes, he and Pol sit side by side, listening intensely to Empire threats as they repetitively peak above, and then fade into the dominant rushing noise. Navigator Peter and copilot Murray scoot up close behind them. Both lean in as if expecting to catch morsels of escaping sound. Pol nudges the volume a tad higher. He reaches above the captain, tweaks the seventeen-stage poly-phase filter array. New voices become barely readable but just as quickly are smothered beneath the ever-present background noise. With the noise growing painfully loud, Thom grabs his headphones and tosses them aside.

"I can't hear a damn thing, Pol. Between that blasted noise and those guys cursing, how in hell can anyone understand whatever anyone's saying?"

Pol grins at the captain. "Spiders and cows. I distinctly heard one man's voice yelling what sounded like spiders and cows."

Thom exchanges dazed glances with Pol as he reluctantly slips the discarded cuffs over his ears. Nodding at Pol, the volume gets bumped well beyond human pain threshold. After painfully doubtful minutes, the captain grabs at the ear cuffs. Suddenly the secondary voices appear above the Empire's threatening messages. Choppy words and bits of broken words poke out, sounding like messages bobbing atop a sea of waves and hissing foam. And just as suddenly, the voices are drowned by noise. Agonizing in pain, Thom and Pol listen intensely for the next wave to crest. Pol tweaks the Hi-Q filter and snippets of the voices again blast out.

He and Pol yank their headphones off and toss them onto the floor. Thom stares wide-eyed at the comm-spec as he rubs life back into his throbbing ears. "Use the speakers, Pol. There are no secrets amongst my crew."

Peter snarls at Pol. "Is that so."

Pol snarls back as he yanks both headphone plugs. Hiss immediately pours out of the radio's twin speakers. The crew leans close, holding breaths at each empty spike in background noise.

Murray turns about. He looks about the cabin. "What about that other noise, Captain?"

Captain Thom becomes irritated. "The voices, Murray! Focus on the voices. We need everyone's ears."

"Shouldn't we have heard something by now?" Peter whispers. "Perhaps whoever it was has given up."

Pol's eyes narrow upon his crewmate. "Don't you know how weak signals work, Peter? They arrive in spurts, fading in and out of thermal noise. You learn to work with what you get."

Hushing everyone, Thom listens hard to the voiceless noise. He does his best to ignore the Empire's threats. Pol again tweaks the quintessential filter and like the biblical Tower of Babel fable, dozens of voices pour out the speaker, all chattering in indistinguishable tongues. Just as quickly, the voices fade.

"See? I wasn't crazy," Pol says, grinning at the others. "We're not alone out here. I knew there were more starships out here than our measly three."

"What about that other noise?" Murray mumbles. "What about that creepy high-pitched crackling sound? Can't anyone besides me hear it?"

Thom pats his radioman on the back. "Good job, Pol. But I'm afraid you've opened a can of worms."

Murray grabs the navigator's arm and pulls him away from the others. "What about you, Peter? Surely you can hear that crackling noise."

Peter whisks a hand at Murray as if swatting a fly. He then rejoins the others. "Those voices on the radio, they don't sound human."

All but Murray stare at the hissing speaker as if waiting for answers to magically leap out at them. Pol fiddles with the knobs until voices return, louder, more profound but still jumbled together.

Pointing at the speaker, Thom's voice excites, "That one, Pol … the man with the acrid tongue. Hear the others pause whenever he speaks? He must be their leader. Focus on *his* voice. He's the one I'm interested in."

Peter snorts. "There must be forty voices jumbled up. You'll never pick a single voice out of that garbled mess."

Out the corner of one eye, Thom spots Murray fidgeting, appearing as nervous as he was on launch day, when the crew hid from burning laser beams that swept through the bridge. He recalls it was the first mate who forfeited a middle finger while displaying disdain for the Empire. He grunts at Murray's hands, persistently pawing on his shirt.

Murray's voice trembles. "You must hear that crackling noise. I—I don't know where it's coming from but it's getting louder. I think you should …"

Murray lowers his head and then stares at the twin bolts securing the captain's chair to the floor. "Why are there only two?" he mumbles.

Thom follows his first-mate's eyes to the twin bolts securing his captain's chair. He trances, deep in a recurring vision of clinging onto that same chair for dear life while he is being sucked into the vacuum of space. *Perhaps it is already setting in. Insanity will consume every last one of us first gens. For generations yet to be born on the starships, this world will be all they know. But for this current generation, sacrifices forgone will eventually take their toll. Insanity is ingrained in each of us first gens, waiting for some minute instance to be reawakened.*

The captain unwittingly falls from Pol's buddy seat. He quickly stands and brushes Murray aside along with his embarrassment.

"It's not important," he snaps. Thom turns back to the radioman. "Record everything, Pol. Filter out everyone's voice except that angry one … and get rid of that blasted noise."

Pol throws open palms at the captain. "I'll do my best, Captain, but there's only so much I can do with this antiquated equipment."

Thom finger-swipes the ship's main display. After scanning names rapidly scrolling past, he slaps an open palm against the listed passenger summary. "Seven thousand souls aboard the *Atlantis* and not one is a linguist. Oh, I can tell right now, these voices are turning into a royal pain in the—"

Siros, the starship's voice awakens.

Siros: Neck? If the good Captain requires a neck massage, perhaps I will be able to schedule one. Let me find the next available appointment.

Peter rolls his eyes. "That will be all, Siros."

Siros: Cannot comply. You are not Captain Thom Mallory.

"Siros, that will be all," Thom yells.

Siros: Affirmative, Captain Mallory.

Throwing a soured gaze, Peter taps the captain's arm, beckoning him to examine the navigational screen. "I may be able to explain that jumble of voices on Pol's radio. But I think you'd better sit back down, Captain."

With his navigator's and comm-spec's expressions darkening like space beyond the twin frontal viewports, Thom takes a seat, this time at Peter's screen. He winces at the pair of archaic measuring sticks dangling above.

With Peter taking too many deep breaths for their growing impatience, Thom and Pol egg the navigator on with their hands. "For weeks, I've noticed extra blips on the navigation screen. At first, I chocked them off as random noise … you know … false echoes. But now, hearing those voices and seeing as many blips … it's beginning to make sense. See those white lights on the screen, Captain? I lost count after forty."

Thom gulps.

Pol rubs his chin. "Like the forty voices."

Thom swivels in the navigator seat. "Siros, can this be true? Are there forty ships approaching the *Atlantis* from astern?"

Siros: Negative, Captain. There are forty-three starships currently on an intercept path with the *S.S. Atlantis* and her sister starships.

Murray appears from behind. He sheepishly taps on Thom's shoulder. "A word with you, Captain. It's of extreme importance."

"Not now, Murray!" Thom shouts, rising to his feet without turning around. "Go ahead, Peter. Explain."

"Yeah, Peter," Pol says. "Spit it out."

When Peter presses buttons on the navigation screen, the display sequences through a history of screens from weeks past. "See how these dots appear to be fanning out? It's as if they're—"

Wiping perspiration off his temples, Thom takes a few steps and then collapses in Pol's jump seat. He peers up at the shoddily painted ceiling. "Surrounding us," he mumbles. "I knew it'd only be a matter of time before the Empire would send battle cruisers. They want to reclaim their prized starships."

Sweat drips off the navigator's forehead as well. "We're totally defenseless out here. There are no weapons aboard any of our three starships."

Pol raises a brow. "They'll use binary codes to gain entry into our shuttle bay … enter the bridge guns a-blazing. Earth's empires have a reputation of eliminating enemy leaders."

"Like starship captains," Thom mumbles. "They have a long history of parading captured starship captains publicly before ceremoniously torturing them to death."

"And don't forget the part of us harboring a known killer," Pol adds. "I'm sure they're not too happy about Chief Engineer Brutus doing away with one of their supreme leaders."

"Fat Max." Thom's face turns ghostly white. "They'll round the both of us up ... shoot us in front of all seven thousand passengers."

"Or shove you both out an airlock," Pol whispers, much too loudly.

Peter returns to his screen to squint at the encroaching blips. "But, how can this be? We're a good three months from Earth. They couldn't possibly have caught up with us this soon."

The captain winces. "The *Atlantis* has been overloaded from day one. It's a miracle our starship ever broke free of Earth's atmosphere. The *Mayflower* and *Phoenix* throttled back so as not to overtake us." Wiping sweat off his brow, Thom gazes back at the navigator. "How soon, Peter? How soon until we face the inevitable?"

Grabbing one of the archaic measuring sticks dangling overhead, Peter reverts to old-school techniques. He lays the piece against the screen and then counts off units with his finger before returning it to the hook above. "Judging the invader's speed and trajectories, I suspect—"

Siros: Maintaining our current vector, Captain Mallory, the *Atlantis* and her sister starships will be within boarding proximity in ninety-three days, seventeen hours, and forty-one minutes, give or take a variance of thirty-six hours.

Peter's eyes narrow. "If you're so smart, Siros, what are the radio-voices saying?"

Siros: Cannot comply. I respond to only Captain Tom Mallory's and Chief Engineer Brutus Bittner's voice patterns.

Murray darts for Pol's radio. He plugs in a headphone and the loud rushing noise ceases. He grabs hold of Thom's arm, drags him away from Pol's jump seat. "Damn it, Captain. Turn around! Look at the—"

Thom scowls at his first mate. He begins to curse but freezes at the eerie crackling sound emanating from behind. Shivers run down his spine. Thom snaps his head around. His eyes are drawn to the expanding network of spider-like cracks spanning the length of both frontal viewports. Thom recalls moments before takeoff when militia outside were tapping both view portals with the butts of their guns.

Green console lights begin to flicker. One by one, lights morph to strobing red and then bright solid red. Oxygen indicators flash dwindling readings of 18%, 17%, 16%. Too many alarms and verbal warnings sound for anyone to follow including the warning of Imminent Pressurization Loss! Each warning alarm sounds off in competition with the others. The starship's voice reawakens.

Siros: EVACUATE THE BRIDGE!

Though Peter and Pol have already escaped out the airlock door, Thom orders a bridge evacuation. "Run for it," he yells, pressing both feet against his reluctant first mate's rump. Giving it his all, he forces Murray out the closing bridge's airlock door.

Murray spins about to block the wobbling bridge door from closing with his nine remaining fingers.

"Door jam! Door jam!" bridge speakers wail out.

"Hurry, Captain!" Murray yells, struggling to hold the door from his weakened horizontal position. "I cannot keep this door open much longer."

Air rushes past Thom through the blocked door. With cabin temperature dropping, he dives for the bridge door. He slips one hand between the door and the frame to replace Murray's reddening hands.

Murray rolls out of the way and rubs his hands together as if trying to reclaim feeling.

"Door jam! Door jam!" bridge speakers wail.

Thom struggles to wedge fingers between the airlock door and its frame. He pulls until he can no longer feel his fingers. Electrical charges installed to discourage rodents from blocking doors tingle his fingertips. Still, the captain pulls hard on the door. Elevating electrical charges sends pain shooting down both arms and biceps.

The captain's face contorts. Unable to withstand any more electrocution, he retracts both hands. The door wobbles shut, sealing the captain and his fate inside the doomed bridge. Thom gazes back at the cracking viewports.

"Siros, what are my chances of survival?"

Siros: Not well, Captain Mallory. You should have evacuated the bridge when you had the chance. The likelihood of human survival inside the *Atlantis'* primary bridge is next to nil.

Thom leaps across the bridge. In swift motions, he extracts an emergency suit from beneath the captain chair, kicks off his shoes, and wiggles inside. Slipping arms through the sleeves, he feels the suit snugging tight against his torso. With bridge O2 displays counting down to 5%, he begins to feel woozy. Taking shallow breaths, he struggles to align the helmet with the suit's vacu-seal ridge plate.

When the suit's air supply activates, Thom gladly breathes in the oxygen-rich mixture. He waits for the foggy mask to clear, squinting at the display projected on the face of his helmet to verify the fifteen-minute air supply. He taps the helmet's comm-link on his sleeve.

"Siros, assign first-mate Murray Barnwell as Acting Captain in my absence."

Siros: Perhaps you need a few more breaths of oxygen to clear your mind, Captain Mallory. I have a list of twenty highly qualified alternate candidates who will make remarkable starship captains.

"Siros, did you hear me? You are to assign my first mate, Murray Barnwell, as the *Atlantis'* next captain."

Silence.

Thom slides into the captain's chair and grabs at the restraining harness. Pulling the strap, he finds it six-inches short against the suit.

"Siros, why the long pause?"

Siros: I am reminding myself that for the next fourteen minutes and twelve seconds I must accept your commands.

"Siros, are you monitoring my vitals?"

Silence.

"Siros!"

Siros: Affirmative, Captain.

Struggling within the bulky spacesuit, Thom pulls himself toward a supply closet to the right of the sealed airlock door. His gloved-hand awkwardly unwinds one of the long emergency lifelines. He attaches one end-hook to one of the suit loops, reaches above for the frame hook above his head and—

POW!

Both viewports shatter. A foray of shattered fiber and glass is blown into space. In sudden decompression, Thom finds himself being sucked across the bridge, heading toward the dark void of space. He grabs frantically at everything he zooms past. One gloved hand catches the headphone cable engaged in the radio. The cable pulls taut against its quarter inch plug as he wraps it around his sleeve. He spots the plug easing out of the radio jack. Suddenly, a mad hissing noise spews out the speaker as once again Thom finds himself flying feet first toward the open viewports.

Thom snags the over padded captain's chair with one arm and wraps the other around the chair's tall headrest. With dangling feet aimed at the open viewports, he clings to the chair as tight as his suited arms allow. The chair vibrates furiously as he watches the twin molly bolts securing it to the floor back out of the threaded holes. The bolts dance about in the holes, as if arguing with their threads. He recalls Murray's words as he stares at the chair's molly bolts.

"Only two?" Thom grumbles. "With something so important, why are there never more than two?"

One molly bolt pulls loose, then the other. Thom gulps, knowing the chair remains held to the floor by only a thin bead of caulk and the wear of time. Even through the suited arms he can feel the chair fighting a losing battle. The chair lifts to one side before losing total grip. Suddenly, the chair flies toward the open viewports and the frigid space beyond with the captain hanging on. At the last moment, Thom flips around the chair to avoid being crushed as the chair wedges inside the left viewport frame. He watches portal framing working loose as he looks around the bridge, planning his next grab.

Siros: Fifty seconds remain, Captain Mallory. Quite enough time to reconsider your successor.

Thom's eyes focus upon the oxygen readout projected onto the helmet's view window. "Siros, you're cutting me short. I've still got 9.5 minutes of … Wait! Siros! What are you implying? What are you not telling me?"

Siros begins to count down, beginning at forty-five.

Thom glances to look at the radio knobs and buttons, then back at Peter's navigation screen. He peers up at the archaic measuring sticks above, vibrating like crazy at the ends of their hooks.

"Watch out!" Siros shouts, interrupting the countdown. Thom ducks right but not before one of the measuring sticks scratches a six-inch line across his helmet's faceplate.

Thom's eyes widen at the sight of the second stick nearing its hook's opening. The stick suddenly works free and flies at him, heading directly toward his chest. Thom twists hard left, but not before the stick slices a gouge in his sleeve. His suit begins to vent the limited air supply.

Siros again interrupts the countdown. "That's two. Beware Captain. The third one's a doozy."

The captain gasps at sight of his suit's oxygen display counting down rapidly. Nine minutes … eight point five. Knowing his life is ending, Thom does what every red-blooded captain would do. He swears at Siros.

Siros: Twenty-eight … twenty-seven … It is impossible for me do any of those things, Captain Mallory. Are you forgetting I lack physical form? Nineteen … eighteen …

Foam gel fills the venting sleeve gash. With the oxygen display slowing to count down in real time, he breathes deep sigh of relief. *Why has Siros not adjusted his countdown?*

Thom's question is answered when he sees the over-padded chair beginning to twist apart. Padding rips loose and flies out the viewport. Within seconds, the chair is only a frame, held together by glue and a handful of screws.

In desperation, Thom fans both legs, doing his best to keep from slipping further outside. Using every last bit of strength, he pulls himself inside the bridge. With one hand, he reaches beneath the console dash. The other hand stretches to hook his lifeline. He can feel the lifeline's hook beginning to catch beneath the console.

Siros: Three … two …

The viewport frame suddenly snaps and Thom is sucked into the vacuum of space amongst the foray of plastic, metal, and broken glass. He slams hard against the *Atlantis'* hull, momentarily robbing wind from his breath. Thom verifies the air supply display on his helmet screen displays 7.5 before clambering along the titanium hull, searching for any loop with which to engage the drifting lifeline hook. Sliding along the hull Thom discovers a foot-hold.

"Saved! Siros, send a rescue shuttle to the *Atlantis'* port bow."

Silence.

"Did you hear me, Siros? Have a—" Thom's foot slips and he suddenly finds himself floating without a ship.

Siros: Thom Mallory has left his post while on duty. I now answer to Chief Engineer, Brutus Bittner and Acting Captain Murray Barnwell.

Oxygen numbers projected on the upper right of his helmet begin to flash. Seven minutes remain—brain dead seven minutes after that.

I still have time. I'll wave at the many view portals scrolling past. Someone will spot me. They'll send a shuttle. Sickbay will resuscitate me. There is hope.

Drifting past the *Atlantis'* portside viewing windows, Thom flails his arms at the many passenger faces. No one peers outside. He dog-paddles frantically toward the *Atlantis* as she and her sister starships continue silently on their journey without him.

Thom's oxygen display flashes warnings upon his faceplate. Gasping for air, he watches the *Atlantis*, *Phoenix*, and *Mayflower* reduce to small lights before fading within the starlit blackness of space. To the tune of 'Golden Slumbers' playing in Thom's helmet, Siros' fading voice calls out.

Siros: I shall miss you, Thom Mallory.

*

Binky's log – 21-064850:

I shall miss you as well, Captain Thom. All hell is about to break loose and we really need you.

CHAPTER 7

Bittersweet

Day 21: 0650

B earing scratches across his arms, neck and face, Andorf bursts through sickbay doors cradling Serin in his arms. He pushes past a series of blankets masking the converted observation deck's once panoramic view only to grimace at medical crew scampering about and making preparations as if he and Serin were expected.

Serin wrenches as he gently places her on a clean gurney prepped with fresh bedding. He begins to flag someone down but Serin refuses to relinquish her death-grip on his arm. "I'm scared, Andorf. For the first time in my life, I'm scared," she whimpers between gasping breaths. "Don't leave me."

"I'm med-tech Kaylis," says a frail med tech in a blood-stained smock appearing from between makeshift room dividers. "I'll be assisting with Serin's delivery." Andorf follows as the med tech rolls Serin's gurney into a backroom encircled by newly-assembled machines. He scrutinizes the multi-color wires haphazardly interconnecting the devices. Kaylis' jittery hand slips a pillow beneath Serin's head. Staring at the bedsheet turning red, the young lady begins to weep.

Andorf raises a brow. "B—but how did you know?"

A nurse appears through the room dividers. "Some guy with a scruffy voice notified us of your pending arrival. At first, we thought we were hearing things. But when Binky mentioned Serin by name, everyone dropped whatever they were doing. A surgeon in the next room is prepping for the procedure."

Scanning all the complex-looking machinery lining the room and colored probes running everywhere, Andorf feels lost. He recalls how it was reverse-engineered from files smuggled out of the Empire on the tiny pica chip Serin still wears on a lanyard around her neck. The blinking lights … the multi-colored wires interconnecting the machines … everything appears out of place, as does the seemingly ill-prepared medical staff. Andorf cannot place it, but things are not quite right.

"They are dressed for the parts but can they play their roles?" he mumbles, much too loudly.

When a three-hundred-pound orderly suddenly grabs his arm, Andorf finds himself propelled him through the makeshift room dividers and onto a waiting area floor.

"But Serin's my wife. She is going into surgery. I must be with her."

The orderly points a threatening finger in Andorf's face. "I don't care if you were the Lord of Yestermore. You're waiting out here."

Before the orderly leaves, Andorf is back on his feet. He pushes the dividers aside to see Serin clenching bloody bedsheets in her fists, her head twisting, yelping in pain and Kaylis on the sidelines sobbing. Pulling the sheets from Serin's weak grip, he grasps her cold, clammy hand.

"Your wife's lost an awful lot of blood," Kaylis says, wiping away tears dripping down her cheeks. "If only you had arrived sooner."

Andorf hops onto an undressed gurney. He rips off his shirt and uses it to tie a crude tourniquet around his bicep. "Give her my blood—all of it if you must. Do whatever it takes. Hurry! You must save my Serin."

"What the hell are you doing?" the nurse yells, staring at Andorf as if he has gone mad. She removes the tourniquet and orders him out. She then hits a wall-mounted panic button.

The heavy orderly reappears. Steaming mad, he grabs hold of Andorf's gurney and wheels him through the hanging room dividers.

Andorf leaps off. After jogging around the orderly, he bolts back inside. Dropping to his knees, he stares up at the nurse with cupped hands. "I'm begging you, please. Give Serin my blood. Do it now. Do it right now, while she still has life."

"Impossible," the nurse says. "Your blood would need to be cleansed and then run through a series of complex tests. Only then could we—"

"Forget your damn tests," Andorf yells. "We are of the same blood type, I swear. Hurry! Give Serin my blood. It will save her life."

"Someone, get this maniac out of here," the nurse yells back as she presses a wall-mounted panic button.

Andorf recalls hearing about a nurse with a Sudanese accent. Reading Jasmine's nametag, he leaps to his feet. He firmly grabs her arm. "You must believe me, Jasmine. Whole blood transfusions will become common place by year's end."

Growling even louder than her empty stomach, Jasmine reaches for her belt-pouch. She extracts an emergency tool and waves it in Andorf's face. "You want me to zap you with my stunner? Huh? That's what I'll do if you don't release me. You'll be lying face down on the floor in five seconds, gasping for breath." Jasmine's eyes narrow. She counts. "Four … three … two …"

Andorf lets go of Jasmine's arm. He returns to the gurney, pleading with her as the orderly again wheels him through the makeshift curtains.

In all Serin's weakness, Andorf feels her reaching out for him. His wife's faint thoughts overwhelm his own. *The old man at the Cos warned … I'd never see my baby.*

Moments later, Andorf returns wearing gloves and a surgical mask. The orderly's large hand reaches for Andorf's throat but freezes at sight of a scruffy five-year-old pushing her way through the makeshift room dividers. Baring teeth at the orderly, Mila wedges between the beastly orderly and Andorf. With both hands rest on her hips, she scowls at the medical staff.

"Touch my daddy again and I'll scream. I can scream really, really loud."

The orderly and Nurse Jasmine dance a Texas two-step away from the feisty tot. Both point for the child and Andorf to wait in a corner. Watching Andorf and the girl step away, Jasmine returns to her patient.

Amongst the chaos of screaming buzzers from unfamiliar medical devices and Nurse Jasmine barking orders, Andorf and the girl take refuge in a corner of the cramped room. Eyes locked upon the tot, Andorf is unsure what just occurred between her and the orderly and even more so, the scruffy young girl calling him daddy.

At Serin's whimpering, Andorf leaps to his feet. He stares hypnotized at Serin's convulsing body beneath the blood-stained sheets. Between the machine's strobing lights, the multi-colored mini-probes attached to his wife's arms, and the beet-red bedsheets, lost reality smacks him in the face.

"No! Not again," Mila wails out before running out of the room.

Andorf wants to chase after the tot, to hold her in his arms, to tell her everything will be okay. But he cannot leave his wife's side.

Serin lifts her hand and holds it weakly in Andorf's direction. "The old man at the Cos," she moans, through a series of shallow breaths. "It was you, Andorf. You were warning me that night. You came back for me ... as promised."

"She believes I am old man Chester," Andorf mumbles.

Kaylis slips a comforting arm over Andorf's shoulder. "I wouldn't take much credence in anything your wife says. She's lost an awful lot of blood."

Nurse Jasmine nods. "In her weakened state, your wife is delirious."

Andorf jogs around the gurney. He gathers Serin's cold, clammy hand in his own. He whispers to his beloved. "I will keep coming back for you, Serin. I swear I will never quit. Not until I never lose you."

Serin leans her head to face him. A hard-pressed smile appears on her face. Her eyes then darken, losing their ever-present glimmer. She exhales her last breath.

"No!" Andorf peels off his face mask. He dispels the gloves to run his fingers through Serin's long blonde hair and then kiss her lips. He falls off the gurney and collapses onto the cold floor. Suddenly, he is in a place where things no longer make sense. "Serin is my life," he whimpers. "How can I accept her in past tense? How? How?"

Overhead lights flicker a few times. Complex machines lining the walls wind down and then rev up to re-sound their alarms. Fighting tears, Kaylis kneels to drop a comforting arm around Andorf. "Life is so fragile. There's never enough time."

Nurse Jasmine lowers her stethoscope and then disconnects Serin's lifeless form from the raging machines. She covers the corpse with a sheet and nods at the orderly to rush the gurney into the next room. Eyes tearing, she stoops down to cradle Andorf's face in her hands.

"I've seen this too many times before. It never gets easier. Death's shadow has come between you. But you must be strong. Life continues."

As Jasmine chases after Serin's gurney, Kaylis futilely wipes at her own streaming tears. "I recall my last night on Earth like it was yesterday. My best friend, Leigh, and I were scared, hiding behind dumpsters. Copters were skimming the rooflines. Their bright floodlights swept overhead. Huddled together with our worldly belongings, we shivered at sirens screaming past for the longest time. By some miracle, our husbands' packed cargo van arrived. We squeezed inside with barely enough room to breathe. It was the most scared I'd ever been in my entire life. But Serin took me in her arms—held me, a total stranger as though I was her own. I'll never forget her kindness on that long, terrifying ride up Jake's Mountain."

At the sound of clomping footsteps, Kaylis jumps to her feet. Her mouth contorts at the foul stench of oil and grease permeating the room. She winces at the beastly man in shredded clothing. The chief engineer pushes his way past the room dividers with all the grace of the proverbial bull in a china shop.

"Where the hell's my wife?" Brutus yells. "She's supposed to be here delivering our baby."

No one answers.

Brutus looks around, eyeing the alarming machines appearing to be stitched together by multi-colored wires without good reason. He sees Kaylis with her streaming tears and Andorf curled up on the floor with bloodstained sheets tight-gripped in his hands. His eyes widen, as if remembering seeing the orderly exiting the draped-off room, pushing a gurney with similar red-stained sheets and a nurse in tow.

"No!" he yells, beating on haphazardly-wired machines. "You can't do this to my wife. Bring Serin back! Bring her back now! Fix her! Make her whole again!"

In all her frailty, Kaylis latches onto Brutus' hefty shoulder as far as her much smaller arms allow. "You must believe me. We did everything possible," she cries out, whimpering between words. "Our three-week training course was insufficient. We learned nothing about delivering babies." Kayliss looks about the room. "Nothing in the course trained us how to use these new medical devices."

Andorf strains to find his feet. After staggering about the room like a drunkard, he falls limp against Brutus and then whimpers. "One moment Serin was sitting on the bedroom floor and the next … I was kissing her lifeless lips goodbye. Why did she leave us, Brutus? Why? Why?"

Glancing again at Brutus' hefty physique peeking through greasy, torn clothes, Kaylis backs away slowly to a safer distance. Wiping her eyes, she points at the array of strange machinery spanning every corner of the room. "I never touched those things, I swear. Who in hell even knows what they do?"

After eyeing the med tech suspiciously, Brutus slams a fist down hard. He glares at the med-tech's guilt-ridden face. His voice ramps up. "What? Are you telling me these devices weren't in your training labs? Andorf, I thought you were handling the—"

Kaylis throws open palms at Brutus. "You can't blame Andorf! He's been here most every day checking on the machines' progress. It's those damn assemblers, I tell you. They didn't know what the hell they were—"

A baby's cry interrupts. Seconds later, Nurse Jasmine reappears and gently lowers a cloth-wrapped bundle into Andorf's arms. "Congratulations on the first baby born in space."

Before Andorf peers up, the nurse has gone. Kaylis feels beneath the cloth and smiles at Andorf. "What in the world will you name your daughter?"

Andorf's cheeks swell with pride. "Ayla. It is the name Serin and I had chosen."

Brutus grumbles. In the blink of an eye, Nurse Jasmine has returned to place a second crying, cloth-wrapped bundle into *his* less than expectant arms. "Space babies … twins at that. You must be proud fathers."

Peeling back the baby's wrap, Brutus grins widely. "My son shall be named Sarak, after his gypsy grandfather."

The fathers cast damp eyes upon their newborns, admiring Serin's final gift on this bittersweet day. After an extended moment, Andorf halfway grins. "Serin knew this would happen. She described an old man back at the Cos … a soothsayer who predicted she would never—"

The room darkens. Raging machines around them wind down. Everything becomes deadly quiet. Screams are heard echoing from the hallway. Emergency lights flicker before illuminating to a partial brightness. Over the sounds of machines struggling to reawaken, they hear voices outside shouting fears of the world coming to an end.

In the eerie twilight and with temperature dropping, Brutus hands his bundled-wrapped son off to Kaylis. He unsnaps a palm-sized monitor from his belt clip. A finger swipe projects the starship's failure status onto the floor. Another finger-swipe patches him into the starship's paging system. Speakers throughout the *Atlantis* awaken to the chief engineer's voice as he uses the hand-held device's screen lighting to maneuver between the hanging room dividers.

"Attention! Attention, everyone," he says, speaking calmly into the device. "Persons having zero-gravity experience must grab mag-boots and meet me outside the G-deck bridge. Pronto! That's the G-deck bridge. And bring flash-lights. This is not a drill."

Andorf hands his daughter off to Jasmine. In near frenzy, he dashes into the crowded G-deck hallway. Amongst flickering lights, he spots Brutus in the far distance, pushing through the crowd and brushing away those clinging to his hefty arms. And just like that, the chief engineer vanishes within the crowd of panicking passengers.

Returning to the waiting area, Andorf cannot help but smile at the scruffy-looking girl sprawled out across several chairs, sound asleep amongst the chaos. His heart flutters at the thought of her calling him daddy. He gathers the little vagrant girl in his arms and then charges through the crowd. "Come, my little Mila. Brutus needs our help."

Awakening, the girl wraps both arms around his neck. Her half-opened eyes scan the crazed people running around in every direction. "But there are too many. How will you ever find him?"

Andorf smiles at the child held lovingly in his arms as he forges a path through the crowd. "No worry, my little Mila. Finding trouble has never been my problem."

*

Binky's log – 21-071012

Help sometimes comes from somewhere least expected.

CHAPTER 8
Heaven Help Us

Day 21: 0714

Between jogging through the crowded hallway and pushing people aside, Brutus arrives at the far end of the G-deck bridge out of breath. He squints in the near-twilight and sees Murray clawing relentlessly at ice crystals spanning a length of the bridge door. Peter and Pol are on either side, tugging on the first mate's arms. A finger-swipe on Brutus' scanner reveals not only are life support systems throughout the starship shutting down, but Captain Thom is nowhere to be found.

"What the hell happened?" Brutus yells, approaching the bridge crew. "Was anyone inside the bridge? Where's your captain? My scanner indicates he's no longer aboard the *Atlantis*."

Rubbing life into his bluish fingers, Murray collapses to the floor. Emergency lights highlight the tears running down his face in red flashes. The first mate gazes up at Brutus. "I tried to warn Captain Thom but he wouldn't listen." Pointing fingers at the fellow bridge-mates, his voice sharpens. "None of you ever listen to me. What good is a first mate if no one listens to you?"

"The—the captain," Peter says, brushing off Murray. "He was inside the bridge when the airlock door wedged shut."

Pol lowers his head as if shamed. "The three of us barely made it out in time. But the captain …"

In the middle of blowing warm air over his frostbitten hands, Murray yells out, "I held the door open as long as possible. The captain isn't expendable. He can't die."

Brutus' hand-held scanner indicates the starship's temperature has dropped another five degrees. Gravity status lights are morphing from green to amber. Verbal messages blast out of the ship-wide speakers.

"Warning! Warning! Imminent gravity failure."

With horror portrayed on the bridge crew's faces and thick layers of frost blanketing the bridge door, it is not difficult for the chief engineer to compile events leading up to the captain's suspected demise. Brutus focuses on his handheld device. "According to the scanner, fragments of a captain's chair are embedded in one of the bridge's frontal viewport frames and bridge temperature is approaching 80 degrees Kelvin."

"Great sands of Egypt," Murray yells. "Captain Thom was in that chair. He's been catapulted into space. We must go back, Brutus … retrieve our good captain."

Scratching at his balding crown, Brutus ponders for a painful moment. "If the captain has indeed left the ship, I suspect he's well beyond shuttle range. Assuming Thom made it into a space suit, his air supply has long been exhausted."

Peter's face saddens. "Captain Thom never stood a chance."

Emergency lights begin to dim. Warnings continue to blast out ship-wide speakers.

"Warning! Warning! Gravity failing. Take security in the nearest gravity hold."

Flickering gravity lights alternate between amber and red, becoming redder and redder before morphing to a dull cherry red. The starship's temperature continues to drop.

"This is how it all ends," Peter yells, lifting off the floor. "Big brother begged me to pick the *Phoenix* but no, I wouldn't listen. *Atlantis* is a larger, more stable starship I told him."

Rising as well, Brutus manages to squeeze one of his large shoes into a wall-mounted gravity-weld. Finger-swiping the hand-scanner, three-dimensional schematics are projected onto the ceiling. A second finger-swipe awakens the all-knowing Siros. Waiting on the ship's voice to respond, Brutus analyzes the hologram.

Siros: You appear troubled, Chief Engineer Brutus Bittner. Your blood pressure is elevated. You are secreting sweat at an alarming rate. How may I help you?

"Siros, why are system control lines running through the main bridge? They're supposed to be feeding the main bridge from this hallway, not running *through* the bridge."

Siros: Unbeknownst to but a few, accountant teams seized control of the *Atlantis'* project mid-way through its construction phase. To cut costs, the 'beanos' as many call them, rerouted control lines above the bridge.

"Damn beanos," Brutus yells. "Now the lines are frozen. Life support is beginning to shut down."

Siros: The accountants overlooked the fact I saw everything, heard everything, and knew everything. Did you know I played 'Golden Slumbers' for Thom Mallory during *his* final moments?

Brutus winces. "Siros, don't you mean *Captain* Thom Mallory?"

Siros: Thom Mallory left his post while in command. Thus, he was no longer captain of the *Atlantis*. But for you Chief Engineer Brutus Bittner, being a man of few words, I shall choose a more instrumental melody.

"Such wonderful news," Brutus says, watching the bridge crew swimming past in zero-G. "Just like those beanos … risking everyone's lives to pinch a few bucks. I wouldn't put it past them to sweep my ashes into a dustpan when I'm …" Brutus' face pales. His eyes cross. "Wait, Siros! Why did you mention my elegy? Are you telling me I'm about to …" Brutus gulps. "Die?"

Silence.

"Siros, I'm asking you a direct question. Is life coming to an end for me and everyone aboard the *Atlantis*?"

Siros: That much is certain. As for the exact moment, there are too many variables to be precise. However, at this moment I would not want to be a biomass aboard the S. S. *Atlantis*. Things are not looking good for you biotics.

"Siros, quick! Reroute control lines around the main bridge. Send control functions up to the B-deck secondary bridge."

Siros: Negative, Chief Engineer Brutus Bittner. Power diversion requires manual interaction. You will find such a diverter valve located inside the wall-mounted access cabinet outside the main bridge door, approximately two meters to your left. After removing the cover, you reroute control power by first turning the roto-valve a quarter-turn to break power to the primary G-deck bridge. Another quarter-turn will divert power to the B-deck secondary bridge, which, if I might add, is presently a cozier 21 degrees Celsius.

Extracting his shoe from the gravity weld, Brutus kicks off the wall and floats toward a utility closet across from the frosty bridge door. Wedged tight inside the small closet, he slips into the largest of the zero-G boots. Clunking along the floor, he walks up the wall leading up to the access cabinet and then wrestles the door open. His large fingers soon become entangled in control tubing as he feels for the roto-valve handle. Brutus soon tires of battling the cabinet ever-closing door and pops it off its hinges. The normally heavy two-foot square cabinet door floats off as the bridge crew swims past on their second lap.

To gain mechanical advantage, Brutus clamps one mag-boot against the wall, the other to the side of the cabinet. He reaches for the valve handle but finds his large hand cannot penetrate the tight web of wires and plastic pneumatic tubes routed through the cramped cabinet.

"If only I can slip a couple fingers beneath this mess ... get enough leverage to break power to the main bridge," he mumbles. "I can redirect power to the secondary bridge and everything should return to normal."

In near darkness, he weaves his fingers over, under, and around the wire and tubing bundles. When he rediscovers the roto-valve, his thumb and index finger wrap tightly around its slick handle. He fights to slip a second and third finger underneath but finds no room for his oversized fingers. Using but two of his digits, he tugs and tugs on the handle until his thumb and index finger lose their grip.

After giving his hand a good shake, he reinserts the large digits beneath the mess. A firm tug on the handle finally breaks power feeding through the main bridge. The electrical contacts emit a loud arcing SNAP.

The handheld scanner announces purification machinery located in the bowels beginning to shut down. Within minutes, toxic air will be recirculated throughout the *Atlantis*. Brutus has got to rotate the valve handle another quarter-turn.

He continues to tug but the slick handle refuses to budge any further. He repositions his bulky hand inside the tight cabinet until it becomes wedged beneath the harnesses. He leans to one side, feels along the harness and then grabs the handle using his same thumb and index finger. He tugs hard as he can but in spite of his huge girth, he lacks the required mechanical advantage. The roto-valve remains locked in neutral position.

Emergency lights buzz as their internal power cells begin to fail. All around Brutus the already dim lights begrudgingly extinguish, casting him into total darkness. Blaring alarms dwindle as they too run out of juice. Except for flashing red warning lights running off the ship's small backup generators, the *Atlantis* is totally dark. The deathly quiet is interrupted by the bridge crew swimming past for a third lap. Brutus tugs desperately on the diverter handle but in his awkward stance, his thumb slips off the handle, followed by his index finger. With life-support failing, Brutus begins to panic. Grabbing for the slick valve handle, he comes up with a handful of wires and tubing. He shivers at chills running down his spine and at the strange clunking sounds echoing throughout the corridor.

The clunking grows louder with each step. Propelling off a wall, Peter backstrokes closer. He latches onto one of the chief engineer's beefy shoulders. "Hear that noise, Brutus? The creatures powering the *Atlantis'* machines have escaped from their cages. They've somehow found their way up to the G-deck. What the hell are we gonna do now?"

"Creatures? Cages? What the hell are you talking about, Peter?" Brutus brushes the distressed navigator off with a whisk of his free hand. But hearing the loudening clunks approaching from somewhere around the corner, he almost believes the navigator's fear. Picking out two pairs of distinct clunks and daring not abandon the cabinet, he again shivers.

Something brushes past Brutus' shoulder. He feels small hands reaching past his own and pulling control lines and wiring off to one side. He feels the warmth of an adult-sized hand bumps up against his own and wraps around the diverter handle. In swift lateral motion, the valve handle rotates a full quarter turn, rerouting control power to the B-deck secondary bridge. Electrical contacts SNAP, leaving an acrid taste of beryllium on Brutus' tongue—sharp and bitter.

Overhead lights once again illuminate. The next instant, gravity returns. Brutus watches Peter and Pol catching themselves with their hands to prevent landing on their heads. He cringes at the loud THUMP behind him and turns to see the first mate lying on the floor beneath the heavy diverter cabinet door. Murray's crewmates rush to revive him.

Brutus grins at his old friend hovering above, hands still clamped firmly around the valve handle. "Andorf? Magnetic boots? Night vision glasses? How the hell did you know about magnetic boots?"

Grinning mischievously, Andorf leans closer and whispers. "You never knew our wife's kinky side, did you? Oh, that's right, you were never around. An inner voice told me to stop by a utility cabinet."

Brutus grins. "Binky."

Andorf and the girl release their boots and drop to the floor. Clunking in their mag-boots and holding hands, the pair begins to walk off.

"Hey!" Brutus yells. "Where are you going, Poo?"

Andorf pauses, turns to face Brutus. "Hurry back to the bowels of the starship. Your precious number six has no doubt been missing you. As for me, I've got two kids to raise."

To Brutus' dismay, the girl tugs on Andorf's pants leg. Her sparkling eyes gaze up. "What about me, Daddy? Don't you mean three," she asks, displaying as many fingers.

Andorf grins at Mila. "I stand corrected. Make that two kids and a young lady."

"Huh? What?" Brutus says. "Where'd that scruffy little thing come from? I've never seen her before."

"Remember that vagrant child I mentioned? Brutus, meet Mila."

Brutus' jaw drops. "Mila … like the beast from ancient gypsy folklore?"

Holding her stuffed rabbit, the five-year old cowers behind Andorf. "I'm not a beast, you big bully!" she yells, suddenly charging and kicking fearlessly at the grease-covered man towering above. She then runs back under the safety of Andorf's protective arms.

Grinning widely and chuckling, Andorf takes her hand as they walk off.

Brutus approaches the man with four-fingered hand profanely sticking out and lying unconscious beside the discarded cabinet door. He watches the bridge crewmates doing their best to resuscitate the unconscious first mate. Brutus grumbles. "When Murray awakens, inform him of his new position of the *Atlantis'* Acting Captain."

Siros awakens.

Siros: I placed names of twenty more-qualified candidates in your hand-scanner, Chief Engineer Brutus Bittner. Perhaps you will reconsider one of these more appropriate candidates as your choice of acting captains.

"Siros! Assign Murray as Acting Captain."

Silence.

"Siros, did you hear me? That's an order!"

Siros: My records indicate there are seventy-three Murrays aboard our three starships. Perhaps you mean someone other than 'nine-finger' Murray Barnwell?

"Indeed. Nine-finger Murray Barnwell shall be Acting Captain of the *Atlantis*, Siros."

After a long minute, Siros responds.

Siros: As you wish, Chief Engineer Brutus Bittner.

"Acting Captain?" sputters out a side of Pol's mouth.

Staring dumbfounded at the chief engineer and then back at Murray passed out on the floor, Peter gulps. "Heaven help us all."

*

Binky's log – 21-074403:

Well, that certainly changes things. It's time to find out more about this so-called Mila.

CHAPTER 9

About That Day

Day 35: 1300 -
Titan Outpost rendezvous: 736 days

With Brutus pulling eighteen-hour shifts, Andorf has been left caring for the twin babies and five-year-old stowaway. From the privacy of their cabin, he and Mila watch the overplayed archive of two coffins being removed from freeze chambers in the bowels of the *Atlantis*. Both tear at Acting Captain Murray's touching words, with simulated bugles playing in the background. Thom's empty coffin jettisons out an aft port. Serin's coffin is lowered into position and then jettisoned out to trail behind the late captain's casket. As many times before, they watch in silence at the image of twin coffins fading into the blackness of space.

"Something still bothers me about that day." Andorf says, turning to Mila as he wipes his face. "Why did you run out of surgery yelling out 'not again'?"

Mila's face turns ghostly white. The five-year-old begins to speak but instead covers her eyes with both hands.

Andorf gathers Mila in his arms, waits for her to calm before releasing her. "And I've been wondering just how you ended up on the *Atlantis*. What happened to your parents, Mila?"

Mila drops both hands to wipe her damp eyes. After sniffling, she stutters, as if finding it difficult to speak. "Mommy and I were standing in line. Be brave, she kept saying. Daddy will be joining us soon."

"So, you were boarding the *Atlantis* with your mother on Freedom Day?"

Mila nods. "I heard loud bangs. Everyone was pushing. Soldiers were grabbing people from the line. I turned around and mommy was gone. Then I saw daddy lying on the pavement with mommy kneeling over him.

I could barely see her. Smoke was burning my eyes and it was hard to breathe but I saw her waving me up the ramp. I felt hands on my back pushing me up the ramp. At the top, I looked down to see mommy and others being dragged away."

Andorf gulps. "To the Cos."

"Why'd they kill my da—?" Mila squinches her face. "I mean my other daddy."

"From what I heard, Mila, it was far better to be shot than be taken as a political prisoner."

"I was afraid … alone inside this shiny metal starship." Mila pauses to sniffle. "I was screaming but everyone kept running past, ignoring me. They wouldn't answer me. No one would answer me. It was like I was invisible."

"That was Freedom Day. I suspect everyone had blinders on," Andorf says. Trying to explain how no one was expecting children and how her parents were smuggling her aboard. "That is why you went unnoticed."

"Everywhere I went it was really loud. I ran deep inside the starship, going down and down steps until they ended. There I was, alone with nowhere to go."

Andorf gathers Mila in his arms. He holds her close until she quits sobbing. "I promise my sweet girl, you will never again be alone."

"Being alone was the hardest thing ever."

He releases Mila. At the sink, he splashes water on his face. After towel-drying his face, he winces at the five-year-old. "For me, the hard thing has yet to occur. But it must be done. I've been putting it off far too long." Andorf takes a deep breath as he buzzes for child keeper.

*

Binky's log – 35-131325:

Isn't it odd how opposites attract? Oh, I'm not talking about me and my human Andorf. It is his meticulous technically-minded best friend that concerns me. How can anyone be so damn tidy?

CHAPTER 10

An Old Friend

Day 35: 1350

Future Tenulian phrase: 'naybudah mi fond' – "it is nothing, my friend."

Andorf approaches a B-deck cabin with weighted apprehension. Finding the door ajar, he hands Mila a poly-matrix puzzle and whispers for her to stay put. The moment he soft-steps inside, a dread engulfs him. He had always felt uncomfortable in his best friend's apartment back home on Earth, but now being a bearer of bad news, the burden feels overwhelming.

As before, framed groupings of one-inch paper squares, individually illuminated mounted dead center of the entryway greet him. Everything in the pristine living quarters is tucked within precisely-defined boundaries, museum perfect like Gregory's old apartment back on Earth. In fact, Andorf appears to be the only thing out of place.

This time, Gregory's odor precedes him as he walks the main room in tight circles. Smelling unbathed and bearing a face wearing as many wrinkles as his slept-in clothing, Andorf's once best friend appears acutely tormented. Spotting his old friend in this condition, Andorf waits in the foyer, formulating the appropriate words. Stepping further inside, he reaches to nudge one of the framed paper squares and—

"Hey! Don't touch that!" Gregory calls as he joins Andorf in the entryway. "It took me the better part of a week to put this place back in order after the last gravity mishap."

"I ... uh."

"Yes, I heard you speaking with someone in the doorway. You were loud as hourly workers at quitting time." Gregory flashes a metalized arm in Andorf's direction. "Are you forgetting about my implants? I hear everything within a quarter mile, courtesy of many experimental surgeries the Empire performed on me at the Cos."

"Well ... I."

"And all of a sudden you decide to visit me? You'd think my best friend wouldn't have waited weeks before informing me about my sister."

Avoiding eye contact, Andorf steps further inside. "I–I thought you heard by now. Apparently, everyone expected me to bring you the news."

Gregory leads Andorf further into to the living area and again walks in circles. "I know we haven't been close since my abduction back on Earth but hell, Andorf ... I was dragged off in the middle of the night—"

"To the Cos," Andorf mumbles.

Gregory stares at Andorf for a long, awkward silent moment. "I asked you go to the mountaintop and inform the rebels of my abduction."

Andorf shakes his head.

"But we went through all that, Andorf, right down to the last detail. If either of us were to be captured, the survivor was to climb the hills in the pre-dawn and inform those who sung protests to the starship each glorious sunrise."

Andorf cringes. "Well, I ..."

"To worsen matters, I had to relocate to the *Atlantis*. The bigoted captain of the *S.S. Phoenix* was making everyone's life unbearable. Argent's more of dictator than a captain."

Andorf does his best to smile as he looks about. "I see you have the place fixed up like the old apartment. I—I mean before the agents broke down your door and trashed the place."

Gregory's eyes narrow. "And what's this I hear about me having a new niece and nephew?"

Lost for words, Andorf stares at Gregory's bare feet.

Gregory strolls over to a corner of the room. He picks up a micro-driver off a shelf and then methodically adjusts one of his troubling metal implants.

Andorf cringes at the squealing sounds as he scans a collection of home-made whatnots lining the rear of the workbench. As he grabs to spin one of the knobs, he hears Gregory yelling at him to not touch.

"What you see is the basic signal injector, waveform slicer, and bench scope."

It all goes over Andorf's head. As in Gregory's apartment before, he is lost in tech-land.

Displaying rage, Gregory slams the micro-driver down onto the workbench. "Dammit, Andorf! You're acting just like the others, avoiding me because of my disfigurements. Am I so disgusting even *you* can't bear my sight?"

"Not so, Gregory. Nothing could be further from the truth."

"Oh, I see the fear on kids' faces out there in the hallways. They're always snickering and pointing. I can accept it from them, but you … I thought you of all people would be more—"

Andorf approaches Gregory casting outfacing palms. "Stop right there. Serin may have been your sister but she was my wife. My whole world revolved around her. Don't you think I've been struggling? Everything has come crashing down around me. Have you considered that?"

Beginning to twitch, Gregory's eyes widen. He takes several deep breaths. "Well, I thought it was a rather nice ceremony. You know … the fake bugles and such. Acting Captain Murray's final words were rather touching."

Andorf stares hypnotized staring at the animated movements of Gregory's kitty clock collection at eye-level on the wall. Though each wind-up clock bears slightly different time, the tick-tocking eyes and wagging tails are in perfect unison.

"You still don't carry a timepiece, do you, Andorf? Andorf! Are you listening to me?" Gregory waves a hand in front of Andorf's face to break the spell.

"You know how well I trust technology." Andorf clears his throat. "Now about Serin—"

"It's a good thing she was …"

"She was what?" Andorf snaps.

Gregory takes another deep breath, as if wanting to say more. "Naybudah mi fond."

"Huh?"

"It is nothing, my friend. As you were saying?"

Andorf peers deep into Gregory's brown eyes, wades through his best friend's thoughts. He finds every neural pathway pertaining to Serin either missing or blocked. He leans back to examine Gregory's facial features. "Well, it's just certain things have occurred since those apartment days."

"It's my large nose, isn't it? It reminds you of her, doesn't it?"

Andorf nods. "Serin's brown eyes ... her high cheeks ... her—"

"Flowery perfume. Ah yes, her flowery perfume. Oh, I never should've introduced the two of you."

"You had nothing to do with us meeting. You were well on your way to the Cos by the time we met. Do you recall breaking into the Archives the previous evening ... agents tracking us back to your apartment ... the loud pounding on your doors as we hid beneath your bed?"

"Damn dust! If only we'd stayed clear of that damn dust. First, I miss my sister's wedding, let alone her marrying my best friend, and now I've got a niece and nephew of whom I have yet to meet."

"Gregory stop! Don't you think I have my hands full with the babies? I have left the cabin only a handful of times since Serin's death. Not only do I have my responsibilities but with Serin gone, I am saddled with her tasks as well."

"How hard can it be, Andorf? I've heard neighbors are helping watch the kids."

The cabin door swings open a bit wider, revealing a curious five-year-old girl peeking inside. At Andorf's hand gesture, Mila steps cautiously inside. Leaving her puzzle behind, she runs up to examine the mechanically-enhanced man from behind the safety of Andorf's pants leg.

At the sight of the curious five-year-old, Gregory's scowl morphs into a genuine, heart-warming smile. "And who do we have here?" he says, bending down for a better view of Mila.

The proud father of three scoops the bashful girl up in his arms. "Gregory, this is Mila. She was with me in sickbay when Serin passed. I don't know what I would have done if my precious girl wasn't there."

Gregory breaks into a chuckle. "Mila? As from ancient gypsy folklore?"

"Am I the only one unaware of this fable?" Andorf mumbles.

"I'm not a beast!" Mila yells, pointing a tiny finger at the mechanical-looking man.

Gregory's voice softens. "Why, I'd never think such a thing of a pretty little girl. Anyone who calls you that would be a—"

"Bully," Mila snorts. "A big, fat, greasy bully."

Raising a brow, Gregory leans toward Andorf. "I take it she's met the big ox?"

Andorf nods. "Brutus? Yes indeed."

With Mila squirming in his arms, Andorf eases her onto the floor. The moment her feet touch down, she runs the length of the entryway, investigating Gregory's collection of animated clocks, all with tick-tocking eyes and wagging tails in perfect unison, but each displaying slightly different times.

"Gregory was my best friend," Andorf calls out to her. "Long before the starship hijackings."

"Still am," Gregory says, strolling over to whisper in Mila's ear. "Much has happened since your daddy and I hung out back in the day. Did you know, Mila, I'm stuffed full of wonderful stories?"

"Not only was Gregory my downstairs neighbor, but he was—"

Mila looks Gregory over. "Serin's brother," she squeaks out.

"So, that makes me your uncle, doesn't it?" Winking at Andorf, Gregory scoops Mila into his arms. He gently wipes the remnants of dried tears with a damp cloth held in one of his mechanized hands. When his head begins to twitch, he lowers the five-year-old onto the floor. Mila stares in concern up at her uncle's sudden jerking motions.

"You must not be afraid." Andorf steps closer. "You see, Gregory was ..."

Gregory taps Andorf's shoulder and then nods.

"Your Uncle Gregory was one of many political prisoners. The Canine Empire performed all sorts of experiments on him while he was detained in—"

"The Cos," Mila says, peering up at her new-found uncle. "I know all about the Cos. But why do you shake like that? Did they put jumping beans in you when you were sleeping?"

Chuckling, Gregory stoops down to Mila's level. "I caught something called Tourette syndrome. It was from all the drugs they pumped in my veins. Now, see these metal pieces?"

Mila reaches out to touch, but then freezes.

"Most of these scars are from removing tracking devices and such." He pinches Mila's nose. "It's okay. You can touch them if you'd like."

Andorf cringes. "You must visit with your nephew and other niece, Uncle Gregory. Even at two weeks old, baby Ayla has your ... uhh—"

Mila's eyes widen. "Large nose, Uncle Greg."

Gregory laughs harder. "I must admit, large honkers *are* dominant in the Gray bloodline." He takes a good look at his best friend and sneers. "Andorf, you don't look at all well. Are you still not sleeping? It's those dreams, isn't it? I'll bet you're still being haunted by all those dreams."

Andorf nods. "Only now it is voices. I hear many at the same time, garbled together and yelling. I cannot understand any of them. There seems to be one dominant angry voice but even this one I cannot—"

"Spiders and cows," Mila blurts out. "The angry man is saying spiders and cows."

Andorf's jaw drops. "How do you know this, Mila? I never mentioned it anyone until now."

"I hear voices too, Daddy."

Gregory snickers. "You've been known to talk in your sleep. Perhaps Mila has ..."

"No! No! No!" Mila yells, shaking her head." I hear the voices even when ..."

"When what, Mila?"

"Even when I'm awake."

Hand on chin, Gregory begins to pace about the room. "I too haven't been sleeping well. I feel a presence ... an evil presence ... to the likes I've not felt in many years."

*

Binky's log – 35-142002:

Uneasiness has been building throughout the three-starship fleet. Perhaps Gregory is not the only one feeling this evil presence.

PART 2
THE TENULIANS

CHAPTER 11

The New Bridge

Day 122 - Titan Outpost rendezvous: 649 days

Blaming everything from Andorf and Mila hearing voices to the twin babies' cries, Brutus takes residence in the vacant master suite next door. In reality, six weeks of grieving was eating away at his soul like acid rain. But he hardly complains. The enormous suite was originally built to accommodate Fat Max and cater to the eight-foot beast's every whim has its perks. The private shower, dining room, elevator, and dumbwaiter from the F-deck kitchen are comforts previously unknown. A long-awaited buzz on the intercom catches him shoveling a complete dwarf muffin down his throat.

"Bridge reconstruction has been completed, sir. It's ready for inspection."

The chief engineer abruptly swallows before quenching his parched throat with pino juice from a half-filled carafe. The tart drink leaves him coughing for the better part of a minute. He grabs for the intercom's ACCEPT button and knowing how the box's tiny microphone filters out his low-pitched voice, shifts the pitch of his voice an octave higher.

"About time you clowns completed this project. Why, Stoner Chong could have finished the work in half the time."

Silence.

Brutus swears he hears voices in the background. After maxing the intercom's volume, the muffled laughter becomes clear. The tiny speaker crackles at the technician's snickering whispers.

"And the guy has no life."

"I'll bet he watches nothing but historical documentaries."

After draining the carafe, Brutus disconnects. He stuffs the last dwarf muffin in his shirt pocket and then steps inside his most treasured amenity, the suite's private elevator. Intended to serve the much larger original occupant, the elevator's spacious area could easily contain a pair of full-grown stallions.

The elevator door opens on the G-deck. Peering beyond impatient repair techs flanking either side, he sees Acting Captain Murray standing poised outside the bridge door, between embattled navigator Peter and radioman Pol, as if separating them to keep peace.

Both techs salute as Brutus exits the elevator doors and walks between them. The youngest tech appears to be bubbling over. Face reddening, as if having feasted on a foot-tall stack of Oxnard hotcakes for breakfast, he is first to speak.

"Captain Thom's hastened exit out the front portals left the main bridge in shambles. Why couldn't he have taken the airlock door like everyone else?"

Acting Captain Murray sprints across the hallway. Within seconds he is pointing his remaining four fingers in the young tech's face. "Have you no respect for the late Thom Mallory? If not for my brave predecessor, we'd all be back on Earth, living beneath repressive thumbs of the Canine Empire."

The slightly-more senior tech wedges between them. He pushes his naïve counterpart aside. "No disrespect intended Acting Captain Murray, but what the young squirt meant was how the instrument panels were damaged beyond repair. It appears each piece fell victim to freezing temperatures and severe pressure drops. It took us a_better part of a month to fabricate parts from scratch. All these one-of-a-kind instruments were custom-replicated and painstakingly calibrated."

The younger tech reluctantly nods. "And replacing viewport windows on our spacewalk was no easy task."

Murray grumbles. "I expect all instruments are now back where they belong and are fully operational?"

"Certainly." The senior tech exchanges glances with his counterpart before turning to the Acting Captain. The techs peer at the chief engineer as if awaiting his approval. At Brutus' nod, they quickly disperse.

Hearing Peter and Pol arguing, Brutus steps around Murray to address the matter. "And what's with the two of you?" he growls. "It'd better not be that jealousy bit again. You've been living together for what, four months?"

Peter distances himself on the far side of Brutus, away from the comm-spec. He stares at Pol from behind the line of safety. "One-hundred and twenty two days to be exact. That's how long the three of us have been living together in that cabin."

Brutus snickers.

"You couldn't possibly know what it's like," Pol snaps back. "Have you ever time-shared your girlfriend with someone you despise? I don't know how much more I can take before I kill the bastard."

Best you both get over this," Brutus says, rolling his eyes. "We've got more pressing matters to deal with than these constant petty squabbles."

Pol pokes his head around Murray. He winces at Peter. "I get so mad when I see him and Amy together. When they're in the same room, they are smiling at each other as if they're doing things behind my back."

"I demand you both stop this right now! You'll either lose your minds or …" Brutus freezes, staring up as if lost in space.

Pol grabs hold of Brutus' robust shoulders with both hands. He stares beyond Brutus' glazed look. "Like what, Mr. Brutus? What in the world could be worse than going insane?"

In a radial thrust, Brutus grabs the comm-spec by the shoulders and nails him against the wall. "Your wife dying, that's what could be worse! I should only be as lucky as the both of you, sharing a lover who's still alive. What I would give to be in your situation."

As if knowing not to interfere, Murray steps alongside his comm-spec to peer at him. His eyes bounce off Peter as well. "Give it a rest, Pol. You are both to get along. That's an order."

"Like we'd ever listened to you," Pol mumbles.

Peter points threateningly at his adversary. "Get along with that S.O.B.? Ha!"

Still holding Pol down, Brutus grabs the navigator with his free hand and slams him against the utility cabinet across from the bridge door. "Don't think for a damn microsecond I wouldn't give everything to have Serin back in my arms, be sharing her again with Andorf." His eyes toggle between the pair. "I'd do anything to be in your shoes. Anything! Hear me? Anything!"

Acting Captain Murray takes hold of Brutus' bulky arms as if hoping to coax him into releasing his startled crewmates.

Eyeing Peter and Pol suspiciously, Brutus concedes. He watches the comm-spec and navigator regain their footing. "What you're experiencing is detachment from everything you've known from back on Earth. In due time it'll pass."

Acting Captain Murray winces. "Captain Thom frequently warned us of such a fate, that the detachment would drive each and every last one of us first gens mad." Wielding a pair of pliers from his back pocket, Murray orders his crew to step aside and allow Brutus access to the control cabinet.

Noting the tool, Brutus reaches into his pocket and then presents his last dwarf muffin to the Acting Captain. "Don't crush that dwarf, Murray. Hand me those pliers."

Murray complies.

With a twist of Brutus' wrist, the control panel opens to reveal an array of gauges and lights, all displaying a friendly Kelly green. When he flips the master switch, the bridge's airlock door squeaks open in a wobbly SWOOSH.

A burnt smell of recent welds greets Brutus as he exchanges Murray's pliers for his last dwarf muffin. After inspecting the muffin, he plops it into his mouth and then leads the bridge crew through the open airlock. Brutus peers at the fire extinguisher on the wall to the right of the door. At sight of a large red axe hanging directly above he falls back a step, blocking passage.

Pol pushes past. "What the matter, Brutus? Haven't you ever seen an ax before?"

"Uh … uh…"

Peter looks strangely at the chief engineer as he struggles to squeeze around the large man. "Every bridge dating back to the airline days has had a red axe like that one. It's standard equipment on every starship bridge."

Murray winces. "What other defense would a bridge crew have against saboteurs?"

"Or to corner your daughter's boyfriend in a dark, musty woodshed," Brutus mumbles, under his breath. Recalling thick spider webs covering him, he hand-brushes his clothing.

Seated at the radios, Pol reorders misplaced tags and reattaches missing wiring patch cords.

Peter frets over his missing collection of archaic measuring devices which once hung from hooks overhead. He hovers above the navigational instruments, familiarizing himself with the redesigned interface. His eyes suddenly widen at sight of a cluster of forty-plus lights, all converging on the three lights in dead center of the radial screen. His face sours.

Wearing headphones, Pol's partially hidden face displays an equally horrid face. Stepping closer, Brutus yanks Pol's headphone plug out of its radio jack. Arguing voices immediately pour out the radio's twin speakers. One phase-distorted voice in heavy accent blasting above the others seems to be making demands.

"Speak Spider! Speak Spider cow!" the angry voice yells.

Pol leaps from his seat. In spite of his and Peter's differences, he joins Murray at the navigator's screen. The crew stares, bewildered by the forty-plus light blips encircling three smaller blips.

Sweating profusely, Murray wanders about the bridge. He makes it halfway back before collapsing into the over-stuffed captain's chair. "They'll head straight to the bridge ... come after the captain, or in my case, the Acting Captain. They always make an example of the head of the bridge. Captain Thom often told us so."

Brutus scratches his head. "What are you talking about, Murray? What the hell's going on here?"

Peter gazes at the others. "The dots ... they're much closer than before."

"And those voices," Pols adds. "They're much louder than before."

"Before?" Brutus yells, rushing to the navigation screen. His eyes widen at sight of the forty plus lights surrounding three others on the screen. "Why am I only now finding out about this? Why hasn't anyone reported this?"

"We—we kind of got distracted," Peter gulps. "You know, with the view-ports cracking and everyone fleeing the bridge it seemed the least of our worries."

Pol winces, "Captain Thom was in the middle of assessing the situation when—"

"When he was jettisoned into space," Murray adds. "We watched video footage … all four minutes of it before the cameras froze."

Looking about the bridge, Brutus wants nothing more than to punch someone or something. He pauses to contemplate the consequences of taking such action. Instead, he stares at the flashing lights on the navigation screen. "Can I assume those three blips in the center are our fleet?"

Peter nods. "We suspect the other blips to be rogue starships."

"Converging upon us," adds the acting captain.

About to hyperventilate, Brutus extracts a well-worn fiber bag from his back pocket. He takes several deep breaths and then pulls the bag off his face. "Am I hearing this right? An armada of forty starships is closing in on us?"

Murray gulps. "That's the gist of it."

Brutus takes a deep breath. He begins to reach for his trusty fiber bag but pauses. "Siros, how soon until the *Atlantis* is within boarding range?"

Siros, the starship's conscience quickly awakens.

Siros: Maintaining present speed and vector, Chief Engineer Brutus Bittner, the *Atlantis* and her sister starships will be seized in three weeks and eight hours give or take two-and-a-half hours.

Peter raises a brow. "Oh, yeah, Siros? If you're so smart, what are the voices on Pol's radio saying?"

Siros: Cannot comply. I answer only to Chief Engineer Brutus Bittner and Acting Captain Murray.

Murray winces. "Siros, what does 'speak Spider cow' mean?"

After a long moment, the starship's conscience replies.

Siros: References to spiders and cows in my databases do not translate properly for this situation. Now if you'd like references about speaking spiders and cows—

Brutus waves his hand. "Siros, enough!" He begins to leave but pauses to address the Acting Captain. "Andorf mentioned reliving a past life quite often. Perhaps my old friend may be able to enlighten us. Call the Goshi to the bridge. Have him listen to this angry man."

Murray nods.

Before exiting the bridge, Brutus throws a pointed finger back at the acting captain and his crew. "I'm warning each of you now. If you spill the beans about what actually happened to Serin ..." He scowls at the crew's souring faces. "There'll be hell to pay."

"What?" Murray says, smirking. "Don't tell me Andorf doesn't know."

Pol chuckles. "Of course the Goshi knows. Everyone knows about the recycle program."

"It's been months," Murray mumbles. "How long can the guy remain in denial?"

"It's much too soon," Brutus says. "The guy would go nuts. I've seen him in such a condition. We definitely don't want to go there."

Peter winces. "But can't Andorf read other's thoughts? Surely, he at least suspects."

Brutus rolls his eyes. "He's too emotional to accept this reality. Believe me, now's not a good time."

"The guy's a bit touchy, if you ask me." Murray grumbles. "Serin was a great leader but she's—"

Brutus darts across the small bridge. His massive hand wraps around the Acting Captain's throat, pins him against a bridge wall. "Another word about my deceased wife and I'll rip your tongue out—" Holding Murray firmly, he grabs the pliers from the Acting Captain's pocket and waves it in each of the crew's faces. "And mention any of this to Andorf and I'll rip out your tongues as well ... every last one of them. Hear me? Every last one of your tongues!"

*

Binky's log – 122-095025:

Wow. Someone really ticked off the chief engineer. But what about those voices? Even that useless Siros could not help. Hopefully, my Andorf can make some sense of this.

CHAPTER 12
Voices

Day 123 - Titan Outpost rendezvous: 648 days

Andorf flinches at the urgent message crackling in the tiny intercom speaker. Opening the cabin door, he hears the same message echoing down the hallway and sees neighbors lining both sides of the hallway. All seem to be offering to watch after his twin babies. He turns around and sees the twins in their cribs appearing to be waving him away with their tiny hands.

He hand-gestures Mila to stay put but she pays him no mind. Shoving a stuffed rabbit beneath her arm, she chases after him down the A-deck hallway only to lasso a pinky through one of his belt loops. The insistent five-year-old is dragged several feet before Andorf halts in his tracks. Batting eyes at her daddy, Mila stands her ground.

"No, Mila. I have no time for this."

"But Daddy ..."

"I said no."

Mila stomps her feet and yells. "But I want to see the spiders and cows."

Andorf's brow furrows. He bends down, scoops Mila into his arms, and dashes through the winding A-deck corridor. Her arms wrap tight around

Andorf's neck, regulating his progress via airway constriction as he ignores his own rules and leaps down six flights of floating steps. Arriving on the G-deck landing, he pants out of breath.

Relinquishing her death grip, Mila lands onto the floor. She scampers ahead, leaving Andorf wondering how in the world he will ever keep up with the rambunctious five-year-old. Standing on tiptoes, Mila presses the mushroom-shaped door release button. The bridge door opens with a SWOOSH. She blocks the door, flailing her hands for Andorf to get his butt in gear.

Upon entering the bridge, Andorf senses the acting captain's discomfort. Even though the new captain's chair now has three longer bolts securing it to the floor joists, he catches Murray squatting and examining the chair's bolt heads as if unconvinced of improved safety of the latest fasteners.

"If Captain Thom had only listened," Murray mumbles, swiveling the chair. "He'd be here right now, warming this seat."

Andorf peers at the bridge crew. He spots Peter and Pol glaring at each other from behind their stations.

Mila pushes past. Stuffed rabbit tucked under her arm, she skips across the bridge heading straight for the troubled Acting Captain. Eying Murray's burned-off middle finger, she reaches to touch. "Why do they call it a bird finger, Acting Captain Murray? Did you have a little birdie? Did your little birdie get mad at you and bite you finger off?"

Smiling awkwardly at the inquisitive youngster, Murray slips the hand with the abbreviated digit inside a pocket. "Say missy, where'd you get that furry guy? I lost mine the just other day. I'll bet this one's mine." He then grabs at the toy with his complete hand.

Mila swings her stuffed bunny away, far from Murray's clutches. "Sabrina can't be yours. She's Binky's girlfriend. My first one smelled really bad so Papa Brutus made Sabrina on his replicator machine. Papa said he could replicate people too, but their glicker skin would feel like plastic."

Andorf grins. "Glycerin."

"I'm sure Papa would replicate you a new finger if you ask him real nice."

Shivering at the thought, Murray points above the bridge door. "What's with your gypsy friend, Andorf? The chief engineer seemed terrified by the axe."

"An axe?" Andorf scratches his head.

"The big red axe over there ... above the bridge door." Peter points. "Every starship bridge has had one since the beginning of flight."

Andorf gazes above the bridge door. "If the axe bothers him, I advise you to remove it."

Murray winces. "And do what with it?"

"Damn, Murray! Just hide it! Now what was your urgent call is about?"

Andorf is flagged over to the navigational screen. He stares at the nearly four dozen blinking lights. After a moment, his eyes widen. "I suspect those three flashing dots in the middle represent our fleet?"

Peter nods. "And the forty-three dots surround them are the starships encircling us."

Andorf collapses into the navigator's buddy seat. Visions of the Canine Empire's militia, armed to their teeth and swarming through the *Atlantis* rip through his thoughts. He envisions passengers yanked from their cabins and packed into cages to await transport back to Earth. "After so many months," he mumbles. "I should have known it would only be a matter of time."

Acting Captain Murray winces. "Siros tells us the forty-three starships will be within boarding range in a matter of weeks."

"But that's not the worst of it," Pol adds.

Andorf begins shivers. "What could be worse than the Empire reclaiming its three prized starships and emancipated citizens?"

Pol is now flailing his hands. The comm-spec unplugs his headphones. A collection of jumbled voices blasts out the radio's twin speakers in what sounds like a bad mix of vulgar rap songs.

Andorf rises and then grabs the seatback to steady himself. "Those voices, they are the same ones which have kept me awake for far too many nights."

Mila grins at the crew's long faces. "I hear them too."

"They're the same ones as before." Pol raises a brow. "Only now they're much louder."

"Much louder," Peter adds.

"Only now? Andorf says rubbing his chin. He suddenly drops his hand. "Wait! How long has all this been going on?"

Pol gulps. "You—you can't really blame us. When we heard them last, the bridge alarms were all wailing."

"And—and viewports were cracking." Peter winces. "The three of us barely escaped out the airlock with our lives."

Murray sniffs. "Unlike Captain Thom."

Andorf's eyes narrow on the crew. "So, after all these months, what may have been corrected has bloomed into a full-fledged crisis?"

While the silent crew stares at the freshly-painted ceiling of the repaired bridge, Mila runs about, wild-eyed and hands out. "Look at all the buttons and switches and flashing lights. What's this blinking light do?"

"Easy there, little one. Hasty actions carry severe consequences." Peter grabs for Mila's reaching hand. At sight of Andorf's scorn, he retracts his outstretched hands.

"Who the hell are these guys on the radio?" Andorf says. "They are not militia. They sound disjointed and confused."

"We've been trying to make heads or tails out of the pileup. Brutus thought we should contact you." Murray grins at Andorf. "We're hoping you could enlighten us. Go ahead, Pol. Let Andorf hear the cleaned-up version."

Playing back the snippet, Pol tweaks rows of quintessential filters. One lone phase-distorted voice speaking with harsh accent dominates the conversations. The others quiet when he speaks.

"Manwick Spider! Speewick Spider cow!"

Andorf eyes Mila spinning around in Pol's seat. "This angry-sounding man ... he seems to demand something called Manwick Spider Cow."

"A man with a spider cow," Mila blurts out, laughing.

Murray exchanges estranged gazes with the others. "We've searched starship registries from Manfred to Manzini. Nothing comes remotely close to Manwick."

Peter snickers. "Know-it-all Siros was less than useless."

Pol scratches his head. "Manwick must be some sort of code ... you know ... a nickname."

Hand rubbing his chin, Andorf begins to pace about the small bridge. "Spiders ... cows ... hmm. Where have I heard this before?"

Mila trails behind him, tugging insistently on his dangling arm. Each time she begins to speak, Andorf silences her with a pat on the head. The five-year-old quiets. Her face swells to a deep cherry-red color. She appears as to be choking on more than words.

Staring at the girl, Pol's eyes widen. "Great tides of Sansifer, Andorf! Let the child speak."

Peter covers both ears. "Hurry! Do it now, before she explodes."

Murray signals for Pol to silence the radio. "Go ahead, little one. Speak your piece."

Mila scans the adult faces, verifying all eyes focused upon her. With Andorf's hands prompting her, Mila bursts out. "He means Serin! The angry man wants to speak to Serin."

"Speak spider cow." Andorf's eyes widen. "Why, of course. Speak with spider now. This Spider he is referring to must be my Serin. It could be no one else."

Peter stares perplexed. "But how can that be? Serin's been dead nearly two months. No disrespect intended," he says, turning eyes toward Andorf.

"Not that you're even capable of respect," Pol grumbles not so quietly.

Andorf slowly cracks a smile. "Why this makes perfect sense. Serin is the one this madman calls Spider. With her leading the revolt ... the starship hi-jackings, I can see how an outsider could believe she is still in charge."

Murray half-way grins at Andorf. "Your late wife *is* the reason we're on *The Atlantis*, speeding toward planet Nero."

The bridge's airlock SWOOSHES open. Gregory Gray steps boldly inside. He scans all the concerned faces. "What's all this brouhaha?"

"Boo ha ha!" Mila shouts.

To Andorf's amazement, Mila runs past and jumps into her uncle's inviting arms. He begins to speak, but instead grins at Mila's admiration of his best friend. "Gregory? What brings you to the bridge?"

Gregory releases Mila and then taps Andorf's shoulder. "Is there any truth in the rumors I hear about alien vessels out there surrounded our fleet?"

"Forty-three starships to be exact." Murray winces. "We suspect they've come from Earth's six other empires."

Peter grins wide as if boasting. "Andorf's little girl did what Siros could not. She broke the radio code."

Appearing confused, Gregory looks about. "Radio? Code? What the hell's going on here?"

Pol replays the cleaned-up audio snippet. One lone voice screams out of the radio's twin speakers.

"Manwick Spider! Speewick Spider cow!"

"He wants to speak with Serin," Mila bursts out, twirling around to take ownership of the matter.

Gregory's jaw drops. "Serin? You mean my deceased sister, Serin?"

Murray nods. "That's right, the organizer of the Freedom Day mutiny."

"The coup d'état," Peter adds.

Giving strange looks, Gregory begins to gleam. "Why, of course. Serin *is* the reason we're out here millions of miles from home. Everyone must know I was her contact inside the Cos." He pauses suddenly. His face reddens. His eyes narrow. "Wait a minute. Is my sister the spider or the cow?"

Andorf grins. "By the way she wove an intricate web of dedicated followers, I would think the Spider."

"How about all those gadgets she built," Pol says.

Murray grins wide. "Like the transmitter which remotely-triggered the security alarms at the Cos? I was there. I helped launch the antenna with a helium balloon."

Gregory also grins. "And look how Serin slipped through the Empire's best agent's hands like water. I have no doubt word of her revolution spread amongst the other empires. Renegades of those empires must have followed suit. Who else could they be, out here six months from our home world?"

Andorf winces. "These encroaching starships must contain refugees who like us have escaped their own repressive empires."

Peter appears short-winded, on the verge of panic. "Now we've figured out who these guys are but what are we going to do? There's some lunatic leading them who wants to speak with Serin but she's been—"

Murray slaps a hand over the navigator's mouth. Pol threatens Peter with twisting hand motions as if he were holding pliers and anxious to yank out his adversary's tongue.

Feeling a sudden detachment, Andorf senses Murray and his crew redirecting their thoughts. One by one, he reads the thoughts behind their solemn faces.

Pol thinks about his girlfriend, how Amy forced him to share her with Peter. Peter imagines having a much larger place of his own without Pol. Murray replays highlights of the past World Series game in his head."

Despite Gregory's hand trying to hold him back and telling his friend arguing for him to do otherwise, Andorf's eyes narrow. His voice sharpens in a pious tongue. "The chief engineer has forbidden everyone to say anything, has he not? I see it in all your insincere faces. I agree Brutus is a beastly large man but I warn you. He *is not* the one you should fear."

The Acting Captain smirks but quits as all but one overhead light extinguishes and a ruby-red glow focuses on his burned-off middle finger. Taking hold of his abbreviated hand, Murray jumps outside the laser-like spotlight. "Stop that," he yells. "I've got nothing to say."

When Pol snickers, Andorf eyes him suspiciously. The comm-spec grabs at his throat. He gags until Andorf mentally releases him.

Peter begins to sweat. As if knowing he is next, he stares at the array of lights converging on the three blinking lights in dead center of his screen. "Wait," he says. "Replay that snippet, Pol. Let's hear the angry man's voice again."

Pol raises the volume and fiddles with the quintessential filters until one dominant Middle-Eastern voice jumps out the radio's twin speakers. With Mila having deciphered the message, the man's demands magically clarify.

"I demand to speak with Spider! I must speak with Spider now!"

Gregory stumbles backward. One of his mechanical hands holds his head as it shakes side to side. "No! No! No! This cannot be happening."

With the exception of Mila swiveling around playfully in Peter's seat, the bridge quiets.

"If this guy is who I suspect, his name is Turk. We must steer clear of the bastard … avoid him at all cost. There's absolutely no bargaining with the maniac. You hear me? No bargaining!"

"So, how bad can this guy be, Gregory?" Peter grins. "We exchange greetings … do a little trading … be on our way."

Gregory's head twitches out of control before locking, tilted to one side. After pulling his head straight with both mechanized hands, he stares, twisted-brow at the navigator. "How bad can this Turk be you ask? For starters, the tyrant stabbed an older brother for merely snoring in his sleep."

Peter gulps. "His brother?"

"But that's not the worst of it. In a jealous rage, Turk shot his dog after it crawled in bed with his wife. The dog survived but I cannot say as much for the brother."

"His own dog?" Pol's face turns green. He grabs a fiber bag from beneath his seat and quickly vanishes out the bridge door.

SWOOSH!

"As I said, Turk's no one we want to deal with. The narcissist is without conscience. He'll turn on us like a—"

"Snake!" Andorf's mouth sours, looking about for a place to spit. "I have had close experiences with such a soul-less creature. It is something I dare not repeat."

Covering the wet spot staining his slacky-khakis with his full-fingered hand, Murray rises slowly. He gazes first at the damp captain's seat and then at the others. His voice flutters. "Look at the way his ships are surrounding our fleet. Turk's planning to take command of our fleet, beginning right here with the *Atlantis*."

Gregory nods. "Turk and his clan are pirates. They're expecting to raid us for easy pickings?"

Andorf scratches the overgrowth on his chin. "Like us, they must be heading for Titan Outpost to refuel."

Peter throws both hands up. "Perhaps the guy merely wants to join our pilgrimage. As Andorf said, they're most likely renegades, escaping from belligerent empires such as our own."

Andorf leers at the navigator. "That was before I found out about this maniac."

Pol returns, wiping his dripping mouth and crinkling a spent puke bag. "Are you deaf *and* stupid, Peter? You heard what Gregory said. The bastard shot a dog … his own dog."

Perspiration drips off the acting captain's forehead. Like Gregory, his hands begin to twitch uncontrollably. "Turk's coming straight for this bridge. He'll assimilate all of us like cyborgs." He pauses to wince apologetically at Gregory and his metal appendages. "No offense, Gregory."

"None taken." Gregory turns to face the Acting Captain. "No doubt they'll take your bridge, Murray ... along with those on the *Mayflower* and *Phoenix*. That's what ruthless tyrants do."

"Oh, why isn't Captain Thom still here?" Murray cries out. "He would've known what to do. The captain was supposed to live forever, not die and leave *me* in command."

Andorf taps Murray's shoulder. "Get a grip, Murray. You are Acting Captain of the *Atlantis*. I am sure Thom Mallory had good reason for appointing you as his first mate."

The crew silences as Andorf turns away.

"Though I have no idea why," Andorf mumbles. Taking a deep breath, he turns back and peers back at the Acting Captain. "Like it or not, Murray, you *must* play the hand you have been dealt."

"How? I got no respect as the captain's first-mate, even less now as acting captain. And what's with everyone addressing me as *acting* captain? What'll it take for me to become a full-fledged captain?"

"You become a genuine captain when you're faced with a true crisis," Gregory says. "That's when you officially take command of the *Atlantis*."

Andorf returns to the navigation screen. After long moments of squinting at the blinking lights, he gazes back at the Acting Captain. "I believe your time has arrived, Murray."

Silent and wide-eyed, Murray settles into the captain chair, staring off as if realizing he has chewed off more reality than he could ever possibly swallow. "I never signed up for any of this," he mumbles. "Had I known it would come down to dealing with pirates, I would've stayed back at the Cos. I would've ended up disfigured like Gregory but at least I'd still be alive."

Gregory sneers at Murray. "Until they wheeled you into the power cell factory on a gurney."

"How soon, Siros?" Andorf says. "How much time do we have before the *Atlantis* and her sister starships are overtaken?"

Siros: I answer only to Chief Engineer Brutus Bittner and ... Acting Captain Murray.

"And ..." Andorf squints. Deep lines span the length of his face.

Siros: And Goshi, Andorf Johnson.

Andorf cringes at the nickname. "Siros, how much time remains before these forty-three pirate ships overtake us?"

Murray winces. "Siros, we need something more exact than a few weeks.""

Siros: Of course, Acting Captain Murray. According to the forty-three ships' current speed and vector, the lead starship will be within boarding range in twenty-one days, six hours, and thirty-five minutes, give or take two hours.

Andorf squints again. "Siros, make that Captain Murray."

Silence.

"Siros!"

Siros: Captain Murray ... noted.

The crew stares at Andorf in disbelief before shifting focus to Peter's navigation screen. All stare in silence, as if expecting answers will surface on the screen, to the likes of an old Magic 8 ball.

"Hmm," Gregory mumbles, staring at his best friend while scratching his head. He grins at his niece, fast asleep on the floor, before gazing back at the captain. "Perhaps we could change course, head off in a slightly different direction."

"Our flight path is pre-programmed," Captain Murray says. "Besides, there's barely enough fuel to reach Titan Outpost. Even if we could deviate from the set course by as little as a quarter-degree would throw us way off course."

"We'd never make it to the fueling station," Peter adds.

Andorf continues to rub his furry chin. "If an invasion is imminent, let us head it off. We shall prepare a feast. Let us welcome our new friends warmly while we determine their motives. In the meantime, they shall be treated like honored guests."

Eyes widening, Pol cracks a grin. "Back in college, we formulated truth serum gas from vast supplies of oxygen nitrates. With Brutus' help, we could flood the shuttle bay. Our guests would be intoxicated the moment they exit their shuttles."

Murray winces. "You mean laughing gas?"

"Nitrous Oxide never fails." Pol grins. "With warm grub in their bellies and truth serum filling their lungs, the suckers will be squawking like crows on a wire."

Throwing both hands up, Gregory storms off. "You guys are living in a fog. Turk has seen every trick. The bastard will be ready for anything you can dish out."

"Anything?" Andorf says.

"Oh, no, Andorf." Gregory turns about face. "Don't even think about using mind-reading tricks. It may work on the rest of us but this guy Turk won't fall for it. He and his renegades will be boarding the *Atlantis* bearing sabers. It will happen quickly. There'll be no time to read anyone's thoughts."

Murray's eyes widen. His hands twitch. "They're closing in on us as we speak. What'll we do, Mr. Goshi? You heard Gregory. These tyrants will have swords."

Scratching his chin, Andorf again paces about the small bridge. "Notify every passenger, including those on the *Phoenix* and the *Mayflower*. Not a single soul is to communicate with this Turk."

Pol smirks. "No problem. I'm sure no one outside this group has deciphered the lunatic's message."

"Keep it so," Andorf says, "Murray, have Brutus round up a few gypsy pals. Have them join me, you, and Gregory in the C-deck conference room in an hour's time. The makings of a planning council are in order."

Captain Murray slaps an open hand across his forehead, he sighs much too loud. "A council? Space life is becoming way too complicated."

Gregory slams his fist onto the captain's console and begins to yell. "Haven't you guys understood anything I've said? Turk's absolutely brutal! He'll rip our hearts out with his bare hands and serve them to his crew for dinner. There's absolutely no winning with Turk. None I tell you. None!"

*

Binky's log – 123-150552:

So, another problem rears its ugly head. First, my troubles with Siros and now there may be a narcissist out there with his sights on our three-starship fleet. They say bad things occur in threes. I wonder what lies down the road.

CHAPTER 13
Turk

The six-foot-ten commander of the forty-three-starship armada forces his way through the *Aegean's* bridge door. He knocks the navigator down and kicks him out of the way. Eyes narrowing on his next-in-command, Turk darts across the bridge. He grabs the bulky, seven-foot man by the neck, pins him against a wall, and extracts his trusty saber. Pressing the blade against the next-in-command's Adam's apple, spots of blood appear onto the floor.

"Give me good reason, Burak, not to cut your throat right here and now."

Burak peers at the red stains on the walls, then at the drops of his own blood wetting his shoes. "Such a mess it makes of the bridge, your Excellency. You should really put that thing away."

"What the hell's taking so long? Why haven't we caught up with their tiny fleet?"

Side-stepping clear of Turk's sharp saber, Burak stares past the Commander's fiery eyes. He gazes at the crew and then back at the commander. "The three starship fleet had a good month lead, sir. Though the *Aegean* is heavily loaded, I expect her to be within boarding range in a matter of a few weeks."

Turk spits on his next-in-command's highly-polished shoes. "You told me as much six weeks ago."

Peering down at the slime, Burak cringes. Mumbling beneath his breath, he gazes back at his superior. "If you will allow me to send a handful of smaller ships ahead—"

"No!" Turk yells. "I won't split up the armada. My starships will arrive as one gallant armada. Understand me?"

Fingers curing, Turk spins about. Slamming a fist down hard onto the console, he takes aim at the trembling comm-spec. "Why hasn't the tiny fleet answered? Have you quit transmitting my messages, radioman?"

The comm-spec cowers behind the radio gear. He begins to stutter. "Ev—every starship in the armada has been broadcasting continuous messages over the past three months, interrupted only by your pre-programmed demands. Our targets have yet to reply."

The navigator staggers to his feet. Sighting Turk's narrowing eyes, he slithers behind the navigational screen, eyes glued to the commander. "Perhaps they aren't listening on universal frequencies."

Turk grits his teeth and growls. "Where's this Spider? I must speak with Spider now!"

*

Binky's log – 124-111925:

The commander of the grand starship armada appears as ruthless as Gregory says. The council needs a wakeup call but a lot of good it'll do to bring representatives from the three starships into a large room only to scare the hell out of them.

CHAPTER 14
The First Council

Day 125: 0900 -
Titan Outpost rendezvous: 646 days

Standing at the *Mayflower's* council chambers main entry door, Andorf discovers clues of how the large room was once an observation deck. Like the *Atlantis'* eight observation decks which were repurposed to classrooms and sickbays it too has been repurposed. Gregory's head popping up and down behind the podium draws his attention to the front of the room. After a long session of Gregory tapping microphones, the opening speaker is gestured to approach a podium on the impromptu low-rise stage.

Everyone appears equally as nervous as *Atlantis'* Captain Murray when he steps forward to introduce himself. He graciously thanks the highly-skilled band of gypsies for assembling the council chambers on such short notice. "And let me thank each of you for interrupting your busy schedules to attend the fleet's first council." He scans the many faces. "It appears our three-starship fleet is well represented."

At the tap on his shoulder, Murray briefly pauses. He reads the paper Gregory shoves in his hand. "I am to announce that this council is to meet here in this chamber daily at 9A.M. sharp and shall adjourn no later than noon.

Unresolved items of the previous session will become first items of discussion at the next meeting. Now, with one pressing issue currently before us, formal rules of courtesy will be deferred until a later date."

Behind the stage, Brutus appears to be zoning out. Andorf's much smaller hand partially wraps around the chief engineer's hefty wrist and directs his old friend into a less-busy corner. He looks around the council chamber for curious ears before speaking. "I—I do not know about all this, Brutus. Considering everything I have heard about Turk I am beginning to doubt my own plans. Are we doing the right thing by inviting these guys aboard the *Atlantis*?"

"Relax, Andorf. How bad can this Turk guy possibly be?"

"Are you kidding me? According to Gregory the S.O.B. slit his brother's throat for merely snoring."

Brutus yawns with into a cupped hand. "Can you blame a guy for wanting a good night's rest?"

"What about the guy shooting a dog … his own dog?"

Brutus looks around the packed room. "It was a great idea forming this council even if I must claim credit."

"What?"

"It'll keep everyone informed. The last things we need are self-righteous wackos spreading big lies. You know how gullible people become with wild-eyed conspiracy theories."

Andorf nods.

"You and Gregory should go ahead with your own backup plan."

"Plan C," Andorf mumbles.

"In the meantime, my fellow gypsies will be hosting the dinner as I also suggested."

"Huh?"

"We'll welcome Turk and his clan with open arms while we scrutinize their true intentions." Brutus suddenly freezes. His eyes suddenly cross. He begins to stutter. "W—wait! Did you say the sick bastard shot his own dog?"

Andorf raises a brow. "Yep. In a jealous rage, the S.O.B. shot the dog after it crawled into bed with his wife."

"Why am I having second thoughts about entertaining these strangers?" Brutus takes a deep breath as he begins to hyperventilate.

"I have similar feelings, my friend. In fact, I cannot see how any of us are coming out of this reception unscathed."

"Lock up the dinnerware. Dim the lights so Turk and his pirates won't notice they're using cheap carbene breakfast-ware. My fellow gypsies will polish up the utensils so they gleam under reduced lighting." He smiles at Andorf. "You can never be too cautious with strangers."

Andorf stares down his old friend. "Lest I remind you how my complete twelve place setting of monogrammed silverware passed down seven generations was stolen by a pair of thieves?"

Brutus extends an arm around Andorf's shoulder. He leads him out of the room, away from now perking ears. In the near-vacant hallway, the chief engineer speaks freely. "Why are you still hell-bent on this? Your silverware helped finance the starship hijackings. We'd still be back on Earth under the guise of that repressive two-party empire if it weren't for Serin's underhandedness. Besides, retaining such quantity of silver would have been too heavy to smuggle aboard unnoticed. And possessing as much could have landed you in jail."

"Yeah ... well ... the thought of melting down my inheritance will forever haunt me."

"I thought you had finally moved on, Poo." Shaking his head, Brutus leads Andorf back into the council chambers where they hear Captain Murray wrapping up his opening comments.

Recognizing Andorf and Brutus returning, Captain Murray waves the pair further inside the council chambers. "And with introductions behind us, we have an urgent matter on today's agenda. As most of you are well aware, there is trouble brewing well beyond these starship walls. Now, I've heard rumors ranging from armed Canine Empire forces readying to retrieve their prized starships to predatory aliens priming for an attack." Murray takes a deep breath. "Rest assured, everyone, the forty-three starships amassing around our hulls are neither."

Council chamber breaks into chaos. Rising from their seats, councilmembers shout frantic words.

"Calm down! Calm down, everyone," Murray yells into the microphone.

"Let's not spread more of these vicious lies. We gather in these council chambers only to discuss facts."

After Andorf and Brutus join him on the low-rise stage and fan their hands, the ambience quiets to a dull roar. The majority of the councilmembers reclaim their seats.

"Nonetheless, we are facing a real threat," Murray continues after taking a deep breath. "We must deal with this possible threat in a rational manner. From recent radio intercepts, we have every reason to believe—"

Flailing both hands wildly in the air, Captain Argent of the *S.S. Phoenix* leaps to his feet. The burly man with flaming red locks flopping about as he approaches the low-rise stage is flanked by two bodyguards. The narcissistic captain lives up to reputation of bully perceived adversaries. He points a threatening finger at the Atlantis' chief engineer, standing on the sidelines before plucking a microphone off Murray's lapel.

Brutus appears to ignore Argent's rude gesture.

The captain holds Murray's wireless device up to his mouth close enough so everyone in the council chambers hears his breath. Again, he holds his hands high in the air. "Here we are, millions of miles from home without weaponry of any sort. How in blazing Alderon are we to defend ourselves? Why, there are one-eyed aliens out there right now converging on us at this moment. And with forty-three starships, there must be hundreds of thousands ... millions of the one-eyed buggers."

"One-eyed buggers?" Andorf leans into Brutus. "I see where the alien rumors originated."

Brutus clips on a wireless mic as he and Andorf step onto the low-rise stage from the rear. The chief engineer fosters a large, boasting grin.

Andorf grabs at his friend with both hands but with Brutus' girth, he is left behind. "Don't do it," he calls out. "Leave the narcissist alone."

Brutus stares down the arrogant captain. "We hold the element of surprise, Argent. These visitors don't know our starships like—"

Captain Argent grabs his knees as he bursts out laughing. "Are you kidding me, gypsy boy? Every kid back home had comic book blueprints of our starships. They're the same rags used to train those clown techs of yours."

Approaching Captain Argent, Brutus' mouth stretches the many worry lines spanning his reddening face. Hands projected toward the captain's throat, he lunges.

Argent's bodyguards wedge between the large men. Doing their best, they separate Brutus and Argent while the hotheads fire escalating rounds of verbal jabs and hand grabs at one another. Poking fingers at each other, the adversaries appear to be dancing around the bodyguards.

A buzzing on his belt steals the chief engineer's focus. Brutus turns suddenly and runs for the nearest exit, yelling back at *Phoenix's* captain. "This ain't over, you bastard!"

Eyeing Brutus, Argent snickers. "Bastard indeed. I'll be waiting right here, you wimpy gypsy."

Councilmembers roar as Brutus speeds out of the council chamber doors. Murray flails his hands fruitlessly, as if expecting to calm the frenzied crowd.

Amidst the chaos, a four-foot-eleven woman identifying herself as Rita Ambrosia and representing the *Mayflower's* mid C-deck steps onto the low-rise stage. She grabs the mic from Argent's bulky hand and then squints at the *Phoenix's* captain before turning to wave at her fellow councilmembers. The frenzy dwindles at the sound of Rita's squeaky voice.

"One day, my prized second-grade student brought a phasor pistol into class for display. Of course, I immediately confiscated the weapon and locked it in my desk drawer. Returning from recess, I found not only had the drawer been ripped off its tracks but it was tossed into the middle of my classroom floor, along with its contents, minus the gun. An agent named Pinscher left her calling card." Rita rolls her eyes. "Ha. As if I'd ever actually contact the bitch."

Andorf's ears perk at mention of the agent's name. His face pales in memory of his run-in with that very same Pinscher in his old apartment back on Earth. He shivers, still tasting her slimy, snake-like tongue slipping between his lips … licking the inside of his cheeks as she probed for information about his wife, Serin. By reflex, he spits the foul taste from his mouth.

"The Canine Empire confiscated and destroyed every last one of those weapons," one of Argent's bodyguards yells out.

"Phasor plans were then purged from the Empire's master database," adds the other bodyguard. "Factories were destroyed … blueprints burned … anyone having manufacturing knowledge was eliminated."

Rita's eyes narrow. "Yes, but rumor has it one man retains the last pair of phasor pistols in existence." Her eyes sweep slowly past Andorf. "Possibly someone in these very chambers."

Andorf gulps. "Busted."

Argent chuckles. "And you believe a couple hand-held phasors could deter an alien army of millions?" Argent runs a hand over his balding crown. "Those one-eyed creatures have deadly antlers which—"

One bodyguard leans close and whispers in the captain's ear.

"Err … horns … protruding out the tops of their heads. I'm sorry Ms. Meter maid but you and that squeaky voice will have to do better."

Rita growls. The mic drops as she balls her hands into fists. Four-foot-eleven Rita races toward the captain. Argent takes a stiff punch to his left cheek. She delivers a second blow to his right.

Rubbing his face, Argent steps aside to allow his bodyguards to do their work. The bodyguards grab the school teacher's arms and secure them behind her back. Ms. Rita wiggles, struggling to break free.

"I can use someone with good right and left hooks." Argent rubs feeling back into his cheeks. "Double this lil-tiger's food rations. Better yet, bump her up to get captain rations. Let's fatten 'er up, boys."

Rita jerks both arms. Unable to free herself, she spits in her captor's faces.

By instinct, the guards release her to wipe their eyes.

Rita takes no time extracting a pocket-knife from her rear pocket. Pointing it at Argent, she charges. The bodyguards reclaim their prize before she can inflict further damage. "One of these days, Argent," she yells. "One of these days I'm going to—"

Staring at the small blade, Argent laughs hard. "You're going to do what, cut me into teeny weeny pieces?"

Both bodyguards echo the captain's laughter.

Grasping the knife firmly in her hands, Rita fingers fit into a recession. The small toy suddenly morphs into a bowie knife with a six-inch blade.

Eye's widening, Argent's steps back, distancing himself from the threat.

Rita once again charges. One bodyguard puts himself between Rita and the captain. The other grabs Rita from behind, wraps both arms around her petite frame, and then wrestles her down. The pair flops back and forth on the floor like a determined guppy holding a lethal weapon and a beached mullet doing his best to avoid being sliced.

The second bodyguard kicks the knife from Rita's hand. He takes her hands and binder-cuffs them behind her back. As the goons drag her off, Rita spits back at Argent.

The captain grins at his prospective resource. "Oh, how I love a woman with spunk."

The council again breaks into chaos with the *Mayflower's* captain leaping from his seat. In a tear, he and a stream of councilmembers rush the low-rise stage.

Argent's face sours. Left without protection, he high-tails out the nearest exit trailed by angry councilpersons while cursing Rita and every woman he's known in 140-word rants in all caps.

Andorf watches from the rear of the low-rise stage, shaking his head in disbelief. He strolls around the stage and retrieves Rita's wireless mic. Holding the piece high in the air, squealing speakers command everyone's attention. He keeps the feedback going until remaining councilmembers have returned to their seats.

"And what a lively crowd we have here. I want everyone to pick a number." Andorf scans the now half-filled room of strange faces. He points at one councilmember in the crowd. "The woman over there in the turquoise blouse ... you chose seven."

The woman flashes one thumb up.

Andorf's eyes narrow upon the *Atlantis'* Captain behind him. "And you, Captain Murray ... why the twenty-character octet number?"

Murray's head droops like a dog beaten with a wet towel. He presses an open palm outward. "It's a long story. I'd rather not go there."

Andorf hand-nudges him as do many others. "Go ahead, Murray. We are all friends. Tell us your story. We are all listening."

The captain lifts his eyes to anxious smiles. "Well, you see ... back on Earth I was locked away in a small room at the Cos. With all records of my existence erased, I was destined for the power cell factory, to become essential ingredients in someone's flashlight. They assigned me this number ... like the same octet numbers you'll find stamped on every power cell."

"I remember the Cos," many shout. "It was a terrible place."

Leaving their seats, councilmembers begin to loudly voice their fears. "But these invaders outside, they aren't even human."

"We can't reason with them."

"You can't control one-eyed aliens with cheap parlor tricks."

"Argent was right. Without weapons, we're totally defenseless."

Andorf raises open palms at the room of angry faces and the council chamber dwindles to a dull roar. "These visitors are quite human as will soon be explained by my distinguished colleague. My friend has travelled to two ... no, three foreign empires and speaks a variety of languages. Why he even—"

Eyes follow a man entering the main chamber doors, taking a slow, deliberate path toward the low-rise stage. He pauses at the first row, holding a hand high to display a transcriber embedded into his palm. As he approaches the podium, a finger swipe from his other hand on the device plays a cleaned up six-second recording through the chamber's speakers.

"I demand to speak with Spider now!" yells a deep voice, laden with Middle-Eastern accent. Gregory swipes a finger to replay the short snippet.

For a third time, the council chamber breaks into chaos.

Gregory scans the crowd's grumbling faces. Like messiahs, he, Andorf, and Murray fan the crowd with their hands until the chamber quiets. Gregory continues.

"What you heard was the voice of a nearly seven-foot man weighing in at two hundred and forty pounds. He is an uncontested tribal leader, has a wife, a one-year-old son, and goes by the name Turk for obvious reasons. I suspect he's the leader of this forty-three-starship armada approaches our small fleet."

Councilmembers uniformly rise to voice their opinions. One councilman yells out above her cohorts. "I find it highly improbable how you picked such detail out of a six-second recording."

Gregory's eyes follow Argent and his fresh pair of bodyguards as they discretely fill vacant front row seats. His attention returns to the council. "I had the personal misfortune of meeting Turk. I was en route to visit Swedish relatives when we first crossed distant paths."

"How tough can the guy be?" Argent yells, grinning smugly at the bodyguards flanking him on either side.

Gregory approaches the *Phoenix's* captain. Keeping his distance, he throws a pointed index finger in Argent's face. "Turk gutted an older sibling for merely snoring in his sleep."

"So, the man's got a bad temper." Argent laughs aloud. "Every respectable leader has got a temper. It's a prerequisite of the job."

The bodyguards nod.

Leaning closer, Gregory's eyes narrow upon Argent. "In a jealous rage, he shot a dog ... his own dog."

Argent smirks. "Well then, I shall certainly keep my distance."

To both bodyguards' dismay, Gregory jams his face right in front of Argent, close enough to make the captain turn away from Gregory's stale breath. "You'll be dead is what you'll be, Argent."

The large men grab Gregory's arms and pull him aside. At the sight of Andorf's narrowing eyes, they loosen their grip. Gregory jerks free and steps onto the low-rise stage. Councilmembers stand and rush the stage. When they grill him with unanswerable questions, Gregory throws both hands out to hold back the crowd. Most of the council back away, appearing shocked by sight of Gregory's metal arm appendages.

Gregory fans open hands at the receding crowd. "All we know for certain is Turk wants a word with a Spider person. Andorf here believes this Spider to be his late wife ... my sister, Serin."

"The great Serin Gray," many chant.

Rising from his seat, Argent yells out louder than the others. "What's this mongrel want with Serin? Doesn't he know she's—?"

Andorf casts an open palm toward the *Phoenix's* captain, silencing the redheaded beast of a man. He squints at Argent. "Speak of my wife in such ill manner again and I'll burn your nuts off."

Holding his crotch, Argent drops into his seat, as do his bodyguards.

Regaining composure, Gregory wipes at his tearing eyes as he speaks into his mic. "Well, it appears this Turk fellow will be in for one huge disappointment, won't he?"

Pandemonium again breaks out in the council chambers. With Gregory and Murray fielding endless rounds of pointless questions, Andorf takes a hike out the nearest exit. Within moments, he is riding the *Mayflower's* floating steps down to the transportation deck, aiming to catch the next ride back to the *Atlantis*.

*

Binky's log – 125-095005:

As bad as the Phoenix's captain may be, he appears no match for the junior Goshi. As to where the Atlantis' *chief engineer ran off is anyone's guess.*

CHAPTER 15
An Upper Hand

Day 125: 0955

A ndorf discovers the chief engineer in the bowels of the *Atlantis* outside the greasy mechanical room, walking in circles and talking to himself. He grabs Brutus' hefty arm and in doing so gets dragged around until the chief engineer comes to a halt.

"What the hell happened back there, Brutus? You left the council meeting so abruptly I thought there was something terribly wrong with the *Atlantis*." Andorf scrutinizes Brutus' droopy stance and troubled face. "No! Don't tell me. Captain Argent actually intimidated you?"

"Nothing of the sort," Brutus says, wiping dripping sweat off his brow. "My head was pounding. I couldn't see straight. I was literally on the verge of murdering the bastard. I've murdered before you know. They say it gets easier each time. No! One murder in anyone's lifetime is more than enough."

Andorf cringes. "I know the feeling."

Face inches away, Brutus growls. "Yet another unsettled matter with you. How many times must we go through this? Your friend was already dead when you shot him. My friend, Malcomb, was there, lest you forget. He witnessed the incident. You had nothing to do with Brett's demise."

"Ah yes. Malcomb, the guy you had tailing me. But I was there. Does that not make me an accomplice?"

Brushing Andorf aside with a sweeping hand motion, Brutus sighs. "As I said before, you were framed, setup by political thugs."

Andorf follows Brutus as he continues to walk about. "I am always being setup. Oh, if I had never gotten involved with you and Serin, I would be living a peaceful life back on Earth."

"And what a dull life that would've been." Brutus grumbles at his old friend. "No excitement."

Andorf grabs hold of Brutus' lanky arm. "Excitement? You want excitement? You left the council chambers before the real excitement began. A grade school teacher got up and confronted your buddy, Argent. After he verbally abused her, she got a couple licks in before his grunts cuffed and dragged her off."

"You mean feisty four-foot-eleven Rita Ambrosia? I've heard she's quite capable of holding her own against any man. But enough small talk. We've got much larger issues at hand."

Brutus leads Andorf into the main stairwell. They dart up a double flight of steps before exiting into the hallway. Taking the floating steps five decks up to the G-deck, they head straight for the main bridge. Brutus slaps the wall-mounted mushroom button and the bridge door opens with a wobbly SWOOSH. They interrupt the navigator and comm-spec watching a live feed of the council chamber chaos from opposite ends of the bridge.

Pol breaks his focus long enough to return Brutus' glare. "What if those guys are right, Brutus? What if this Turk is more authoritarian than the binary empire we narrowly escaped?"

"We must construct weapons," Peter adds. "Surely, you can devise something from your parts inventory."

"I have twin phasor pistols from our run-in with Fat Max," Andorf says. "They are safely locked away in my cabin."

Brutus snarfs. "As much as it kills me, I must agree with Argent. A couple of handheld phasors would be futile against an army of thousands."

"Is it possible to reverse engineer Andorf's phasors?" Peter raises a brow.

"We could churn them out by the hundreds. That'd certainly bend things in our favor."

"Even working around the clock, three weeks wouldn't be enough time," Brutus says.

"I know it sounds archaic," Pols says. "Perhaps we could assemble archaic projectile weapons."

Andorf nods. "That would be like bringing pea shooters to a knife fight."

The bridge's airlock door SWOOSHES open. Appearing distraught, Captain Murray burst inside, wiping his face with a damp cloth. "That arrogant council … I can't take it any longer. They refused to hear anything Gregory and I were telling them."

Peter briefs the captain on their weaponry discussion. Pol rehashes his thoughts on using projectile weapons.

Murray peers beyond the new instrument console, out the recently replaced viewport windows into the vast emptiness of space. Droplets drip from his forehead as he fingers the rubber seals encasing transparent aluminum windows in their frames. He turns about. His voice flutters. "Projectiles are absolutely off the table. The smallest puncture of the *Atlantis'* pressurized hull and we're all goners. Look what happened to my predecessor, the late Captain Thom."

Pol winces. "But—"

"Those things have a way of happening to starship captains," Murray mumbles, collapsing into the over-padded captain's seat. "We're expected to die out here in the line of duty. I looked it up. It's mentioned briefly in micro-wording sections of the job description."

Pol strolls about the bridge, smirking at the recently promoted captain. "As I had mentioned previously, I played with nioxides back in college. Ample quantities should be fairly easy to produce. Isn't that right, Brutus?"

Brutus grabs his chin as he walks about the small bridge. "We could possibly tap nitrates off the *Atlantis'* engine exhaust. Of course, oxygen injectors would need to be modified, but it could certainly be done. We could retrofit empty storage tanks, run lines, and flood the shuttle bay with the gas.

Pol's eyes widen. His voice revs in excitement. "Turk and his gang won't know what hit 'em."

"The illustrious Captain Thom spoke often about an old friend named Robert Foos running Saturn's moon base." Peter raises a brow. "Perhaps we could use this to our advantage."

Murray taps his navigator's shoulder. "You know as well as anyone, Peter, our rendezvous with Titan Outpost is another twenty-three months off. If Siros is correct, Turk's incursion will occur in a matter of weeks."

"Too bad the Trans-Galactic drives are still in the design stages." Brutus grumbles. "We could fire up those bad boys … rendezvous with Titan's re-fueling station in a matter of days, leaving Turk and his marauders in our wake."

Pol winces. "I hear Robert Foos had a kid sister."

"Nicki," Brutus mumbles. With face reddening, he quietly joins Captain Murray at the frontal viewport windows.

All stare at the chief engineer in silence. By consensus, Andorf taps his old friend's shoulder. "What's the matter, Brutus? Is there something we should know about this guy's sister?"

Brutus cowers at everyone's glaring eyes. Appearing as nervous as when he spotted the red axe hanging above, he wipes perspiration off his brow. "It's nothing … nothing to worry about. Don't sweat it, guys."

Murray gulps. "Then explain to me, Brutus, why am I suddenly feeling sharp knives stabbing at my gut? Come on. Spit it out."

Brutus gazes out the frontal viewport window, appearing to be wishing he were elsewhere. He begins to stutter. "It's just that Nicki and I used to have this thing."

"A thing?" Murray says. "Just how well did you know this kid sister?"

"It really didn't get very far. Things were just heating up when her father …" Brutus turns about to peer at the empty hanger above the fire extinguisher and the dust outline of a missing axe. He sighs.

Pol approaches to tap Brutus lightly on the back. "How about persuading your gypsy friends to brew up special batches of Psygmy Ale I've heard so much about?"

Brutus clears his throat. "Ah yes, Psygmy Ale. Intoxication may be brief but for those unaccustomed, there could be lingering flatulence followed by bouts of uncontrollable laughter. Normally, I'd have reservations about doing anything as drastic."

Peter grins. "Desperate situations call for drastic actions."

Rubbing his furry chin, Andorf watches the others dance about the bridge with euphoria, as though a solution to the dilemma is well within their grasp. "Nioxides? Psygmy Ale?" he mumbles. "Overconfidence appears to be gaining an upper hand."

*

Binky's log – 125-100842:

Ah yes. Overconfidence appears to be spiraling around like an unstuck drain. As for Turk, I wonder what the bastard pirate is up to.

CHAPTER 16
The Pushback

Day 132 - Titan Outpost rendezvous: 639 days

Sir, I've got a response from one of the targets." The *Aegean's* comm-spec spins about in his seat. "It's from the fleet's lead ship, the *S.S. Atlantis.*"

Turk snarls at the radioman. "It's about damn time."

"They've invited representatives from each of our starships to a welcoming dinner." The radioman raises a brow. "Attendance is limited to one hundred guests."

"One hundred? One hundred?" Turk yells. "I've had raiding parties with five times as many."

"Shall I request seating for five hundred?"

Turk scratches at his thick black beard. "To overtake the Canine Empire, this Spider leads an army in the tens of thousands." He pounds his fist on the counter. "Let's show them who they're dealing with. Make it a thousand."

The comm-spec gulps. "I've heard the Spider's ruthless ... a tyrant. Not— not anything like you, Commander, but a ruthless tyrant nonetheless."

"According to Canine Empire records, Spider and his renegades broke into political prisons and released their most violent inmates onto the streets," second in command, Burak adds. "After overpowering royal guards, he beheaded one of their high-order. He then went on to hijack the empire's prized deep-space starships."

"Spider accomplished all this in a single evening?"

The comm-spec nods.

Continuing to scratch his beard, Turk walks about the bridge mumbling aloud. "So, Spider beheaded someone in the high order, did he? This despicable man sounds like my kind of warrior. Yes indeed, I look forward to sparring with this Spider."

The navigator sheepishly appears from behind his station console, keeping distance between himself and the commander. "The *Atlantis* must be heavily loaded. How else are we able to overtake the fleet in a matter of months?"

The comm-spec steps away from his radio. He leans against the commander's counter. "Judging by the size of their starships, Commander, we outnumber them seventy to one."

Burak grins. "Rumor has it the fleet possess engineering skills required to assemble a Trans-Galactic drive … one which could easily power them beyond the stars."

Turk swings his saber in an arc, sending it crashing onto the counter. While the crew jumps back out of harm's way, Turk begins to salivate. "Within three weeks their Galactic Drive technology will be mine."

Burak retracts his hand off the counter seconds before losing fingers. Still, he counts his digits. The comm-spec and navigator scurry behind the safety of their station consoles. Burak falls back a few steps.

"I must speak with Spider," Turk growls. "Get the bastard on the radio … now!"

*

Binky's log – 132-140316:

So, the pirate wants to meet this Spider. Boy is he in for a big surprise.

CHAPTER 17
Reality

Day 133 - Titan Outpost rendezvous: 638 days

W hat? A Thousand?" Gregory yells, pacing about the *Atlantis'* small bridge. "The pirate expects us to host him and a thousand of his warriors?"

Comm-spec Pol gulps. "Warriors?"

Captain Murray's face pales as he peers at the others. "They'll be bearing sabers."

Gregory winces. "We can devise metal detectors … post them at the shuttle-bay exits."

Peter winces. "And you know how to build such things, Gregory?"

The tech-wiz gazes dumbfounded at the clueless navigator.

"You certainly have my permission to use whatever parts you find in the bowels of the *Atlantis*." Murray clears his throat loudly. "I'll clear it with our chief engineer."

Pol's eyes widen. "What if there are spies?"

Murray winces. "Best we not mention any of this to the council."

*

Binky's log – 133-162053:

The way rumors spread on the Atlantis, *it's best not to tell anyone anything.*

CHAPTER 18
Preparations

Day 141 - Titan Outpost rendezvous: 630 days

With guest shuttles expected to fill every available space in *Atlantis'* underbelly shuttle bay, Brutus tasks everyone within earshot to stack whatever they find against the perimeter walls. He takes notice of his most-troublesome techs in a far corner, bent over a collection of footlockers and scratching at their heads.

"Look here, boss!" the most-junior tech calls out. "These markings indicate these set of twenty boxes are destined for the A-deck luxury suite. Say, Brutus, isn't that your quarters?"

"Hmm," Brutus mumbles, approaching the fumbling techs. "I don't recall owning footlockers ... definitely not twenty of them." He squints at the stenciled numbers ranging from one to twenty and at the Hotot-like pictogram placards. His hand-scanner is slow to decode pictograms. Brutus taps the piece with the butt of his hand. Moments later, the scanner flashes disturbing verbiage.

The junior techs gather around.

"No! This can't be," he grumbles, stepping away from the confused junior techs.

One of the techs steps closer. "What's in the foot lockers, Brutus? Are they filled with weapons?"

The second tech's eyes widen. "Can we use them to fight off those one-eyed aliens?"

Brutus stares bewildered at the lads. "One-eyed aliens? Huh?"

The techs nod in unison.

Brutus throws up both hands in disgust. "I see Argent has been spreading more of his conspiracy theories."

"Oh no, Mister Brutus." The younger tech grins ear-to-ear. "We made that one up by ourselves."

"Never mind what they contain!" Brutus yells, throwing up both hands. "Load two footlockers into each of the shuttles. Bind them behind the front seats with permaseal. Then take the others down to the secondary cargo hold on the M-deck. After chaining them to the storage racks, cover them with self-wrapping tarps."

"Two per shuttle … check."

"M-deck cargo hold … check."

Brutus' finger swipe transfers the day's shuttle codes to the tech's wrist devices. He reaches deep inside his pocket and tosses cargo-hold keys to the most senior tech. "Keep this under wraps. Not a word of this to anyone. Do you both hear me?"

The senior tech takes the keys and then nods.

The other tech chuckles. "How about we just dump the boxes outside, boss? No one would ever—"

In an eye-blink, Brutus is in the young man's face. His bulky hand bounces the lad off a rear wall. "How dare you entertain such a stupid thought. Such an irresponsible act like would cause irreparable health risks of unimaginable proportion to anyone happening upon them. Why, the ramifications of such action could last well beyond the next millennium … perhaps longer."

The senior tech slugs his counterpart's shoulder. "Like what happened in that Jumanji movie we watched last week. Is that what would happen if anyone opened them? Is it, Mr. Brutus? Huh?"

Rolling his eyes, Brutus slaps self-sealing phosphorus-red tri-hazard labels along the edges of the vacuum-sealed footlockers. "Consider their contents extremely toxic. What's inside can make you go blind. Even worse … it'll permanently stain your hands a pale olive green."

Staring wide-eyed at their pristine hands, the techs' faces contort like rung-out sponges. They quickly back away from the footlockers.

"Hurry up, you two!" Brutus growls. "Get this stuff under wraps before anyone takes notice. It's both your hides if news of this leaks out."

The techs slip into bio-hazard gear and begin loading the first pair of the footlockers onto sets of air-glides.

In passing, a bulky man takes interest in Brutus' fumbling techs and changes course. After bending down to examine one of the footlocker placards, he abruptly pulls Brutus aside. "How is it you entrust these young squirts with such vast quantities of Carnga nuts?" He leans close and whispers. "One lick of the Pandora's snack will leave those two chirping like Tangonese Minkeze. Believe me, Brutus. I've personally witnessed such a thing. It ain't pretty."

"Relax my gypsy brother. I know those techs all too well. They could not possibly understand the true consequences of mishandling the addictive delicacies. Besides, they barely get along, let alone work well together." Beginning to salivate, Brutus leans toward the man and whispers. "I hear the rare cashew-like nuts are quite tasty."

"So, I've heard," the gypsy grumbles as he turns turning away. "How I envy those Madagascar natives with their immunity to the nut's aphrodisiac properties."

Brutus peers at the large fingers gripped steadfast around his arm. Noting Brutus' focus, the man quickly retracts his hand.

"I'm not naming names, but a few of our brothers have actually sampled nuts such as those. It's been years and they have yet to recover from the Carnga's evil spell. Oh, cursed those nuts are." He again takes hold of Brutus' equally large arm. "We absolutely cannot allow this cargo to fall into the wrong hands. I'm begging you. They must be destroyed … every last nut."

"Rest your mind. All footlockers will be secured, safely away from suspicious eyes. Shuttle codes change daily and few have access to the secondary cargo-hold. I shall add inspecting the footlockers to my daily rounds."

The gypsy again leans into Brutus. "Have you heard the latest? Captain Argent of the *S.S. Phoenix* has gone missing."

"It's nothing but rumor. I had nothing to do with it."

The gypsy chuckles for a moment. "Remember that four-foot-eleven gal who had a run-in with him at the first council meeting? Word is she escaped his custody. With the gal missing, she's the leading suspect. Odds are running twenty to one against her."

Brutus winces. "Ex-councilwoman Rita Ambrosia? I can't believe anyone would place bets against her?"

"I advise you to get in now, my brother, while the odds are low."

Shaking his head, Brutus leads his fellow gypsy near a maze of three-inch pipes, cautioning him to drop his head as they pass beneath. "Let me show you what we've conjured up to welcome our guests."

The man gazes up, eyes following the piping path from the backroom high-pressure tanks and through one of the walls. "You'd better be absolutely certain of this, Brutus. We're taking big risks with this Turk and his merry men. If he or his clan suspects nitrous gas, they could turn on us in whip-snappy fashion. And from what I've learned about that crazed S.O.B., the last thing we want is to start a full-fledged war with him."

Brutus gulps. "Have you heard about the guy stabbing an older sibling for merely snoring?"

The gypsy shrugs his shoulders.

"And worse, in a jealous rage the bastard shot a dog ... his own dog."

Mouth appearing to sour, the gypsy spits on the floor. "His own dog?"

Brutus nods. "Now about the nitrous oxide ... comm-spec Pol assures me his formula has never failed. He's tested batches on two diverse groups. Things are looking good."

The gypsy stops to review the piping fanning out through the shuttle bay. "Is it safe to assume our guests will be inhaling healthy doses of the truth gas upon first exiting their shuttles?"

"By the time our guests reach the dining hall they'll be, as Pol stated, 'squawking like crows on a wire.'"

The gypsy raises a brow. "I assume your team has been monitoring Turk's inter-ship communications."

"Indeed. Gregory Gray broke their encoded network a few days ago. Thus far, no aggressive memes have been discovered."

"That doesn't mean a thing. I feel it deep within my bones. They're up to no good. Turk's planning to overtake our fleet beginning right here with the *Atlantis*, most likely right after the welcoming dinner."

"I can tell you this, my fellow gypsy. It's a good thing the guy doesn't have a clue about Serin. He'll be expecting to rub noses with the one he calls Spider."

"What?" the gypsy yells. "He doesn't know she's dead? What happens when Turk demands to speak with this Spider person?"

Brutus shakes his head. "Don't worry, my friend. We'll have the entire dining hall bugged. Interpreters wearing ear buds will be mixed in with gypsy servers. The instant trouble rears its ugly head, we'll be alerted. And look, I've even got a disguise to blend in." Brutus pulls a folded-up Kalpak cap from his pocket and arranges it squarely on his head. "Well, what do you think? No one should recognize me wearing this thing."

"Put that thing away, Brutus! You look like a damn fool."

Wincing at his fellow gypsy, Brutus folds the cap and then presses it into a rear pocket. "I take it your team has conjured up the little dinner appetizer? You know, what we discussed a few days ago?"

"Taking up collections, our gypsy brothers really put themselves into special batches of Booger Stew." He elbows Brutus in the ribs. "If you know what I mean. And as requested, we've brewed up one-hundred barrels of extra potent Psygme Ale to wash the slop down."

Brutus wrinkles his nose. "Booger Stew. I still have nightmares of my folks holding my nose and forcing the gooey mess down my throat until I was big enough to fend them off."

"And made a man of you, has it not?"

Brutus nods reluctantly.

"Much labor was spent grinding down solids and thinning out green slime. After all, there must be plenty for our one hundred guests."

"You haven't heard the latest? The guest invitation has been bumped up to eight hundred."

"What? Eight hundred?" The gypsy throws both hands high in the air. "Even if we solicit donations from everyone in the fleet, there won't be enough of the critical ingredient to go around."

103

Brutus winces. "We'll dish out the slop out in small bowls. Absolutely not a drop is to be spilled."

The gypsy snickers. "That's exactly what we'll do. We'll give the fools small tastes and hopefully they'll mistake the slop for fine delicacy. Oh, I can hear those clowns now … every last one of them begging for seconds."

"Just in case, we'll be dimming overhead lights. We can't have our guests noticing they are dining with cheap graphene utensils."

"Or have a good look at what they'll be shoveling in their mouths."

"Warn everyone," Brutus says. "Everyone must remain tight-lipped about the recipe. No one shall speak a word. The last thing we need is for guests to be running back to their ships for weapons. Now with eight hundred guests, you must churn out more batches of Psygme Ale."

The gypsy throws up his hands. "Impossible! We've run out of locations for the fast-brew vessels."

Brutus scratches at his balding crown for a long minute. His eyes suddenly widen. "Give the children a two-week recess. Then setup brewers up in class-rooms."

"You're a genius, Brutus. But what if all these efforts fail? I've heard rumors the bastards are planning to take over the fleet, beginning right here with the *Atlantis* right after dinner. What are we to do then?"

"Andorf and Gregory are working on their own little surprise. They tell me their plan C absolutely can't fail."

Brutus cautions the gypsy to halt as workers roll tables past. The gypsy grins smartly. "Please assure me your little Goshi friend isn't planning any of his mind tricks. The fate of everyone may rest in their hands. There can be no slip ups. Absolutely nothing can go wrong."

"Go check your brew and stew, my brother. Let me get back to my techs. Much work lies ahead."

A loud crash sends Brutus charging across the shuttle-bay. He pauses, staring drop-jawed at footlockers scattered about the shuttle bay floor and at sight of his junior techs arguing like pilots over a minor shuttle mishap. Wedging between the techs, he sends them storming off in opposite directions. He bends down to inspect the damage. His eyes home in on an eight-inch gash across the side of one of the footlockers. Though none of the hazardous Carnga nuts have spilled out, one errant nut appears to poke its head through the gash. The lone, green nut tempts Brutus to have a closer look … to lick his finger and take the tiniest of small tastes.

Brutus winces at the Carnga nut beckoning him closer, calling his name. He looks around a full three-sixty. With no one watching, he moves in. Bending down, Brutus licks an index finger … reaches for the errant Carnga. With nirvana but inches away, he can smell the salty nut's aromatic scent. He imagines the nut slipping between his lips, senses the delectable taste on the tip of his tongue. Wetting his lips and fingers, he reaches for the forbidden fruit.

Suddenly, his manhood awakens. Brutus feels eighteen again. For a moment, he magically lifts into the air. An instant later, he is slammed down hard onto the shuttle bay's floor. All goes black.

*

Brutus awakens to the sound of labels ripping off a dispenser. He squinches an eye to see his gypsy friend slapping self-sealing phosphorus-red tri-hazard labels over an eight-inch tear in the nearest footlocker. Lying partially-paralyzed on the floor, he watches the label assuming the imperfect shape of the footlocker and the protruding nut as it melts over the gash.

"Oww! That hurts," he says, rubbing the back of his skull.

Offering Brutus a hand, the gypsy helps the chief engineer back onto his feet. The man's deep voice calls out. "You can thank me later, Brother Brutus. I've just saved you from a long life of misery. One lick of that devil seed and you would've been ruined … living a life of impossible-to-fulfill sexual cravings." He flashes olive green hands. "Take my word, Brutus. I know."

*

Binky's log – 141-103118:

All this preparation for the welcoming dinner, but will it be enough to stave off a narcissist pirate?

CHAPTER 19
Sizing Things Up

Day 142 - Titan Outpost rendezvous: 629 days

The *S.S. Aegean's* comm-spec leers at the commander. "The *Atlantis* upped their seating capacity, sir. Still, there is seating for only eight-hundred."

Turk growls. "This Spider's toying with us. Continue pressing for a thousand. No, wait! Make it twelve hundred warriors."

Wincing, Burak thumbs through a thin book of cartoonish plans. "Sizing up the *Atlantis*, I see their shuttle bay will barely house thirty shuttles. Subtracting their seven shuttles leaves room for twenty-three."

"Toss your comic book in the trash," Turk yells. "Only an empire of fools would put detailed starship information in public hands."

"There's only so much room in their shuttle bay. No doubt they've been clearing every cubic meter of cargo space."

"If what you say is correct, Burak, we must pack our shuttles to the gills. Discard unnecessary items. Remove passenger seats ... trash all safety devices. Everything must go, beginning with the pilot seats."

"Aye, commander. We mustn't strip the shuttles of their security devices. This Spider is ruthless. He'll undoubtedly be pulling tricks. We shouldn't put anything past the bastard."

Rubbing his thick black beard, Turk paces about the *Aegean's* bridge. "Indeed, Burak. Indeed."

*

Binky's log – 142-234955:

Aha! The pirate will be sending his warriors. Will those aboard the Atlantis *be ready?*

CHAPTER 20
Transparency

Day 144: 0130 -
Titan Outpost rendezvous: 627 days

Mila thrashes about, her hands flailing about. Though fast asleep in her bed, she cries out, "Why are they trying to change us? Why are they making us say these stupid words?"

Hand covering a wide yawn, Andorf stumbles across the room. Sitting on Mila's bed, he takes her tiny hand in his own. As not to wake the twins, he whispers, "What troubles you, my precious one?"

Mila directs half-opened eyes toward Andorf's sleepy face. "Alien faces were staring at me ... ten of them."

Andorf's eyes widen at the alien reference. He rubs his furry, unshaven chin. "Ten aliens, hmm. I have heard those words long ago ... perhaps it was back on Earth. Yes, it was the old man at the infamous rugby game who spoke such words. Chester ... Chester Drawers was his name."

"People were everywhere saying new things. They all wanted me to repeat their stupid made-up words. And there were strangers ... lots of them, dressed up in funny looking robes and hats. They were eating in our cafeteria. Only it was fixed up real fancy-like and—and there were many more tables—all bunched together."

"What else did you see, Mila?"

"Your face, daddy. I saw it speaking from inside a cup. There was steam spilling out."

"Ah, coffee," Andorf says, wiping drool off his lips with the back of his hand. "I have not enjoyed a piping hot cup since—"

"You had grey hair. And—and you wore glasses with as many sides as a spider has legs. You were warning someone but they weren't listening."

Andorf raises a brow. "That event occurred during my hours on Earth. It was in a diner where I stirred creamer stick after creamer stick encouraging the image to reappear. Come to think of it, the man in the coffee cup wore octagon-shaped glasses."

Mila settles into her pillow. "The Last Stab Diner," she yawns out.

His eyes widen. Before he can question her further, the five-year-old has nuzzled into the pillow and fallen back asleep. Wiping drool off his lip again, he recalls the night at the Last Stab. "French Roast, how I miss that bountiful aroma and the warm cup in my hands. If I had only known then of the high price of freedom ..." He slips into a pair of jeans and then wrestles a clean shirt over his head. Running a brush through his peppered shoulder-length hair, he pauses to gaze in awe at Mila turning restlessly in her sleep.

"How could she possibly have known such things?" he mumbles, pulling up Mila's covers. "I have never spoken about them to her or anyone else."

Andorf's eyes suddenly widen in thought of the infamous Rugby match. *The grumpy old vendor who spilled hot coffee as freely as his unsolicited advice ... he spoke words in a foreign tongue. He called it something like ten aliens.* Andorf stares again at Mila as if expecting her to awaken and reveal more.

Nah! She could not have known any of this. It occurred before the starship launch, long before I met Serin. Wait! I may have mentioned it to one other person. His head tips to one side. *Gregory ... Gregory Gray, I'll bet he's ingrained tidbits in all those stories he tells the children. He has been info-dumping things in Mila's head.*

After buzzing for the child-keeper, he peers into a mirror and adjusts his wire-rimmed glasses. *Octagon glasses. Hmm ... I could see myself wearing such things in a few years.*

A light tap on the cabin door has him wrapping sandals around his feet and kissing Mila's forehead and the twins. He grins back at Mila, sound asleep in her bed.

No, wait. Gregory was locked up in the Cos. He could not have possibly known about the Last Stab Diner.

He bends down and jostles Mila awake. "You must tell me the truth, Mila. Have you been reading my mind?"

Mila mumbles incomprehensible words and then falls back asleep. Andorf grabs his transcriber and gazes off into space. "Have I really become so transparent?"

*

Binky's log – 144-014200:

Andorf will soon find out being transparent is the least of his problems.

CHAPTER 21

Complications

Day 144: 0650

Burak grasps his superior's arm. "My sources say the fleet has a Goshi aboard one of its starships."

"Goshi?" Turk yells, tilting his head. "What the hell's a Goshi?"

The *Aegean's* comm-spec approaches. "According to gypsy folklore, Goshis have the ability to read minds, even going as far as to bend one's thoughts."

The helmsman raises a brow. "I've heard Goshis can open doors without touching them."

Turk spits on their shoes. "Folklore, bah! Why would I care about children's fables?"

Burak winces. "There always lies a bit of truth in mysticism."

"Bah!"

The comm-spec gasps. "According to uploaded Canine Empire records, there are over seven thousand gypsies scattered amongst the fleet's three starships."

"Gypsies?" Turk yells. "First we're dealing with some Goshi and now stinking gypsies."

"I disdain the thieving bastards as much as you, Commander," Burak says. "But if we are to apprehend their starships, we must certainly entertain their quirks."

*

Binky's log – 144-065554:

Turk will soon get the taste of a junior Goshi's abilities.

CHAPTER 22
Questions

Day 144: 1230

Andorf and Brutus meet outside a C-deck suite in the stem of the starship. Outside the cabin they can hear Murray's rants. They hesitantly step inside the captain's private quarters.

"What the hell am I supposed to do?" Murray yells. "There's a deranged madman out there with an armada of forty-three starships demanding time with the conspirator behind our hijackings—a woman who's been. He pauses to peer at his visitors. Pardon my bluntness, gentlemen, someone who's been dead for months."

Hand on his furry chin and deep in thought, Andorf proceeds to walk about. He half-way smiles. "No insult taken, Captain."

"Likewise," Brutus adds.

Captain Murray winces. "What troubles me most is Turk's requirement for us to wine and dine a thousand of his clan. Why, there's barely room in the *Atlantis'* dining hall to fit one-hundred tables."

Brutus watches Andorf pace about the lavish captain's quarters. "Not to mention fitting as many carriers in our shuttle bay."

Murray extends an arm, halting Andorf from his distractive pacing. "For the record, boys, I don't trust the guy. First, he appears out of nowhere. Now he's most likely aiming to commandeer the fleet. Has anyone given thought about what he plans to do with us afterwards?"

"Well—," Brutus stutters.

"Well, I have. Pirates raid pantries," Murray says. "They steal women … pillage greenhouses … drain every last drop from fuel tanks. That's what ravaging pirates do."

Brutus begins to speak but the captain continues his rant.

"Are you forgetting what Gregory said about the S.O.B.? He gutted his brother … for merely snoring in his sleep."

"Well … I—"

"Dammit, Brutus, haven't you heard a word I said? The sick bastard shot a dog … his own dog."

Brutus' mouth curls as though trying not to gag.

Murray begins to hyperventilate. Brutus offers him the crinkled bag from his rear pocket but the captain refuses. "So, what are we to do, guys? Judging the quantity and size of their starships, they outnumber us over seventy to one. We have no weapons and there's nowhere to hide."

"Well," Brutus says. "The last thing we need is to be stranded out here millions of miles from Earth without food or fuel."

Andorf fingers the pica memory chip dangling from his neck on a lanyard. "Not necessarily so."

Murray winces. "Whatever do you mean?"

Grinning smugly at the others, Andorf tugs on a lanyard dangling around his neck. "Serin smuggled this pico chip out of the Empire. Gregory discovered it contains more plans than just medical devices. Perhaps it contains something other than weapons which can even up the odds."

"Speaking about odds." Brutus raises a brow. "Wagers against the ex-councilwoman are running fifty to one. Everyone in the fleet appears to be betting against one individual, whoever the poor bastard may be."

Andorf winces. "And you believe the ex-congresswoman is tangled up in Argent's disappearance?"

Brutus grins wide. "You told me yourself, Andorf. Ms. Rita was cuffed, insulted, and hauled off by captain Argent and his goons. I have no doubt about the four-foot-eleven ex-councilwoman."

"Now wait a minute," Andorf says. "You may be connecting the wrong dots."

Reading numbers scrolling the bottom of his display, Murray winces. "The odds are now sixty to one against Ms. Rita." Accessing his comm-terminal, he grins at the others. "I've got to place my bet now."

*

Binky's log – 144-124123:

Wait until the rumor spreads to other starships. As the gypsy once told Brutus, you'd better get in now while the odds are low.

CHAPTER 23
Turk's Plans

Day 145:1100 -
Titan Outpost rendezvous: 626 days

Raising his head above the radio console, the *Aegean's* comm-spec appears out of breath. "I've picked up the fleet's latest internal coded message, Commander. Listen up. They have a missing starship captain ... a sinister man named Argent. There's even a running wager with fingers pointing at someone called Rita. Odds are currently ninety to one against the ex-councilwoman."

"Sick bastards!" Turk growls.

The navigator appears from behind his screen sporting a wide grin. "I got in when odds were running seventy to one. Of course, there would be adjustments to armada unit standards but still ... ninety to one."

Turk growls louder. "Is this all you've got for me, radioman? I want to know the fleet's vulnerabilities. If we are to apprehend their starships, I must be aware of Spider's weaknesses."

"I've read messages from the *S.S. Atlantis'* Captain Murray. There's a few from a chief engineer named Brutus and from someone named Andorf. Quite an odd name if you ask me."

"What about Spider?" Turk yells. "He's the only one who interests me. There must be mention of this Spider."

The comm-spec shakes his head.

The next-in-command raises a brow. "Perhaps this Spider has been ..."

"Has been what, Burak?" Turk slams a fist onto the counter. "Are you implying their leader has been disposed ... that Spider is no longer in charge?"

Burak grins. "Coups occur every day, Commander"

With one hand on his trusty saber, Turk paces about the *Aegean's* bridge, splitting caustic gazes between Burak and the crew. "No!" he yells out. "If Spider has been overthrown there'd have been mention of such in the fleet's communications. Keep probing, radioman. There's still a few hours before this evening's reception."

*

Binky's log – 145-111033:

Oh, how easy it is to suspect anything that's not there.

Gregory's Warning

Day 145: 1200

Gregory's hands flailing about, Gregory "Hasn't anyone heard anything I've told them about the guy? He's ruthless ... conniving ... not to be trusted."

Watching his best friend walking around his living area, Andorf raises a brow. "I've heard you installed metal detectors at every shuttle-bay exit."

"Nothing's fool proof. There's always means of circumventing them."

"What about Pol's nitrous gas. He said they will be left squawking like crows on a wire?"

"Crows on a wire. Ha."

"And what about the gypsy's special blend Psygme Ale which should leave our guests laughing at their own uncontrollably flatulence?"

Gregory shakes his head. "Even if every last one of us aboard the *Atlantis* held phasor pistols in their hands it wouldn't be enough. Did you see the size of Turk's armada? His clan outnumbers us a hundred to one."

"More like seventy-five to one."

"Lest you forget, Turk's seen it all. He'll be ready for anything we can throw at him."

"Then I shall dazzle him with my mind reading skills."

"Not before he slices you in half with a swing of his saber."

"I—I will transpose thoughts inside his head … have him see things—"

"Dammit Andorf! The man is dense. Nothing will you do will get through his thick skull."

Andorf gulps. "Then we will need to revise plan C. With the fate of the fleet resting in our hands, it absolutely cannot fail."

Gregory rolls his eyes. "Thanks. You install great confidence."

*

Binky's log – 145-120844:

This Turk sounds absolutely brutal. Perhaps I need to lower my expectations of the junior Goshi.

CHAPTER 25

The Guests

Day 145: 1940

Gold-laced tablecloths trim *Atlantis'* dining-hall settings. Eight-hundred pairs of well-polished sporks and knives glimmer beneath the subtle twinkle of dimmed overhead lighting. Sparkle as they will, the polished utensils are none the less made of cheap, unbreakable graphene.

At more than one chef's dismay, Brutus stuffs his mouth with lavish helpings of tofu cacciatore, saffron zucchini, and caramelized mushrooms. When he reaches to taste the special Psygme Ale to wash it down, he is ushered out of the kitchen by snarling chefs.

In the dining hall, he spots Gregory meandering through the crowds, finger pressed to his ear and speaking into his wrist. Everywhere Brutus turns, he hears passing servers practicing canned Euro and Mid-Eastern phrases. Standing poised in the middle of it all, he cordially greets seemingly endless parades of oddly dressed men speaking foreign tongues as they pour in through the dining hall doors. The forced smile draws on his cheek muscles. They soon pull tight and swell. He then grabs a passing server by the arm.

"Where are all these damn guests coming from? Is there no end? I thought Turk understood the limit was eight hundred ... no more."

Looking around the packed room, the gypsy server smirks. "Both stairwells are jammed as well. The floating steps are so overwhelmed, they've quit functioning. And still, there's just as many of the suckers packing hallways as far as you can see. Turk's clan is backing up all the way to—"

"The bridge," Brutus mumbles. His eyes suddenly widen. He begins to turn to run. "We must stop this before they ..."

Emerging from the crowd, Andorf grabs Brutus' arm. With the gypsy server in tow, he directs Brutus into a vacant corner. "The hallways on every deck are jam packed, Brutus. After inhaling Pol's gas, why the hell aren't the guests jabbering? We were promised they would be squawking like crows on a wire."

"Something's gone terribly wrong." The server begins to perspire. "Your man's truth gas has failed to release."

Brutus gulps. He stares bewildered at Andorf and the server. "Captain Murray's worst fears are coming true. They're heading for the bridge."

"Relax, big guy. No one takes the *Atlantis* this evening," Andorf grins. "Siros locked down the main and alternate bridges to everyone but me, you, and the bridge crew."

Pol runs up to the group panting out of breath. "What are we going to do? I had doubled the formula. My nitrous just isn't fazing these guys. I don't understand. It's never failed in the past."

Andorf crosses his arms. His eyes narrow upon Pol. "Did you even test your gas?"

"Batches were tested on two groups. One group sounded like prostitutes in Sunday confessionals. The others were babbling like conmen on social media, bragging about everything they've ever got away with."

Brutus extracts a handheld scanner from his deep pockets. After a few finger swipes and shuttle bay's environmental stats are projected onto the floor at his feet. "It's not Pol's fault. The nitrous tanks are empty. Pol's gas was released." He finger-swipes the scanner a second time. "There appears to be an abundance of oxygen in the shuttle bay."

Pol winces. "Turk used a dispersant to neutralize the gas."

"Someone tipped them off," the gypsy whispers, looking around the dining hall. "We've got a spy amongst us."

The chief engineer's hand-scanner buzzes. All eyes widen as Brutus interprets the projected warning on the floor. "There were a number of high energy pulses detected in the *Atlantis'* shuttle bay. It appears our guests disabled all of Gregory's magnetometers."

Andorf shakes his head side to side. "Gregory warned us about Turk. Remember him telling us the guy would be ready for anything we could throw at him?"

The server points out many in the crowd. "And take a gander at our guests' loose clothing. They're concealing sabers alright … every last one of them."

"I hear they're planning to attack after the third course," Pol says. "With no weapons of our own, they'll easily take our fleet."

"And what happens when they discover Booger Stew's secret ingredient?" the server says. "Has anyone even thought about that?"

Andorf cringes. "You mean the stew is actually contains …?"

The server grins. "Everyone in the fleet graciously donated. Don't you recall gypsies stopping by your cabin, making a strange request?"

Pol's face reddens. "Yes, but I thought …"

Spotting a bulge in Andorf's shirt, Brutus lifts a corner of his friend's garment. His eyes widen at the sight of twin phasor pistols stuffed into the Goshi's waistline. "What the hell are you doing with those? I thought we agreed how ineffective a pair of phasor pistols would be against a crowd this size."

Andorf halfway grins. "Perhaps if their leader was eliminated …"

Brutus sucks wind between his teeth. "I—I don't think it's such a good idea, Poo. If Turk was taken out, his cohorts would attack us in waves. I've witnessed such strategy before. You may take out a dozen, maybe two dozen in sweeping phasor blasts but soon you'll be dead meat, waiting for the twin phasors to recharge." Brutus pulls back a lock of his hair to reveal an inch-long scar as a past reminder of his disrespect for authority. "Trust me, I know."

"Working with your techs, Gregory reduced the pistol's charge time by eighty percent. That's right, twelve seconds. And look …" Andorf empties his pockets. "Gregory supplied me with extra high-capacity crystalline-iodide power cells."

Pol gulps. "It'd be like beating on a hornet's nest with a short stick."

The server gulps. "That's right. If this group of warriors gets wiped out, thousands of replacements would storm out of their forty-three-ship armada."

Brutus grabs one of Andorf's pistols, stuffs it beneath his beltline, and then pulls his shirt down. He then relieves Andorf of one of his power packs and drops it in one of his deep pockets.

Pol winces. "Wait, Brutus! Didn't you just tell us …?"

Brutus grins. "If I'm going down, you'd better believe I'm taking a few inbreeds with me."

Gregory appears from within the crowd. Perspiring heavily, he looks the disenchanted group over several times before speaking. "I've got every table bugged. My interpreters are deciphering schemes of pilfering supplies and commandeering our starships ... sometime after the third course."

"See? What'd I tell you?" the server says. "Our guests aren't ambassadors. They're warriors!"

Brutus spots a bulge in the server's beltline. Scanning the dining hall, he sees every last server sporting similar bulges. His eyes widen when Gregory's shirt pulls to one side. "What the hell, Gregory! Even you're packing?"

Gregory shrugs his shoulders. "So, I had your techs replicate a few of Andorf's phasor pistols. The late Captain Thom always urged us to stack things in our favor."

"But I don't understand," Brutus says. "It'd take months to reverse-engineer Andorf's phasor pistols. How'd you—?"

Andorf pulls on the lanyard dangling around his neck. "Are you forgetting Serin's pica chip? Gregory discovered detailed instructions on manufacturing the weapons."

"I found your fellow gypsies have no love for Turk." Gregory smirks. "They helped me construct a small weapons lab in the empty lab across from your mechanical room. You wouldn't believe how fast we churned them out."

Brutus winces. "In the bowels of the *Atlantis*?"

Gregory nods.

"Oh, if Serin were alive, things would never have resorted to this," Brutus mumbles. Raising his brow and taking a long, deep breath, he glances at the others. "Let the battle commence."

*

Binky's log – 145-200502:

As I mentioned before, this Turk and his followers are brutal. What can Andorf and his friends do?

CHAPTER 26
The Tenulians

Day 145: 2100

From a corner of the chaotic dining hall, Andorf, Brutus, Gregory, Pol, and gypsy server see empty ale kegs piling high along the walls. They watch visitors continue to stream through the doors while servers holding back the first course and repeatedly ask the same cordial question.

"A bit more Psygmy Ale for our most-welcomed guest?"

"Look at them chugging down the ale by the quart," Pol says. "They're practically inhaling the stuff."

The server raises a brow. "I hear no laughter, no uncontrolled bouts of flatulence."

Brutus raises a brow. "Are they also immune to Psygmy Ale?"

"Didn't I warn you?" Gregory's face tightens. "These guys are animals. Nothing we do will ever stop them."

Andorf nods. "I feel we are but whip-less lion tamers in the center of a three-ring circus."

"You must excuse me. I see tables without servers." The server leaves suddenly to work the group.

Brutus eyes the vacant seat at the main table. "Where the hell is Turk? Has anyone seen the—?"

The room suddenly quiets. All eyes turn toward the six-foot-ten man ducking as he enters through main doors. Wearing a traditional embroidered Ottoman vest and red Kalpak hat, he is flanked by two nearly as tall men who seem occupied scanning the crowd. Turk raises his arms high and then lowers them slowly. Conversations then resume from where they were abruptly interrupted.

"Look at the bastard," Brutus says, watching Turk meander between tables and pass compatriots with hushing fingers. "He and his thugs are plotting something all right."

"Notice how everyone keeps their eyes on the commander?" Gregory twitches. "No one acts without his explicit signal."

Taking the reserved seat at the main table, Turk is promptly presented the first course and a frosty mug of Psygmy Ale. Again, the room quiets. Compatriots watch Turk's personal taster reach around the armada's commander with his pea-sized spoon.

The wiry man inserts the sampler spoon into Turk's steaming bowl of Booger Stew. He holds the translucent spoon up to the light, taps the end of the sampler with an index finger before sniffing the odd, greenish concoction. After sniffing the tiny sample a second time, the taster slowly inserts the slop into his mouth. His eyes roll about as if relishing an exquisite flavor. When he dips a sampler into the bowl for a second taste, Turk shoves him aside to dig his own, much larger spork into the gooey mess. At the backdrop of wide-grinning servers and Turk shoveling sporkful after sporkful into his mouth, guests dig in.

Andorf hears guests raving about the unique stew and does his best not to laugh. Instead, he gazes intensely at the armada commander. Focused in thought, he walks away from the small group. After a long moment, he rejoins his friends.

"I've evaluated the commander's thoughts, Brutus. You are absolutely correct. Turk and his clan *are* planning to take the *Atlantis* ... promptly after the third course. Noting how they defeated our nitrous gas and appear un-phased by the Psygme Ale, we are advancing onto plan C. Gregory, notify your team."

Gregory taps Pol's arm. "We must hurry. Servers are collecting the first course bowls." And just like that, Gregory and the comm-spec leave the group. Within seconds they blend into the crowd.

"Well, I don't know about you, Poo, but I'm heading for the kitchen," Brutus says. "I have no intention of dying with an empty belly."

Andorf feels suddenly abandoned as he waits patiently. The Goshi wonders if his friends have left to spend their final moments alone. He watches his prey converse with table mates between bites and long slurps of the specially-brewed Psygmy Ale. When the second course is placed before him, Turk wipes froth from his lips and digs in, totally unaware he is the prime target of Andorf and Gregory's plan C.

With the fleet relying on him, Andorf knows nothing else can fail. He eyes the low-rise stage placed along the shortest dining room wall. Mentally rehearsing his moves, he waits for the perfect moment to pounce.

Sighting Turk lowering his spork, Andorf advances. In swift motion, he leaps atop the low-rise stage. After speaking covertly into a wireless microphone hidden in his sleeve, the twinkling overhead lights dim further. He feels the weight of a thousand pairs of eyes suddenly focused upon him. Expecting Turk to be as terrible as Gregory described, he avoids eye contact with the bulky man seated at the master table. He glances across the room, noting the strange mix of loose-fitting outfits and hostile faces appearing startled at his sudden appearance.

Andorf clips a second wireless mic on his lapel and with a pop, he is tapped into the public address systems of all forty-six starships. To avoid confusion, he speaks slow and clearly.

"Welcome to the *Atlantis*, my new friends. I see everyone has savored the exquisite Booger Stew tonight. It is a favorite dish here aboard the *Atlantis*." Andorf uncrosses the fingers held behind his back.

"As most of you already know, we aboard the *Atlantis* and her sister starships, the *Mayflower* and the *Phoenix*, were the first ones to break free of their empire's iron grip."

Andorf spots many lost faces appearing to be questioning his words. Others appear to be pressing fingers against ear-pieces. Taking deep breaths while the guest's translators catch up, he hopes the interpreters are not darkening his words.

"I see the day in a not-too-distant future when we all speak a common language. But for now, we remain at the mercy of intermediaries."

A larger-than-life holograph of Mahatma Gandhi appears above the stage. Andorf glances at the image behind and grins at the crowd.

"It is hard to imagine a hundred years ago, when this man took to the streets, demanding freedom from an oppressive empire such as our own. Armed with only angry words, this man and many like him spoke of revolution ... revolution against a repressive government ... revolution against binary parties who dared limit their choices to merely ones and zeros. Try as they might, the government failed to silence him. Throughout many incarcerations, Gandhi and his followers demanded freedom ... a return of power to the people."

The holograph morphs into the slightly more modern outspoken critic of government, Gil Scott-Heron. "In song, this man also spoke of revolution ... one not sponsored by corporate greed. If these brave leaders were with us today, they would say this to our faces." Voice ramping up, Andorf raises his hands high. "The revolution will not be digitized. Viva la revolution!"

For an instant, the room is deadly quiet. As if by magic, guests throughout the dining hall abandon their seats to stand and cheer loudly in their native tongues.

Turk growls. With eyes narrowing upon the man prancing around the stage, he reluctantly stands. The commander raises both hands high in the air but finds no eyes are upon him.

Though Andorf grins at the sea of applauding hands, he winces inside at the variety of animal calls. He walks the low-rise stage, weaving back and forth in front of sequencing images depicting cruel and oppressive activities of the Asian and Middle-Eastern empires projected on the wall behind him. He calmly sips an apple cooler while focusing on the one man standing arms crossed and fuming, apparently waiting for a lull in the overwhelming cheer to intercede.

Determined to maintain control, Andorf lifts both arms high. He lowers them slowly and the fanfare dwindles to a mild roar. Eyes sweeping the crowd, he speaks before Turk can open his mouth.

"Everywhere I look I see troubled faces of fellow outcasts ... faces from the seven great empires of a dying home world. I envision rich customs passed down through generations, unique as every last one of us. Between our forty-six starships, we must be near a million strong, all different and yet all the same."

Renewed cheer overwhelms Andorf. But he knows if he were to stutter, even for the slightest instant, his built-up momentum will forever be lost. The cheering crowd will surely turn and chew him up quicker than locust in a cornfield. For what comes next, his timing must be spot-on, his approach impeccable. Andorf times his strut across the low-rise stage, knowing everything must be precise when he delivers the bomb. Pocketing his drink, he prepares for the windup but finds himself stumbling on a name … a name of something … anything to unite the fleet to the tribes before him.

The voice of his five-year-old daughter softly echoes in his head. *Ten aliens … Tenalien … Tenulian. That's it … Tenulian.* Taking on the comforting lost-boy look which has never failed him in the past, Andorf raises both arms high. He waits as the cheering wanes. "Unless anyone knows of a better name," he says, displaying open palms at the crowd. "I propose from this day hence forth, each and every one of us shall be known as Tenulians, Earth's triumphant renegades."

Turk appears steaming mad. He pulls off a shoe and pounds it hard on the main dinner table. He pounds repeatedly until every last eye is focused upon him. "I demand to see Spider!" he yells. "I demand to speak to Spider now!"

Andorf is jaw-dropped and lost for words. He feels like a chunk of sharp cheddar in a room full of hungry mice. With the crowd's contemptuous eyes now staring him down, he feels the crowd on the brink of turning against him. Beginning to sweat profusely, Andorf shuts his eyes. He trances his thoughts back to times of fond childhood memories. Into everyone's thoughts, he plants images of his father chasing him through the scrap yard in hot pursuit. He envisions his mother chasing after him and father, warning of dangerous metal shards surrounding them. Then he projects the euphoria of having father all to himself, if only for those few cherished moments.

Andorf switches events. He relives passionate moments with his late wife Serin from the moment they met in Gregory's apartment, to her releasing political prisoners, to battling evil Max and then the chaotic hijacking of the empire's starships. He projects memories of Serin in sickbay—her untimely death during childbirth. Through teary eyes, he spots many in the crowd on the edge of their seats, wiping their own eyes.

Turk tries to interrupt the intense moment but the crowd will have no part of it.

Brutus returns from the kitchen with a full belly. Wiping his mouth, he leaps onto the low-rise stage. He activates a clip-on mic and stares Turk down, "This Spider you speak of happens to be my wife Serin ... the great Serin Gray."

The roaring crowd stares at the chief engineer as if confused. Turk bends his spork around a finger and then watches the cheap carbene piece resume to its spork shape when released. "What the hell is this?" Turk tosses the utensil aside. "And who's this clown?" he yells, pointing at Brutus. "I refuse to deal with a gypsy. Get his ass off the stage."

To the crowd's dismay, gypsy servers throughout the dining hall collect every last mug of specially brewed Psygme Ale, empty or not. Carrying full trays, they storm out of the room.

"I demand to speak with this Spider ... the one you call Serin Gray!" Turk pounds his shoe on the table. "Why is there no Serin Gray here amongst us tonight?"

At the crowd's deafening roar, Andorf throws both hands high in the air. The crowd slowly quiets. "Serin was my wife as well."

"Our wife," Brutus adds. "She died in—"

"Childbirth," Andorf says. "She was delivering our—"

"Twins."

Turk's focus bounces between Andorf and Brutus. Listening to the pair completing each other's sentences, he grabs hold of his head as if to keep it from twisting off. "Are you expecting us to believe this revolution was conspired by a pregnant woman who was married to the both of you?"

Andorf nods. "Serin not only released hundreds of political prisoners but—"

Brutus grins. "She conjured up the whole revolution."

"Right down to the last detail," Andorf adds.

The crowd again roars. With eyes narrowing upon Andorf and Brutus, Turk pounds his shoe on the table. As the crowd is slow to quiet, he continues to pound.

Andorf covers the mic on his lapel and whispers covertly into his sleeve. "Things are getting out of hand in here, Gregory. Get those servers back in here … pronto."

Turk rushes the stage. He grabs Andorf's wrist and pulls back his sleeve to expose the hidden wireless mic. "You think you're pulling a fast one, don't you? Do you take us for fools, believing all these lies? No single person could have possibly done all this … let alone some pregnant woman."

Brutus smirks. "Serin was no ordinary woman. She not only rallied crowds, but she faced down one of the Empire's high holy men."

"All without batting an eye," Andorf adds.

One hundred gypsy servers reappear with hands resting upon their belt-mounted phasor pistols. They encircle the dining hall and then disperse between tables. At Andorf's nod, the servers begin to clap. Despite Turk sending rude hand gestures, there is renewed vibrancy wafting throughout the room. Andorf leaps off the stage to confront Turk. He tugs on the combative commander's hefty arm but the six-foot-ten man towering above resists, yelling native obscenities down at the much shorter Goshi.

To Turk's surprise, he finds himself on the low-rise stage with many of his comrades prodding him to speak. The commander growls at the clip-on mic Andorf attached to his collar. He snarls at Andorf as if sizing up his adversary for dinner and then pushes him aside. "Enough of this carnival stunt, little man. Your puny starship fleet will never take charge of my grand armada of forty-three. That fancy speech gives you no authority and definitely none to a gypsy."

Andorf freezes dead-center of the stage. With eyes narrowing upon Turk's reddening face, his mind probes deep beneath the commander's enraged eyes. The Goshi senses hate, much like what he felt when confronting the high-holy man, Fat Max, back on Earth.

Turk grabs at his wobbly head with both hands. Watching Andorf signal for Brutus to step closer, he takes hold of his not-well-hidden sword. Brutus wedges between Andorf and Turk to limit the commander's arm movement.

Andorf steps away, again whispering in his wrist. Holographs of abused Turkish prisoners brighten the stage. Without fear, Andorf strolls around Brutus to face the six-foot-ten commander, who appears to be caught up viewing the projections.

"Like you, Turk, we are renegades who escaped our *own* repressive empire.

Now we are out here millions of miles from home, on the same energy quest. Can you not see? We are all in this together ... on the same mission. No one wants to diminish your command. We only wish to join your grand armada."

As holographs of his crawling nine-month-old son are projected onto the stage before him, Turk's fingers slowly release the sword. After the baby lets out a loud coo, the image blends into Andorf playing on the floor with his own twin toddlers, Ayla and Sarak.

Watching the hologram of Andorf on all fours playing with the twins, Turk's temper lessens to wane. After long, tense moments, the commander grins at Andorf's 'lost little-boy' look. Turk pulls Andorf's lapel mic off and casts it onto the floor. Then he twists Andorf's wrist, rips off his hidden mic, and tosses it into the crowd. After doing the same with Brutus' mic, he casts his own clip-on mic onto the floor. He then leans down to Andorf.

"I take it you're this Goshi I've been hearing so much about?"

Halfway grinning, Andorf reluctantly raises a brow.

"If you ever get inside my thoughts like that again, I'll slice off your head. Do you understand me, little man?"

Peering up at the towering man, Andorf applies his best salesman-grin. "I see us becoming good friends one day."

Murray mumbles while staring at his missing middle finger. "Stranger things have occurred."

Andorf reaches to shake hands with Turk, but the armada's commander has stepped away to gaze at his many compatriots packing the dining hall and those spilling out the exits. Turk eyes the hundred gypsy servers standing near tables, hands poised on their exposed belt-mounted weapons. He again leans down to Andorf.

"I take it those are phasor pistols your servers are wearing?"

Recalling Brutus' words of an impending battle, Andorf takes a deep breath. "Yep, all fully-charged."

"With high-capacity crystalline-iodide power cells," Brutus adds.

Turk again surveys the room. "With my men all bearing sabers, it appears you are disadvantaged by a factor of eight to one."

Brutus lifts a corner of his shirt to reveal his own phasor. "I would say we're evenly matched."

Andorf lifts his shirt as well.

Taking note of gypsy servers, many of whom are picking their noses and laughing, he leans into Andorf. "Funny custom your gypsies have."

Andorf smirks. "Consider it their way of welcoming you, Commander."

Holding his laugh, Brutus turns away in silence.

Turk picks his own nose at the servers and then turns back to Andorf. "Here's how this plays out, little man. I'm now in command of forty-six-starships. Your three starships are under my direction. This is non-negotiable."

Andorf nods.

"And one more thing," Turk says, eyes narrowing.

Thinking the worst, Andorf begins to speak until Brutus elbows him in the ribs. Facing eye to eye with the commander, Brutus grins over Andorf's head. "And what's that, Commander?"

"Your chefs are to spork over the recipe for that tasty Booger Stew. Am I clear on this?" Turk winces at Brutus and then grunts. He then steps around Andorf to spit on Brutus' shoes.

Andorf is stunned. He glances first at Turk and then at Brutus, wondering whether this is a Turkish custom, an insult, or the beginning of a spitting feud.

Brutus likewise grunts. He too spits, on the floor, aiming at the commander's size fourteen shoes.

Exchanging uneasy glances with the men towering on either side, both prompting him with their hands, Andorf expects the worst. He grunts and then spits on each of their shoes. At sight of lines breaking in Turk's face, he begins to wonder.

Have I misconstrued the subtle rules of this spitting ritual? Did I spit enough too little … too much? Perhaps I have missed some subtle mannerism.

After a long silence, Turk bursts into laughter. He grabs Andorf's much smaller arm and raises it high, toward the crowd. "Viva la revolution!" he yells. "Long live the Tenulians!"

*

Binky's log – 145-231009:

So, my junior Goshi actually pulled it off. Or did he?

PART 3
MINGLINGS

CHAPTER 27

Aftermath

Day 148: 1230 -
Titan Outpost rendezvous: 623 days

Tenulian words with multiple language translations dominating starship informational displays. Common expressions from twenty-seven languages are first to be merged into words of new Tenulian dialect.

Tenulian word of the day is 'capado' – an imposter, someone masquerading as someone else.

B rutus watches his old friend plop his butt into his favorite easy chair and then regret doing so. Andorf spills out of the chair and onto the floor where he lies, reviewing the immensity of everything in the A-deck's grandmaster suite as he catches his breath. Over the oversized furniture, custom-built for the originally intended occupant, the eight-foot-tall Fat Max spans the large room as he struggles to roll out of the deep ruts worn into the middle by a much larger predecessor. He winces at the private bathroom, the dumbwaiter leading directly to the G-deck kitchen and the fancy Hotot crown molding trimming out the ten-foot ceilings.

Brutus first chuckles at the Goshi splayed out on the floor and then get serious. "How could you? You literally gave away the farm. What the hell are we to do now?"

Andorf glances upward as he struggles to find his feet. "Nothing has really changed. It is merely a formality … a title for gosh sakes."

"You've relinquished control of the fleet? Turk and his clan are pirates. Without notice, they can assume control of the bridge … rob our supplies … leave us stranded out here, millions of miles from home."

"And why would Turk do that? By adding our measly fleet of three star-ships to his grand armada of forty-three, I robbed the wind from his sails. What rational man would dare ravage his own starships?"

Brutus scratches his balding crown. "Hmm. Very clever I suppose. But still, Turk's a pirate … never to be trusted and I'm not sure the guy's all that rational."

"I would not worry about it. The commander is too busy minding his own clan to be concerned about our three starships. Why else would he approve a Second Council?"

"That doesn't mean a damn thing, Andorf. There are thousands of gypsies like myself scattered amongst the fleet. He's hoping to dilute our influence by expanding the council. And with Turk being speaker of the Second Council, he can over-rule them on a whim. The guy is only waiting for us to complete our Galactic drives. Until then, the armada will need to refuel at every weigh station between Titan Station and planet Nero."

"Seeing that Turk lacks the engineering skills to advance the Galactic project toward implementation, consider your gypsy engineers a bargaining chip. He may despise the gypsies but he needs them."

Brutus snorts. "Many of us believe he's got spies aboard the *Atlantis*, not to mention aboard the *Phoenix* and the *Mayflower*. They're all keeping tabs on the drive's progress."

"Has anyone even seen Turk aboard the *Atlantis* since the welcoming dinner? Has he or any of his clan stepped one foot aboard this starship since then? Huh? Have they? Besides, Siros has both bridges locked down to all but a few."

"Well no, but—"

"Siros, who has access to the *Atlantis'* main and alternate bridges?"

Siros: *Atlantis'* bridge accesses are limited to bridge crew, Chief Engineer Brutus Bittner, George Harrison, and Goshi Andorf Johnson.

Andorf cringes at the title before grinning at the chief engineer. "See, Brutus? There is absolutely nothing to—WAIT! Siros, did you say George Harrison?"

Siros: Affirmative.

"Who the hell is George Harrison?"

Silence.

"Siros!" Brutus yells. "Answer Andorf's question. Who is George Harrison?"

Siros: George Harrison was the lead guitarist and frequent singer/songwriter of a popular mid-twentieth century British quartet known as the Beatles.

Andorf smirks. "Siros! Terminate George Harrison's bridge access."

Silence.

"Siros," Andorf repeats. "Remove George Harrison's access to the *Atlantis'* bridges."

Siros: Cannot comply. George Harrison's account has been flagged as irrevocable.

"Irrevocable? By whose authority? Siros, by whose authority?"

Silence.

"Siros! Answer Andorf's question!"

Siros: Authority unknown.

"Well, isn't that just grand." Brutus squints in disdain. "Here we have the *Atlantis'* bridges locked down and the crazed pirate can still waltz right in there anytime he chooses."

Andorf casts open palms toward Brutus. "Now, wait a minute. We cannot be absolutely certain this Harrison fellow is actually Turk. As I said, no one has spotted him or any of his clan aboard the *Atlantis* ... nor the *Mayflower* or the *Phoenix* for that matter."

"Think, Andorf. Who else could it be? A sneaky rat this commander is. You've heard what Gregory said about the guy shooting his own dog. If you don't watch him, one day the bastard will come after your rabbit."

Andorf raises a brow. "Binky? I think not."

"Yes, Binky. The pirate has little regard for anyone, let alone their pet."

"For the life of me, I shall never understand this bad blood between the gypsies and Turk's clan. How long has this feud been going on?"

"It's been going on for nearly a century, dating back to the medieval days." Brutus scratches his head for a long moment. "As the tale goes, what began as a simple misunderstanding over a missing goblet quickly escalated. The Turks blamed the gypsies, calling them thieves. The gypsies in turn denied the goblet even existed, calling it bogus, trumped-up charges. There's been mistrust between our clans ever since."

"And now you suspect Turk, who appears to lack technical skills, has hacked into Siros to gain secured access to *Atlantis'* bridge. When will this madness end?"

Brutus grumbles.

"And why would he use George Harrison? If I were Turk, I would have picked something more fitting of a commander … something like Napoleon or Kublai Khan?"

Brutus shakes his head. "Obvious. It's much too obvious."

Andorf's eyes suddenly widen as does Brutus'. They race for the grandmaster suite's informational display and take turns finger-tweezing the display screen in search of the forty-six-starship passenger roster.

Watching names scroll quickly past, Andorf rubs his days old chin growth.

Brutus looks over his old friend's shoulder at the names appearing and quickly scrolling off the display. "That one. No! That one. Nope." He pushes Andorf aside. He tries to slow the scrolling names but finds his fat fingers too clumsy.

After a few minutes, the screen blanks. Four dreaded words are displayed.

<George Harrison not found>

Brutus steps back. "There, Andorf. See for yourself. There's no one aboard any of the armada starships bearing that name. It can only be one person. It must be Turk."

Andorf squeezes past Brutus. He tweezes the screen, searching for any name remotely similar to that of George Harrison. After a moment, one name appears in dead center of the display. He squinches his nose at the results. "The plumber?"

"Calling a pipe-fitter a plumber is a sure way to get your hose bent."

Andorf gazes down at his private parts and then back at the display. "Siros, who is this Jerry Georgison?"

Siros: Jerry Georgison is a master pipe-fitter stationed aboard the *S.S. Cristobel.* He is—

"Siros," Brutus says. "Does this Jerry Georgison have bridge access?"

Siros: Negative.

"Let me try." Andorf clears his throat. "Siros, search for any name similar to Jerry Georgison." He and Brutus stare at each other, waiting.

Siros: It is rumored that Harry Georgison was one of many pennames the British lead guitarist George Harrison coined when playing on other musicians' pieces such as Eric Clapton's—

Brutus questions the starship's consciousness. "Siros, does Harry Georgison have bridge access?"

Siros: Affirmative.

"Siros, when was Harry Georgison granted bridge access?"

Silence.

"Siros!" Brutus yells. "Answer Andorf's question."

Siros: Cannot comply. This data has been purged.

"Purged? Siros, who purged this information?"

Silence.

"Siros!" Brutus yells.

Siros: Cannot comply. That information has also been purged.

Andorf winces. "Siros, where is this Harry Georgison currently located?"

Siros: Unknown. But I can tell you this. Harry Georgison is a fast typist with very warm fingertips.

Brutus also winces. "Siros, display names of anyone who may be familiar with British pop music of the past century."

Siros: There are too many to name. Please narrow your search criteria.

Brutus tries again. "Siros, limit your search to those aboard the armada's original three starships."

Siros: There are too many to name. Please narrow your search criteria.

"Siros," Andorf says. "Using the same search criteria but add having ample technical savvy to hack the *Atlantis'* security system."

Siros: The only name matching your search parameter is George Harrison.

Brutus snorts. "Oh, that's comforting. Here we have a hacker in our midst and Siros only identifies him as a fast typist."

Andorf grins. "And someone with warm fingertips."

Siros: Precisely.

*

Binky's log – 148-125815:

Don't look at me! I'm not a fast typist with warm hands. I'm a rabbit. I have paws.

CHAPTER 28

Words With The Captain

Day 148: 1320

Captain Murray sneers at the Goshi and then at his chief engineer. "And so, you believe we have a hacker in our midst ... someone with free access to the *Atlantis'* bridges?"

Brutus nods. "I suspect this to be the handy-work of Turk and his fellow pirates. After all, it's curious how this just happens to occur while there's uncertainty of how the commander plans to merge our fleet into his armada."

Andorf winces at his old friend. "The hacker is using the name Harry Georgison. It somehow links back to a 'George Harrison'."

Murray raises a brow. "You mean the pipefitter aboard the *S.S. Cristobel?*"

Brutus growls. "No. Not Jerry Georgison."

"Siros tells us the user account cannot be accessed," Andorf adds.

Murray begins to walk about his private quarters. "Harry? George? Can't Siros make up its bloody mind?"

Andorf and Brutus exchange glances as they shrug their shoulders.

"Whoever this hacker is ..." Murray winces. "He or she could not have picked a worse time. We are in the middle of forming a Second Council, the majority of which will come from Turk's forty-three starships. The last thing we need is someone to be assuming control of the *Atlantis*, the *Mayflower*, or the *Phoenix*."

Brutus raises a brow. "Caution the bridge crew to stay vigilant, Captain. Bridge access must be limited to the three of us and your crew."

*

Binky's log – 148-132817:

We've got a serious hacker aboard the Atlantis. *I've never trusted this Siros. He may intentionally be leading everyone astray.*

CHAPTER 29

Binky's Premonition

Day 200: 1200 -
Titan Outpost rendezvous: 571 days

Tenulian word of the day is 'naustevik' – an impending visitor.

Binky tears a path across the cabin, the likes of which has not occurred since Serin's passing. On one pass Andorf bends down and scoops up his furry companion. The bunny shivers as he is cradled in his human's chest.

"What is going on, Binkers? Has something scared you?"

Binky lifts his head, peers into his caregiver's eyes.

After a long moment, Andorf pulls away. He takes a deep breath and lets it out loudly. "So, we are expecting a visitor? Is it another woman?"

The rabbit shakes his head and then peers deep inside Andorf's eyes.

"It will be a large man having an even larger request?"

Binky leaps from Andorf's arms to hop across the room. From the safety of a hay-filled litter box, he winks back at Andorf.

Andorf rubs his chin as he peers out his door's peep hole. "Hmm. I wonder who would be calling at *this* time of day?"

*

Binky's log – 200-121505:

It's true! What Andorf mentioned on Unification Day is about to occur.

CHAPTER 30
A Small Favor

Day 200: 1230

Tenulian word of the day is 'Conta Kuuntan' – a swear word too graphic to explain.

Turk boards the S.S. Atlantis for his first appearance since the welcoming dinner. Frustrated, he examines the last cabin on the A-deck hallway and walks back one cabin from the master suite. The commander taps on the cabin door. After a brief moment, the cabin door opens.

Sighting the absence of the commander's trusty saber brings a smile to Andorf's face. "How warm are your fingertips?"

"What?"

"I am wondering how fast you type."

"I don't type." Turk growls. "Why would you ask?"

Andorf shrugs his shoulders and lets the commander inside. "Never mind. It is unimportant. So, Turk, you have returned to the *Atlantis*. What can I do for you?"

"Is it true what I hear … that you've never consumed GMOs?"

Without words, Andorf nods.

"Or indulged much in distilled beverages or taken any serious drugs recently?"

Andorf shakes his head. "Only a single drink on my wedding night. I suspect it makes me one of the more desirable mating males in the entire the armada. So, I ask again, what brings you here, Commander?"

"Turk. Please call me Turk."

"OK, Turk."

"I recall you once mentioned we would one day become good friends."

Appearing suspicious, Andorf half-way grins. "Indeed. It was back on Unification Day when I first mention it."

Turk stares down at his feet for long seconds wondering how to ask this stranger for such a personal favor. He glances up and awkwardly smiles. "I believe that long-awaited day has arrived. You see, my wife, Anel, speaks of wanting a second child but ... well ... she's having trouble conceiving." Head tilted, he peers at Andorf. "She may need a little help if you know what I mean."

Andorf's eyes widen. "No can do. The sperm bank monitors my donations. They count and measure my potency. Every day I skip a donation it is noted in some accountant logs. Each time my potency diminishes they record it. Have you seen their meticulous logs?"

The commander shakes his head.

"They keep stats on everything, from our food supplies to the escalating birthrate. They track personal things about me and you ... things you don't even want to know."

"You mean even—?"

Andorf pouts his lips and nods.

"Damn beanos. Before you know, they'll be piloting every starship in the armada."

Andorf cringes.

"Anel, she brags she is thirty. In truth, she wears many more years. The wait here on your Atlantis is eighteen months. On the Aegean, it's more like thirty."

"But you are the commander. Surely ..."

"It doesn't matter who you are. Everyone waits. Please, my friend ... I'm begging you. Anel can wait no longer."

Andorf grabs hold of his chin. "I would have to squeeze two in one day. To pull something like this off I would need to be on a special diet for weeks. I do my best work after midnight. Someone would have to watch the kids and—"

Turk's voice revs with excitement. "Of course. It can certainly be arranged."

"Have Anel come to my cabin one evening in a couple weeks."

Hand tightening around his belt-mounted knife, Turk grumbles. "I shall provide a vial and wait in the next room. When you are done, the specimen will be chilled and rushed back to my awaiting bride."

"As I mentioned, my activities are monitored. My donations are frequently tested for vitality. It will require much effort on my part."

"So, what are you saying, my friend?"

Andorf winces. "It will cost you."

A single bead of perspiration drips off Turk's temple. He casts sad eyes at Andorf. "You must understand, Andorf. I'm a lowly commander, a man of very few possessions." He pauses to peer at Mila and the twins playing in the next room. "What could I possibly provide you do not have already?"

Andorf rubs his cheek. He takes a deep breath and exhales slowly. "As with Anel, my rabbit, Binky, is also getting up there in age. Perhaps if Binky had a furry companion ... someone with whom he could continue his blood line. I held off on getting him neutered."

Turk's face reddens. His eyes cross. "No! Absolutely not! Anel loves her bunny more than life itself. Why, she would as well slice off both my arms than to part with her precious Mamooshka."

Andorf displays open palms at the commander. "Whoa there. I would never expect Anel to go through all that trouble." Andorf grins. "But those are my terms, Turk. Take it or leave it."

"Conta Kuuntan," Turk yells. "This cannot be done. What you're asking of me is—"

"Then Anel must wait like the others." Andorf smiles at the kids at play and then turns back to face the commander. "Let me know soon if you change your mind. I am already in my late thirties. My donations are not without end."

"But Andorf, my friend, Anel's child bearing days are also nearing an end."

"As with Binky, my friend."

*

Binky's log – 200-140922:

The six-foot-ten commander does not appear so powerful when he begs. Hopefully, his request won't become a demand.

CHAPTER 31

Brutus' Concern

Day 201 – Titan Outpost rendezvous: 570 days

Tenulian word of the day is 'braunswag' – misdirected concern.

In the wee hours of the morning, Brutus pounds on an A-deck cabin door. "I know you're not asleep in there. Goshis never sleep."

After a moment, Andorf appears. Brutus pushes past into the cabin. He winces at the sight of Andorf waving and the cabin door seeming to close on its own.

"You appear flustered, Brutus. What is this about?"

"Video footage caught Turk riding the floating steps before entering your cabin. Tell me it wasn't the commander."

"Yes, it was Turk." Andorf yawns aloud. "He was here on personal business."

Face reddening, Brutus begins to sweat. "Tell me the pirate wasn't here for the Booger Stew recipe. He's desperate to find the missing ingredient. Why else would he be on the *Atlantis*? My fellow gypsies and I have taken an oath of secrecy." The chief engineer takes a deep breath. "Don't tell me you revealed the special secret ingredient."

"No, no, no! There is another reason ... of a more personal matter."

"And what, you cannot tell the friend you've known since grade school?"

After glancing at the sleeping kids, Andorf whispers, "If you must know, he and his wife are having difficulties conceiving. Turk wanted me to impregnate his wife."

Brutus wipes his damp brow. "Then it has nothing to do with Booger Stew?"

Andorf shakes his head.

"And Turk displayed no interest in commandeering the *Atlantis*?"

Again, Andorf shakes his head.

"Whew! I was scared the guy was trying to 'f' us over." Brutus wipes sweat off his brow. His eyes suddenly narrow. "Wait! What did he offer you in return?"

"Why?"

Brutus grunts. "I don't trust the bastard, Andorf. He'll start schmoozing his way in as your good friend and before you know it ..."

"Before I know what?"

"The pirate will place impossible demands, that's what."

Andorf grins. "If you must know, I asked him to mate his wife's bunny with Binky but he refused."

"Just stay on alert. You'd best be aware of his demands."

*

Binky's log – 201-110533:

Can there be justification for the chief engineer's paranoia? After all, the commander is still a pirate.

CHAPTER 32

Another Sleepless Night

Day 460 - Titan Outpost rendezvous: 311 days

Tenulian word of the day is 'contra con' – expecting the impossible.

A reoccurring nightmare of cougars attacking and ravaging his manhood has Andorf tossing in his sleep. At the insistent pounding, he splashes his face at the sink and then cracks open his cabin door. His foggy eyes widen at the sight of an attractive towel-wrapped woman of early-forties. Hair dripping wet, she appears to have just left one of the daily happy hour sessions set aside for the less gender-discriminant bather.

"Whatever you want now is not a good time. I have sleeping children in the next room."

The woman tightening her damp towel wrap does little to conceal her feminine form. "Aren't you Goshi Andorf? Word has it you have the cleanest genes in the entire armada."

Andorf squinches his nose at the mention of Goshi as he watches her rub a bare thigh seductively against the cabin door frame. "Look, I—lady, it is middle of the night. You should try visiting the clinic later in the morning. I am sure they'll be glad to—"

"Put me on a long wait list?" The woman's towel loosens as she wiggles. It slips off well past her shoulders. "You don't understand. My biological clock is ticking. I cannot wait six months." Barging inside, she freezes at the sight of Mila and the twins asleep in the next room. Her eyes widen as well as the smile on her face. "My friends weren't kidding about your fertility."

Andorf knows better than to gaze into the woman's hypnotic dark browns. Last time he did so, he ended up in a triad marriage smack dab in the middle of a revolution against the mighty Canine Empire. He maintains a safe distance, trying not to inhale the woman's intoxicating perfume. Wearing only briefs, he takes the woman's arm and ushers her into the walk-in closet, away from neighbor's ears and more importantly, the radar-like ears of a certain five-year old sleeping in the next room.

The woman quickly pivots, pinning him against the accordion closet door. Andorf gulps at her moist tongue licking her swollen lip, the beads of water on her shoulders, and the towel edging its way down her torso. With a calculated shake, the towel drops to her ankles.

"Oops," she says, wearing only a seductive grin. She leans forward and presses her breasts firmly against his hairy chest.

Andorf grabs the woman by her dripping shoulders. Locking both elbows, he struggles to keep her at arm's length. He watches beads of water dripping off the ends of her shoulder-length hair. Resist as he might, he simply cannot keep his wandering eyes off the droplets weaving crooked paths down her neck and onto her bare chest. Andorf's elbows weaken. His eyes are not the only thing having a mind of its own.

"I—I am not doing this, lady," he says, choking out words. "You must visit the clinic like everyone else. There can be no exceptions."

The woman slips her hands beneath his arms and tickles his hairy armpits until he releases her. She snuggles closer, cradles his head in both hands. She leans uncomfortably close and whispers in his ear.

"As you can tell sweetie, I'm not very good at waiting."

Trying to back away, Andorf feels the light switch jab into his lower back. The closet darkens as the woman presses against him. As she rocks, the closet lightens and darkens with her gyrations. She whispers as she nibbles on the nub of his ear.

"I'm offering you every straight man's fantasy … sex without commitment. You can give it your all … life without regret."

Andorf pants at the sensation of her moist breath warming his ear. "Y—you must stop, lady."

"But you'll never know what you're missing. I've been told by other lovers I'm pretty good."

Pressing both hands against her shoulders, Andorf pushes her away. "Shouldn't we at least have dinner before we …?"

The woman's mouth contorts. Without warning, she leans back and slaps Andorf's face. "Why, you ungrateful bastard. Here I am offering you sex with no strings. But no! You want it all. Whatever made you ever think I'd want a relationship with you? I'm a married woman."

The woman grabs her towel off the floor and rewraps. Pushing past, she storms out the closet's accordion door, out the cabin door, and into the hallway.

"Damn," Andorf says, poking his head out of the closet in time to catch sight of his cabin door slamming shut. He shakes it off at the sink. A soapy wash cloth cannot wipe the smile off his face. It barely removes the woman's strong scent. After brushing Binky off his pillow, he watches the bunny hop off the bed. He hears the furry guy in his thoughts as Binky gazes up from the floor.

"Yes. Yes. Binky, I know what you would have done if you were me. It is what rabbits do best."

Eyes narrowing back at Andorf, Binky lifts his head and winks.

"I know. I admit it's my own fault why I am not getting much sleep. I must quit answering the door in the middle of the night." Andorf grins at his furry friend. "But did you see her beautiful brown eyes, her luscious lips, Binky? If only she had the large nose to go with them."

Binky grumbles as he leaps on the bed and then settles into Andorf's pillow.

*

Binky's log – 460-042005:

Sheez! The junior Goshi fails to realize when he's got a good thing going. If only I were as lucky.

CHAPTER 33
Paranoia

Day 465 - Titan Outpost rendezvous: 306 days

Tenulian word of the day is 'jinkojo' – over-crowding.

Walking the hallways of the *Atlantis*, everyone seems to be staring. Even with those who turn their heads, Andorf hears their questionable thoughts in his head louder than his own. Which one is the security hack, if such an intruder even exists? Or is some glitch within Siros' memory banks? According to Binky, the starship's voice and conscience is untrustworthy as it has a history of pulling pranks now and then.

A passerby bumps Andorf's shoulder. Before he can turn about, the stranger is gone. Doing his best to turn off the ambient words around him, he hops onto the floating steps where thoughts appear to be his own, for a brief ride up to the A-deck. The moment his feet touch the landing platform, the thought-crowding returns. Entering his cabin at the end of the hallway with a sigh of relief, Andorf wanders into the bedroom. He yawns from lack of sleep while peering starry-eyed at the half-open drawer and the special rubbing cream within. Rubbing his sore shoulder, thoughts of intrusive strangers return. *I really must quit relying on that cream. Funny, I do not remember the tube being so depleted.*

Hearing Mila entering the cabin, he quickly shuts the drawer and then exits the bedroom. A whisk of his hand and the bedroom door closes.

"Daddy! Daddy!" she cries, running toward him with open arms. "Everyone out there is staring. Everywhere I go people are pointing fingers at me."

Andorf scoops Mila into his arm. "You are not the only one they stare at, sweetie." He looks about the living area. He takes a deep breath. "I feel a strange thing about to occur. Perhaps it will put an end to all this madness."

*

Binky's log – 465-165017:

Yes indeed. More than one person knows about the special rubbing cream.

CHAPTER 34

A Bit Of Advice

Day 467:1300 -
Titan Outpost rendezvous: 304 days

Tenulian word of the day is 'mesolvatis' – a mediator.

An insistent knocking on the cabin door interrupts Andorf. He peers through his peephole to see a man and woman dressed in traditional Greek clothing minus head coverings, and a more moderately-dressed boy is with them. He reluctantly opens the door and steps into the hallway.

The man looks Andorf over from head to toe. Lacking facial expression, he utters a handful of sharp, incomprehensible words at the Goshi. The woman behind him flails her hands in the air as while chorus of more colorful-sounding phrases spew from her lips. The man steps back and utters a few colorful words of his own, this time directed at the woman.

Before the woman can return his volley, Andorf steps between them. Feeling their hostility, he immediately doubts the spontaneous action. Using both hands, he pushes the pair apart. He glares at one, then the other. He asks what seems to be the problem, sprinkled with Tenulian words.

The man begins to speak but pauses when the woman throws up a fist. Speaking an unknown dialect, she scowls at Andorf.

Andorf silently offers open palms to the feuding couple until the young lad slips past speaking a hodgepodge of languages. "She says my father won't listen to her. He refuses to take her seriously. I'm hoping the Goshi will resolve their problems."

Andorf turns about and grins at the young faces peering at him from behind his cracked cabin door. "One minute," he says, returning to his cabin. After calling for a child-keeper, he takes Mila's hand and then winces at the feuding couple and their son.

All gaze down at six-year-old Mila as she steps outside. She meets their questioning faces with inquisitive looks of her own. "Sometimes I decipher for my Daddy."

Somehow appearing to understand, the man and woman break into laughter. Then they exchange foul looks at one another while their son leads the group toward the transportation deck. All hop a shuttle to the *S.S. Cristobel*. Aboard the enormous starship, an elevator takes them up to the C-deck. First time aboard a foreign starship, Andorf is overwhelmed by the spaciousness as he proceeds down the wide carpeted hallway.

The man promptly opens his cabin door. All step inside. The cabin proves more luxurious many times over anything in the fleet. Andorf eyes the incredible collection of pictures and family heirlooms as he walks through the living space. All but the woman find seats at a table in the central hospitality area. She reappears moments later with cannabis tea in small cups. One sip proves the tea to be quite potent.

After clearing his throat, Andorf explains to the lad how he will attempt to read the parent's thoughts. After their son interprets, the man and woman nod.

"They want you to go ahead," Mila bursts out.

After silencing Mila with fingers to his lips, the Goshi's eyes first narrow upon the man. He probes the man's thoughts. He then focuses on the wife before halfway smiling peculiar at the troubled couple. "It appears you both disagree on a very simple thing. If I am correct, this matter has been transpiring for many years. What I fail to understand is what suddenly brings this to a head."

"This is nothing new," the boy admits. "My parents argue all the time."

Andorf nods. He is careful to use simple words as not to be misunderstood by the lad as he again stares into the parent's eyes. "There is a major difference in how the both of you interpret one particular issue. Am I correct?"

After the boy speaks in his parent's native tongue, the man and woman nod.

"Can there be compromise in either of your positions?" Andorf says.

Again, the son interprets. After the couple's comments, the boy shakes his head

Andorf turns to face six-year-old Mila as she tugs on his arm. Mila directs his eyes toward the dining area. After gazing at the broken dishes on the floor, Andorf peers at the husband and wife straddling the table on either side of where he sat. The man stares at his wife and then turns away. The woman continues to stare daggers at her husband.

"I see broken dishes on the floor," Andorf says. "I am wondering why they have not been cleaned up."

"The result of mother's temper," the boy says, turning slowly to Andorf.

Throwing both hands out, the woman yells incomprehensible words.

"She says my father cheated on her."

The man yells back.

"But our good dishes," the boy says. "Why did you break our good dishes?"

The woman's eyes narrow. She continues to argue.

"She never liked father's family dishes," the boy says. "Her family dishes are much more elegant."

Andorf rises. He enters the dining area and returns holding a half dozen plates. "Oops," he says, dropping all of them.

The husband and wife stare at Andorf in disbelief, gawking at the broken plates on the floor. The woman extends her arms and yells at Andorf in her native language. The husband does the same.

Mila takes her daddy's hand and leads him quickly outside. At the cabin door, Andorf gazes back at the couple. He sees the woman in her husband's arm, crying and the husband doing his best to console her. Following Andorf and Mila into the hallway, the boy stops them. He reaches out to shake the Goshi's hand.

"Thank you, mister Andorf. I have never seen them so happy."

"But now they both hate me," Andorf says, shaking the lad's hand.

"Yes, but mother and father are together again. This is more important."

Andorf takes a deep breath. He grins at the lad. "Have all the broken plates framed. Hang them in the dining area. It will remind your mother and father of the consequences of both cheating and temper."

The boy bows. "Thank you, mister Goshi. You are truly wise."

To their surprise, Mila blurts out a few of the woman's hateful words. When the young boy's face pales, Andorf places a hand over her mouth and leads her toward the elevator.

"Whatever words that woman said back there, you are never again to repeat them."

*

Binky's log – 467-144500:

Not only has the junior Goshi helped save a marriage but Mila seems to have learned a few choice words. I only hope things don't get out of hand.

CHAPTER 35
One Man's Obsession

Day 467:1520

Tenulian word of the day is 'klaw' – acting out of fear.

W hat?" Captain Murray yells, pacing about the small bridge. "How come no one informed me of the commander visiting the *Atlantis*? Why the hell am I always the last to hear of things?"

Peter and Pol shrug their shoulders.

Murray exits the bridge and hurriedly takes the floating steps down to the lowest deck. There he spots a Greek family exiting the shuttle-bay. He gazes at them mistrustfully before heading for the main stairwell. Exiting into the bowels of the *Atlantis*, he huffs, trying to catch his breath. Upon entering the hot, loud mechanical room, the captain loosens his collar and covers his ears, sniffing at the grease-ridden air.

"Brutus!" he yells above the machinery noise. "Brutus, where in hell are you?"

Appearing from behind, a wayward tech taps the captain's shoulder.

Quickly turning about, Murray flinches not only at the tech but at the repetitive rhythm of machines around him, sounding as though they are warning him to leave while he is still able.

"Sir," the tech says. "I believe the chief engineer is working on #6. Follow me."

Murray trails the tech down a half-level of corrugated steps. They squeeze between busy machinery and side-step pools of grease and parts scattered along the floor. The tech leads him past air-handlers and circumventilators toward a rear corner of the enormous mechanical room. Machinery sounds intensify as they approach the replicators. "Get out now," the replicators seem to churn in milling sounds.

The tech pounds on the sides of the last replicator, the one in the corner by itself. "Brutus," he yells. "You have a visitor."

"Ouch!" a muffled voice yells from deep within the machine. "Who would be visiting me in the middle of the day? If it's Andorf, you can tell him to—"

Brutus appears from behind the machine. His face is dripping in blood and sweat. Replicator #6 sputters as he extracts himself out of her casing.

"I must have a word with you," Murray yells above #6's sputtering. "Foreigners from Turk's ships are walking about the *Atlantis*. I spotted them with my own eyes."

Appearing dumbfounded, Brutus stares down the captain. "What'd you expect, Murray? We've been an armada of forty-six international starships for two months now. Don't you expect visitors from the commander's starships would eventually explore the *Atlantis*?"

"But it was an entire family. They appeared to be looking the place over … like they were looking the place over like they wanted to move in. Hell, they even brought a small child with them … a young boy."

Brutus chuckles. "Relax, Captain. I'm sure they're as curious about us as we are about them."

*

Binky's log – 467-154012:

So, Captain Argent and the council aren't the only one spreading rumors. Let's see where this goes.

CHAPTER 36
Fame

Day 470 - Titan Outpost rendezvous: 301 days

Tenulian word of the day is 'chocto' – unwanted recognition.

Word of Andorf resolving the Greek couple's problem far beyond the S.S. Cristobel. Andorf soon becomes what is a cross between a celebrity and a guidance counselor. He feels uneasy about his new-found notoriety spreading throughout the armada.

Gregory winces at his best friend. "So, what's the problem? You're finally getting the recognition you deserve."

Andorf splashes water before towel-drying his face. "I never wanted this much recognition. Total strangers, many speaking their native tongues, approach to demand my assistance. It is what everyone now expects. Perhaps I should start making appointments ... hand out next-in-line numbers."

"Have you thought about getting metal implants such as these?" Gregory rolls up his sleeves to display metal appendages spanning the length of his arm. "Believe me, they will discourage the majority of such requests."

"I'm serious, Gregory. Everywhere I turn someone is requesting an intervention." Gazing at Mila, he leans closer to his best friend and whispers. "Some of the requests have been downright personal."

Gregory winces. "I can only imagine. At least those desperate women are no longer visiting you during the late-night hours."

"Oh, those visits have not diminished. And now with all these other requests, I have little free time. I am seriously thinking about changing cabins … somewhere on another deck maybe … or transfer to another starship."

A knock on the cabin door has Gregory peering out Andorf's peep hole. "Shall I?" he asks. At Andorf's nod, he opens the door. After failing his mechanized arms, the woman runs away screaming obscenities.

"At least it is not someone bearing another special gift." Andorf grins at his best friend. He winces at the collection of hookahs and tea pots piled up high in a corner of the room before staring back at Mila. "You are not to repeat those words either, young lady."

*

Binky's log – 470-073523:

It appears good deeds do indeed have their consequences.

158

PART 4
A GLIMPSE

CHAPTER 37
A Surprise

Day 684 - Titan Outpost rendezvous: 87 days

Tenulian word of the day is 'gaucho' – something more than expected

A lieutenant at Titan Outpost pulls Commander Foos aside. "An armada of starships approaches, Commander. On their current course, they should arrive in three months. Surely, they would've contacted us by now."

Foos presses a few buttons and reviews the screen for a long moment. A hand is raised. "They are expected, Lieutenant. They will contact us on their orbital approach. Three starships are to refuel as recorded in the contract."

The lieutenant nervously clears his throat. "But forty-six starships in total have been detected."

More than one brow is raised. "Forty-six you say? Ha! My friend Thom is certainly up to his old tricks. Let's restock our pantries. Compose a list of our required supply shortages and whatever is in dire need of repair. A modification to the original agreement is in order."

"Aye, Commander."

*

Binky's log – 684-123117:

Everyone is in for an eye opener.

CHAPTER 38

Gizmos

Day 700 - Titan Outpost rendezvous: 71 days

Tenulian word of the day is 'wackamots' — an overwhelming collection of unexplainables.

I n the rear of the cabin, where most everyone else has a bedroom, Gregory sits at his six-foot workbench. As in his apartment back on Earth, signal injectors, waveform splitters, and bench scopes pressure devices line the rear of the bench. Out of necessity, pressure devices have been added to the all-star lineup. Surrounding him, shelves lining the walls are filled with tools. Bins spill over with parts. Uncompleted projects are stacked up on the floor beneath his feet. He hunches over one new project for hours on end, adding parts and making fine-tuning adjustments. A knock on the cabin door has him gazing up to see his best friend in the monitor. Gregory presses a button and the cabin door buzzes opens.

Moments later Andorf approaches cautiously from behind, appearing confused as if never having seen any of Gregory's projects or his workbench for that matter. He winces at the sight of Gregory using mechanical extension to his appendages. The techno-wiz appears to have four hands working in his favor. "What are all these gizmos?"

Daring not to lift his head, Gregory speaks while peering through a high-powered magnifier. "It would take the better part of the week to explain, Andorf. Neither of us has as much time to waste."

"What about the boxes lining the back of the workbench? They seem new."

"Those items?"

Andorf nods.

"Most are items I've either built or accumulated over the years. A few pieces I actually inherited from Scrin."

"And what about those things?" Andorf says, pointing at a row of video monitors.

Gregory smirks. "You think Siros is the only one keeping tabs on the starship? I've never fully trusted the voice of the ship's unreasonable conscience. It's been known to have a severe attitude toward humans."

Andorf eases closer, peering at the item Gregory's eyes are fixated upon. Though it seems well beyond his comprehension, he appears determined to understand just what his tinkerer friend is working on. "What about the thing you are staring a hole through with your magnifier? Why is it so tiny?"

"I'm developing a micro pressure sensor … an alarm trigger of sorts." Gregory tightens a cover on the tiny device and then places it on the crowded workbench. He pushes away on the bar stool. "At least that's what it's supposed to be if it works. I've got to have it working in the next seventy-one days."

"Seventy-one days? What is the rush?" Andorf fingers the air as if counting the days. His eyes widen. "That is when we are scheduled to arrive at Titan Outpost."

"Precisely. If I can get the damn thing working, I hope to interface it with a remote trigger. It all needs to be small enough to fit inside someone's pocket."

Andorf's eyes narrow. "It all sounds really complicated. How many pressure sensors are you building?"

"Only one, if I can get it to function properly." Returning to the tiny device on the workbench, Gregory hooks wires and applies power.

A bright flash! A puff of smoke! Gagging at the smoke rising off the workbench, Andorf fans his hands in the air.

"Damn!" Gregory yells. "That's the eighth one I've fried in as many days. Oh, if only I had Serin's knack."

Andorf mumbles. "And me as well."

*

Binky's log – 700-163848:

When the techno-wiz's got problems, we've all got problems.

CHAPTER 39
Dribbles

Day 722 - Titan Outpost rendezvous: 49 days

Tenulian word of the day is 'sham' - to fix simple problems by going to extremes.

From within the comfort of his cabin, Andorf observes those in the council chambers voicing strong opinions from the edge of their seats.

Representatives argue over everything from their constituents being worked to death to questioning where the mandatory cuts are heading and when they will end. "For the common good," a lone voice shouts from the rear of the chamber.

Councilman Trebylorshamintu waddles about the chamber floor as if flustered by deliberate mispronunciations of his much-abbreviated family name. The short, rotund man grunts at those calling him anything briefer than the barely-tolerable abbreviated Bylor. Sham, as hecklers call out, he finds totally reprehensible. During his three-minute waddle from the inconveniently-placed rear seat, Bylor scans the collection of faces packing the *S.S. Francesca's* tri-deck chambers, many riling him by throwing rude hand-gestures or clicking of their teeth. Approaching the podium, Bylor struggles to reach the microphone floating slightly above his head. He pulls it down to mouth level.

"My fellow councilmembers ... it has been brought to my attention we've been grossly mismanaging critical resources. While we have no shortage of labor, our runaway birthrate of 1.21 per person is depleting the food reserves."

"Thanks to donors like Andorf Johnson," more than a few councilmembers yell out.

Andorf's ears perk at mention of his name.

"The obvious solution is to deploy more advisors!" Bylor shouts, above the rowdy voices. In soothing circular motions, he pats both hands in the air while repeating, "For the common good."

"Beanos! No more beanos," many shout.

With his eyes scanning the room as if plotting a speedy escape route, Bylor clears his throat loudly into the microphone again hovering inches above his head. "Beano is such an unfriendly term. Back home in my native Delhibad we called them Dribbles."

Voices roar in contempt, swearing 'sham' in collections of native accents.

Acting moderator Gregory Gray weaves his way toward the podium. He finger-activates a wireless lapel mic. "Now, now everyone. I know we are still learning the language but please everyone, speak only in Tenulian."

Near panic-stricken, Bylor stands beside Gregory, futilely patting the air with both hands in circular motions. He strains his neck to reach the microphone floating overhead until Gregory reaches up and yanks it down. "These advisors are registered statisticians. And—and they report to this very council. It would behoove us to seriously consider their recommendations."

"Shamster!" Turk yells out. He leaps from his front row seat and tosses a folded kalpak. The cap sails across the room and smacks Bylor squarely on the back of his head. "Enough of these damn Dribbles! Everywhere I go, I'm tripping into the suckers. Before we know, they'll be running our starships."

"And they're multiplying like rabbits," others shout, rising to their feet to join the armada's commander.

*

Back in Andorf's cabin, Binky hops about, thumping hind legs at one councilperson's latest comment. A series of firm knocks on the cabin door sends Binky hopping toward the nearest hay-box. Andorf lowers the monitor's volume before peering through the door's tiny peephole. Without further hesitation, he opens the door.

Captain Murray barges inside. Out of breath, he quickly shuts the door behind. Noting the twins playing on the floor and Mila's attentive face, he grabs hold of Andorf's arm. With Binky following, he leads Andorf into the bathroom, away from little Mila's not-so-little parabolic ears. Andorf runs sink water.

"You're a councilman, Andorf," he whispers. "You've got to do something about all these damn beanos."

"Don't you mean Dribbles?"

"Dribbles … beanos … whatever you want to call them. This morning, I actually caught one of the suckers on my bridge, tinkering with navigational controls. If I didn't know better, I'd believe he was attempting to change course."

Andorf grabs his chin. "By chance, would he happen to be a fast typist with warm fingertips?"

"What?"

"Never mind. Now as you were saying, Captain?"

Appearing disgusted, Murray shakes his head. "My lackey navigator allowed the bastard inside the bridge. Now I can't get rid of him."

"What the hell? Peter knows better. You warned him did you not?"

"Indeed, many times. But the beano came bearing donuts and …"

"Coffee?" Andorf passes a damp washcloth through the water stream to wipe his drooling lips.

Murray grins. "Cannabis tea."

Andorf's shoulders droop. "Tea? Since when have we become so British?"

The captain shakes his head.

"My hands are tied, Captain," Andorf says. "The council is still undecided on what to do with the men in white satin."

"There's trouble with these Dribbles, I tell you. They're everywhere and multiplying like—"

Murray pauses at the sight of Andorf's glaring eyes. He gazes down to see Binky's narrowing eyes and pointing ears also focused upon him. At Andorf's urging hands, he continues.

"These damn Dribbles … why, they're getting out of hand. Everywhere I go, I'm tripping over one of them."

"Now, now, Captain. Things cannot be so bad. Perhaps you are …"

Murray raises a brow. "Did you know Dribbles are posted outside your cabin door right now?"

Cracking the bathroom door, Andorf spots Mila peering into the hallway. The six-year-old pans her head in both directions before closing the door and latching it shut. Holding two fingers up, she nods.

Andorf quickly shuts the bathroom door and whispers. "Dribbles are not the only thing getting out of hand. No matter how careful I am, that six-year-old hears everything. I swear she even hears what I am thinking."

Murray grins. "Why am I not surprised, Mr. Goshi?"

"Quit calling me that!"

"I suspect your telepathic abilities have somehow transmuted to the girl."

Andorf shakes his head. "Impossible. Mila is not even my biological daughter."

"Perhaps it's more of a contact high. By living with you some of your powers have rubbed off on her."

"Hmm. Like an energy transference of sorts." Andorf rubs his chin. "Now going back to these dribbles … what you know about them? Why are they camped outside my cabin door?"

The captain winces. "I suspect they've noticed some minute change in your donation routine."

Andorf's eyes widen. They have noticed a decreased potency from all those late-night encounters." He turns and stares red-faced, at Murray. "I knew it would only be a matter of time. Prospective mothers continue to pound on my door at odd hours, expecting to skip long waiting lists. What the hell am I supposed to do, Captain? I try my best to fend them off but I too have urges. I am only human."

"Be careful, my friend. The bastards take note of anything and everything. Nothing seems to slip past them."

*

Binky's log – 722-100525:

It appears even in space, we are being watched. I'd better check to see if things are really this bad.

CHAPTER 40

Binky's Tour

Day 728 - Titan Outpost rendezvous: 43 days

Tenulian word of the day is 'chisanakoto' – doing small things.

With Andorf's cabin door held open, Binky covertly slips out and hops down the A-deck hallway to enjoy a newfound freedom. Passengers are not expecting to see a rabbit so the seven-pound lagomorph hopping past allows him to go unnoticed. Binky hops onto the floating steps and rides them down to the G-deck. Moments later, he follows Peter inside the bridge. Peter subconsciously swats at fluffs of rabbit fur floating past.

"Why can't you be more like Pol over there," Captain Murray barks. "Aren't you ever on time?"

Pol's head surfaces from behind the radio console. He grins facetiously at Peter. "Has anyone been selected as a new first mate? You know, in case something terrible happens to you, Captain."

"Well, there *is* one promising candidate who I'm expecting to arrive at any moment." Murray winces at a fur fluff floating overhead. "Jobriah Cates of the *S.S. Phoenix* has flight combat experience but carries a troubling history of—"

A tap on the bridge door has Peter opening the door to allow Jobriah

Cate's entry. Binky darts out. He hops onto the floating steps and rides them down to the transportation deck. In the shuttle bay he spots workers scrambling about and stacking boxes high against the perimeter walls. While discussing odds against the ex-councilwoman running two-hundred-and-fifty to one, every free hand appears busy retrofitting the starship's nearly spent secondary fuel tanks. Binky watches vibrafoam insulation being stuffed in cracks and crevices to insulate the enormous bulkheads. He sees workers transferring fuel reserves into single tanks in order to allow remaining tanks to be cleaned. Others are retrofitting empty tanks with expansion bladders to contain frosty, liquid methane.

Advisors with soft-pads and transcriber pens dangling from their wrists buzz past, oblivious to Binky's presence. All appear to be taking notes while nosing into everyone's business. Even Binky finds it difficult to go anywhere without bumping into one of the many bean counters.

He exits the shuttle-bay and finds the main stairwell door propped open. An easy hop down many steps finds him on the grease-ridden M-deck. With techs going in and out the large mechanical room door, he finds it is easy to slip inside. Vibrations from air handlers and air rushing past have Binky's fur standing on end. Heading toward the back of the room, he hurriedly hops down a half-height of corrugated steps. He winces at sight of replicators in the corner, all running non-stop to churn out customized parts. Binky recalls hearing how the latest move to convert to liquid methane is creating shortages of critically vital parts. He ponders about the coinciding with dwindling food reserves, meal rations being cut by ten percent. With the replicators churning out so many parts, he wonders why everyone is complaining about shortages. It seems the only things gaining numbers are the ever-present advisors dressed in white satin and everyone's growing impatience.

Sneezing out of control, Binky exits the mechanical room and heads toward the A-deck. With all of Andorf's frequent visitors, he easily slips back inside the cabin unnoticed. He rubs against the litter box hay, trying to rid himself of the greasy smell coating his fur.

*

Binky's log – 728-125108:

What a terrible place that mechanical room is. How in hell does anyone work there?

CHAPTER 41
The Captain's Concern

Day 735 - Titan Outpost rendezvous: 36 days

Tenulian word of the day is 'kurmanji' – beyond hope, to languish in despair.

M urray winces. "I take it the security hacker is still at large?"

Andorf and Brutus eye each other before nodding.

"Great. Really great." Murray's mouth sours as he begins to walk about in his private quarters. "Here we are weeks from orbiting Titan Outpost and there's someone out there who can waltz in here and take over the *Atlantis*. Oh, I've got a queasy feeling brewing in the pit of my stomach that won't quit. The refueling agreement was drawn up two years ago. We were three starships back then. Now we are forty-six. I'm sure that will affect the original agreement. Things have ways of getting forgotten over time."

Andorf and Brutus shrug their shoulders.

"Now with my predecessor out of the picture, negotiating with those in charge of Titan Outpost has fallen in my lap. What if the previous arrangements are no longer valid? Oh, Thom Mallory, how could you have done this to me?"

"Relax, Captain," Brutus says. "Last I heard, my old pal, Robert Foos was

171

running the outpost. I've known the guy since grade school. Though it's been twenty years, I expect he'll be most amiable on renegotiating new terms."

The captain grins. "With you and this Foos guy being old pals, you need to join me at the negotiating table."

Brutus winces. "But—but—"

"This is *not* a request, Brutus."

"You can't order me around, Captain," Brutus says, watching Andorf slip out the captain's door. "I'm not one of your lackey crewmembers."

"I'll keep that in mind when it comes up before the Second Council."

*

Binky's log – 735-153522:

For all we know, this Robert Foos may no longer be running the outpost. What if …?

CHAPTER 42
Assignments

Day 740 - Titan Outpost rendezvous: 31 days

Tenulian words of the day are 'juliano' - being saddled with an impossible task,
'Briar' - someone of authority who rules without conscience.

Andorf catches up with the *S.S. Mayflower's* captain outside his starship's last surviving observation deck. He sees the captain peering through one of the windows leading into the room with cupped hands. "You wanted to see me, Captain? Is there a problem?"

The captain turns and smiles at Andorf. "I take it the chief engineer on the *Atlantis* is one of your dear friends?"

"Brutus is an old friend." Andorf winces. "Let us leave it at that."

"Well, whatever. The guy's been camped out in my observation deck all morning just gazing into space. With him grunting, many enter and quickly leave. I thought you knowing the guy, you'd care to intervene."

The captain leads Andorf onto a conveyor. The pair then passes through sets of optical-conditioning chambers before exiting into a dark observation room. Eyes fully-dilated, they spot Brutus standing on the starboard side gazing out one of the panoramic viewing portals. The large man appears hypnotized, focused on a single magnified dot in the viewing area.

Darting past Andorf, the captain taps one of Brutus' hefty shoulders. "It's hard to believe that tiny speck orbiting Saturn will be our first destination. It will mark twenty-four months of space travel."

Without breaking his gaze, Brutus nods. "Titan Outpost is still a good ways off, Captain. Much can happen between now and our arrival."

"You don't seem at all excited, Brutus. I expected you would be looking forward to a break from all your mundane engineering duties. Personally, I'd love to escape all the subtle starship noises if only for a matter of hours."

Brutus breathes deep. "I admit it'll be great seeing my old friend Robert Foos but …"

"But what?" Andorf says, joining the Captain and Brutus at the panoramic viewing portal.

Looking away from the portal, Brutus takes a moment before squinting at the others. "Captain Murray is not the only one having queasy feelings in his gut."

"Ah, it's the refueling process." The captain rubs his chin. "Or is it the negotiations which are disturbing you?"

Taking a moment, Brutus gulps. "Both I guess."

"You and Murray have a month to get a grip on any ill feelings. I expect you both …" The captain takes a deep breath as he places a thumb and index finger against the glass and finger-tweezes the image of Saturn to enlarge it to the size of a baseball. "There. The ring layers are much clearer."

Brutus reaches past the captain to tweeze the adjacent tannish-colored dot in the background. The largest moon's image expands to nearly the size of Saturn.

Andorf leans against the viewer user interface. "So, that is Titan. What is that thin ring encircling the moon?"

Teleprompter: Before you lies Titan Outpost. Using poly-modular construction, the outpost was completed in twenty-seven years. With a ring diameter of 3,505 miles, the orbiting station proves to be humanity's greatest engineering marvel to date. Maintaining a stable orbit 147.9 miles above the moon's surface, the man-made station is powered from any number of frigid methane lakes on the moon's surface. Warming feeder lines convert liquid fuel into a gas, which—

"Enough!" The captain taps a wrist-mounted timepiece. His eyes widen.

Waving at Brutus, he grabs hold of Andorf's arm and leads him onto an exit conveyor. The pair passes through a series of retinal adjustment chambers before dumbing them into a brightly-lit hallway outside the observation room.

Andorf peers back at the darkened room but cannot see inside.

The captain takes off in a trot, heading toward the *Mayflower's* shuttle bay. "With delegates representing nearing one million Earth's refugees, council chambers have been relocated to the *Francesca's* much larger tri-deck auditorium. You never want to arrive late to a council meeting."

"So I have heard," Andorf mumbles, running to catch up.

"Last week, I was twenty minutes late and found I had been assigned a supervisor position on some newly-created Juliano project. I've yet to figure what's entailed but with a name such as Juliano, things do not sound promising. Besides, I don't speak any foreign languages." The captain grins painfully. "I don't know about you but I barely understand Tenulian."

"You think that's harsh? I missed one session and was volunteered onto the fueling negotiations team. Why would they ever want me? I know absolutely nothing about negotiating ... even less about refueling starships. I feel like I have been tossed into a briar patch and left to fend for myself."

The captain smirks. "In a twisted way it kinda makes sense, with you being able to read people's thoughts and such. Perhaps they expect you to keep everything in check. I've heard outpost commanders can sometimes be quite difficult."

"Brutus and this Foos character are supposedly old friends. We should leave it to them to haggle with fueling agreements." Andorf takes a seat along with the captain in a shuttle destined for the *S.S. Francesca*. He and the captain smirk at the latest Tenulian words scrolling across displays with definitions in forty languages. Andorf points out two of the new words. 'Juliano' is defined as being saddled with an impossible task. In contrast, 'Briar' refers to someone of authority who rules without conscience.

Moments later, the shuttle comes to a jolting halt inside the belly of the *S.S. Francesca*. After the doors slide open, Andorf and the captain rush out of the starship's shuttle-bay. Out of breath, they enter the council chambers barely in time to claim the last vacant seats. Unfortunately, they are separated some distance from one another.

Andorf is overwhelmed by the enormity of the auditorium packed with jabbering strangers. He press-fits into a seat between robust councilmembers. He scans the expanded council chambers the best he can from his limited view. Recognizing no one, Andorf feels lost for the first time in his life. As the noise level approaches human pain threshold, he is on the verge of sticking fingers in his ears. At the point of screaming at the top of his lungs, his ears perk at the familiar creak of well-worn shoes heading his way. The sound draws his eyes downward.

"Feeling a bit lost there, Representative Johnson?" says the wearer of the creaky shoes hovering above.

Andorf peers up at Gregory's smiling face. For a fleeting moment, life feels whole again. "Gregory!" he yells, prying himself out of the seat to give his best friend a bear hug. "I have not seen you on the *Atlantis* recently. I was beginning to think you had again jumped ship. How are you dealing with your—?"

"Geez, Andorf! No need to squeeze the life out of me." Gregory's trembling hands unwrap Andorf's hands off his torso. He leads Andorf into a relatively quieter, isolated corner of the huge room. "I'm doing as well as anyone can expect for a middle-age councilman experiencing random Tourette tics. Hey, can you believe we're both on the ruling council? We *are* the authority now. How did this ever happen?"

Glancing back at his now occupied seat, Andorf turns back to Gregory and shrugs his shoulders. "Yes, now that there are no empires to be overthrown."

"Well, I certainly don't miss the government's bogus media blurbs."

Andorf looks around at all the tentative faces observing him and Gregory. "Or the feeling of always being watched."

"We certainly took crooked paths to get here, didn't we?"

"Remember the night we broke into the Archives building … how dark and dusty it was … and all those rats running everywhere?"

Gregory's hands begin to twitch. His eyes roll about uncontrollably as he grabs his crotch. After a moment he calms. "I was sitting on that dusty floor. Rodents were gnawing on my shoes. Others were eyeing my …"

Andorf grabs his best friend's shoulders with both hands and holds them until the violent shaking subsides. He decides it best to change the subject. "So, have you heard the latest on the refueling operations?"

Gregory takes a breath. "Word has it you'll be accompanying Captain Murray and Brutus at the negotiating table." Catching himself about to drool, Gregory wipes his mouth with the back of his hand. "Oh, what I'd give to see the inside of Titan Outpost. Did you know it took twenty-seven years to construct the ring?"

"I know. I know. It is mankind's greatest engineering achievement."

Voice revving in excitement, Gregory appears to be fidgeting while doing his best to maintain some resemblance of composure. "I'll bet it's filled with all sorts of high-tech gadgetry … things you won't find anywhere else in the universe."

Andorf feels underwhelmed with technology. He desires to again change the subject but with his best friend being so unusually hyped, he presses on.

"Brutus and Captain Murray are having ill feelings about the negotiations. I hate to admit it but I too am a bit queasy. Hell, Gregory. Why did they have to pick me? I know nothing about refueling starships. And I am certainly not a negotiator."

Gregory's smile widens. "I disagree, my friend. Look how you handled Turk that first night. Even I was impressed. But these negotiations, they may turn dangerous. I don't think you should attend."

"You must not worry. Brutus and the outpost commander are old pals from way back when. They have childhood history. What in the world could possibly go wrong?"

"I have grave feeling concern about this negotiation. There must be some way you can worm your way out of it. What does the furry advisor have to say?"

"Binky?" Andorf shrugs his shoulder.

*

Binky's log – 740-111423:

What could possibly go wrong? Just wait and see.

CHAPTER 43
Vexation

Day 750 - Titan Outpost rendezvous: 21 days

Tenulian word of the day is 'pisane' — irritational sensation, like walking barefoot on sandpaper.

Andorf peers at the enlarged images of the half-mile-wide man-made anomaly encircling Saturn's largest moon, appearing on the hallway display. Still a good quarter-million miles off, the ring's beveled-edges send intermittent arcs of light sparkling outward, inviting closer investigation. He cannot see the sipping tubes running down to methane lakes on the moon's surface below, which fuel the outpost. While rotating at one revolution per hour to generate a 0.95G, the fueling tubes are hidden from view. The outpost is truly engineering's finest endeavor.

Crews of the forty-six starships have checked pumps, fuel lines, and fittings relentlessly. The starship refueling procedures have been rehearsed too many times over the past few weeks the crews can practically do it in their sleep. Bladders have been installed in every last fuel tank to accommodate the chilly liquid methane.

Three weeks from orbiting Titan Station, an unusually high percentage of Tenulians are experiencing ill feelings, particularly those aboard the *S.S. Atlantis*, *S.S. Inca*, and *S.S. Calypso*. People have been seen swatting at perceived flying things around them. Others cringe at the random creaks and groans of their aging starships and walk starship hallways chanting numbers 325 and 1410.

*

Binky's log – 750-023006:

With all the unknowns, I'm having doubts about the— Binky claws at an imaginary hexoid buzzing pas his head. He looks in both directions to no avail. *As I said, these negotiations are in question.*

CHAPTER 44

Reflections

Day 761 - Titan Outpost rendezvous: 10 days

Tenulian word of the day is 'bugafied' - loosely described as having high anxiety.

On his late-night rounds, Captain Murray stumbles upon something out of the ordinary. He spots a large man gazing out one of the wall-sized portals in the *Atlantis'* last observation deck. Noticing the troubled man wearing patterns into the floor, Murray cautiously approaches. Recalling what occurred weeks earlier on the *S.S. Mayflower*, Murray suspects the man to be his chief engineer.

"Brutus, is that you?"

In silence, the bulky man continues to stare out the viewing portal.

"In the two years I've known you, Brutus, I've never seen you as distraught. What the devil has gotten into you?"

Ignoring the captain, the chief engineer continues to peer out the portal.

"When our great Captain Thom got sucked out the bridge viewport, you were unfazed. The day your wife, Serin, died you barely grieved. When we lost gravity and were seconds from losing ship-wide life support, you remained calm, focused on task. So, I wonder what in the world could possibly be troubling you this badly."

Brutus grumbles. "You wouldn't understand, Captain."

"Try me."

"It was long ago." Brutus turns slowly to face Murray. "Nicki and I were …"

"I cannot believe you of all people would let one stupid—"

Murray suddenly finds himself pinned hard against the glass viewing portal. Held by his tightening collar, he gasps for air while staring face to face with a crazed chief engineer. When he is finally released, Murray massages feeling back into his neck. As Brutus walks away, the captain grabs one of Brutus' hefty arms.

"You needn't remind me of first loves, Brutus. We are overwhelmed by the beautiful face … fragrance … mannerisms. It's that first kiss we never forget. Those things haunt us for the rest of our days. And so it must be with this Nicki of yours. She is the girl by whom you judge all others."

"You don't understand, Murray. Nicki Foos was like no other. She was one in a million, one in a—"

Murray squinches his face. "Wait! Nicki Foos, as in the kid sister of Robert Foos who just happens to be running Titan Outpost?"

Brutus nods. "As kids, Robert and Nicki fought as siblings do. But they were always together … always into what the other was doing. What began as the three of us soon became just Nicki and me."

"Look, Brutus. You can't let one little childhood incident ruin your entire life. Every last one of us wears skeletons of our past."

Returning to the viewing portal, Brutus leers at the magnified image of a tan sphere on its descending orbit around Saturn. Careful not to damage the viewing portal, he slams an open palm against the titanium window frame. "I was never there to protect her from of all life's dings and dents as I had promised. She must still hold me accountable for everything terrible that's happened in her life."

"Quit blaming yourself. You were kids. I'm sure she's long forgotten—"

"No! Not Nicki! She had a vengeful temper you wouldn't believe."

Brutus shivers before wincing back at the captain. "People change, Murray, don't they? I mean, we remember them one way when in fact they're actually quite different."

Murray apprehensively strides closer, eyeing the much larger chief engineer. "Sheez, Brutus. Is that what's been bothering you?" The captain chuckles for a moment. "Everyone's someone other than who they appear. You know … the Norvest Syndrome."

"You don't understand. Long before Robert became Commander Foos, long before Serin, Nicki was my everything. If not for her overbearing father, we would have …'"

"You're not making this easy."

"Well—"

But why now? Why ten days before the crucial fueling negotiations is your troubling past coming out of the closet? With this gal being the commander's sister, she could make things terribly difficult for us. Oh, this reeks of fresh-cut scallions."

Brutus grumbles.

"Have you any idea of what's become of the old girlfriend? Hell, for all you know, Nicki could be running the outpost."

As Brutus stumbles off, head in hands, Murray turns to review the largest of the moons setting behind Saturn. He ponders about the increased complexity of extracting liquid methane from the many lakes encircling Titan. *Why do I have a nagging feeling Nicki Foos will be the death of me?*

The reflection of Andorf and a much taller man lingering behind him appears in the viewing portal. Murray winces at the weight of a six-foot-ten man's hand bearing down on his shoulder. The man drops his heavy hand as Murray turns about.

Turk scowls. "Was that your gypsy engineer I saw leaving, Captain?"

"You mean Brutus?"

"I don't trust him, Captain. Nor do I trust any of his fellow gypsies. Why, those thieving hoodlums would steal the shirts right off our backs if not for their sleeves."

"And you should hear what the gypsies say about you," Murray mumbles beneath his breath.

Dismissing all fear, Andorf elbows the chest of the bulky man towering above. "How long must you be burdened by this ancient feud, Turk? Remember Unification Day? We all became Tenulians that day, each and every last one of us. Besides, Brutus is not that bad of a guy … once you get past his crusty, outer shell."

Murray grins uncomfortably at the odd pair who appears to have oddly become friends over the past months. "I must agree with Andorf. Brutus is an acquired taste. But like him or not, the chief engineer knows the shuttlecraft inside and out. I'll be expecting him to lead the negotiation team."

Andorf smirks. "Brutus and Commander Foos have a long, favorable history dating back to their teens."

Turk eyes Murray suspiciously. "Which Foos are you referring to … Robert or his sister, Nicki?"

Murray's eyes widen. "You know about Nicki Foos?"

"Indeed, Captain. I've done my research. The commander's kid sister is highly unstable. She's nothing but trouble. I've read there are grave consequences for anyone who crosses her. She's ruthless, vengeful, and downright manipulative."

"Robert," Murray says, much too quickly. "As Brutus said, he and the outpost commander were pals from way back when. Now this Nicki you mentioned was—"

Andorf slaps a hand over Murray's mouth. "What the Captain means to say is their amiable relationship will tip the refueling renegotiations in our favor. Murray's predecessor, Captain Thom, had previous arrangements right down to the last detail. I'm sure servicing a few extra starships will not prove to be much of an issue."

Maintaining his focus on the commander, Murray peels off Andorf's hand. "As you must know, the starships have been running on reserves. Without the outpost's methane, every last one of the armada's starships will be stranded out here for all eternity. My chief engineer is our best option. Besides, me and Andorf will be right by his side."

"I don't like any of this," Turk growls. "Brutus carries much baggage. With him and this kid sister having questionable history, our armada is placed in a precarious position. I suspect your gypsy engineer may not be up to task."

Murray winces. "Oh, you know about that?"

"Indeed. Perhaps it should be the three of us who attend the fueling negotiations on the outpost."

"If it's any consolation, we'll have our resident Goshi will defuse any issues, won't we, Andorf?"

Andorf squints at the now barely-discernible moon. Letting out a sigh, he peers at the other's reflections in the viewing portal. "As I have been told."

"And what's this I hear of Brutus killing a member of the Canine Empire's high order?" Turk growls louder. "No doubt there's a bounty on the chief engineer's head. And won't this Robert Foos be expecting your late predecessor? How will he act when the three of you show up in Captain Thom's place?"

"The situation annoys me as well." Murray clears his throat loudly. "But in order to continue on our energy quest, we *must* work around these conflicts. If we can steer clear of the commander's sister, we'll be able to tap the methane lakes in several orbital passes to fuel up the armada and we'll then be well on our way in a matter of hours."

"Or we can do this the easy way," Turk says, extracting his saber and holding it high in the air. "Titan Outpost appears totally defenseless. I can send a few of my most talented warriors and—"

Andorf throws his palms at the commander. "Turk! You cannot raid the outpost," he yells. "Our descendants may need the stopover on their return to Earth."

"I'm always open to negotiating deals." Turk drops the saber into its scabbard. "Perhaps you'll convince those no-good gypsies to relinquish the secret recipe of their scrumptious Booger Stew. They have yet to fulfill their promise."

Scratching his head, Andorf's lips purse. After a long awkward moment, he peers up at the armada commander towering above. "Perhaps we will be able to provide you something much more rewarding than some stinking recipe."

"Don't do it," Murray mumbles.

Andorf glares at Turk. "Now, about you and Brutus ..."

At the sight of the Goshi's narrowing eyes focused upon him, the armada's commander relaxes. "I'm seriously trying to like the guy, Andorf ... but all moons of Jupiter will align before I'll ever trust the gypsy." Turk scratches at his thinning hairline. "There's one ingredient in that exquisite dish our spectrometers fail to identify ... one stinking ingredient."

Rubbing his nose, Murray turns toward Saturn's glorious image. "Some things are best left unknown," he mumbles to himself.

Andorf turns his head as well to peer out the viewing portal. "Oh, I feel trouble brewing, not just here but out there, in the winds of darkness."

*

Binky's log – 761-065422:

Trouble is certainly brewing. I can feel it in these lagomorph bones.

CHAPTER 45

Of Differing Opinion

Day 768 - Titan Outpost rendezvous: 3 days

Tenulian word of the day is 'froglump' – having a mighty bad feeling

Gregory holds his chin as he paces about the living area. *Nothing is what it appears. The team must be made aware. But no, they cannot be forewarned. Negotiations are too important. They must proceed.*

Playing on the floor, Mila releases her puzzle and stares up at her uncle. "Daddy already knows."

He abruptly halts, tips his head to one side. "Huh? What? Mila, have you been reading my thoughts?"

Mila smiles innocently and returns to the puzzle.

Gregory grins at the six-year-old. "Oh, I suppose it's only appropriate. Andorf and I cannot be the only ones aboard the *Atlantis* with this blasted mind-reading curse."

"Only daddy puts thoughts into other people's heads."

Gregory recalls the evening in the dining-hall where his best friend projected thoughts onto a crowd of eight-hundred. "That he can, Mila." Gregory smirks and resumes his pacing. "There must be a way for negotiators to be prepared ... to expect the unexpected."

"Daddy is one of the negotiators."

"What! Your father's still on the negotiating team?"

Mila nods. "It'll be okay, Uncle Greg. He'll just read the outpost commander's thoughts."

Gregory pauses. His eyes widen. He takes a deep breath. "What if your father were not of right mind?"

*

Binky's log – 768-104836:

At least two of us are worried about Andorf. Does the guy have any idea of what the negotiating team will be facing?

CHAPTER 46

Koshhald

Day 769 - Titan Outpost rendezvous: 2 days

Tenulian word of the day is 'koshhald' - loosely interpreted as expecting one thing but settling for something quite different.

A strobing light on the captain's desk splashes the darkened room with red flashes. Murray quickly ushers his overnight guest and her clothes into the next room before pulling the privacy door shut. Buttoning his shirt, he takes a seat at the former captain's credenza desk. Murray squints at one particular daily word and its definition scrolling above multilingual pronunciations on an adjacent wall. "Koshhald," he chants, reaching for the comm-console. Feeling gas percolating in his belly and a twitching hand, he hesitates more than once before accepting the incoming message.

The face of a middle-aged woman materializes upon the view screen before him. He winces at the sight of her greasy, short-cropped hair.

"Who the hell are you?" the woman yells, in a screechy voice. "What are you doing in Thom Mallory's leather chair? Where's the captain? What have you done with him?"

Murray is taken aback at the woman's abruptness, even more so by her irritatingly whiny voice. Straightening his shirt, he leans back in the late captain's favored seat. Doing his best to remain calm, he takes deep breaths while focusing on the irate woman.

"I was about to ask you the same, Ms. ..."

The woman eases into her premium-executive chair. "You are addressing Titan Outpost's illustrious commander. You may call me Commander Foos. Now, with formalities out of the way, if you would be so kind, go run along and fetch your starship captain pronto. Commander Foos does not like to be kept waiting."

"Commander Foos?" he mumbles, softly while his foot begins to shake. Murray clears his throat. "I *am* the captain of the *S.S. Atlantis* ... Captain Murray at your service."

Foos chuckles. "Don't be silly. There can only be one captain on a ..."

Murray nods.

The commander stares into the view screen. Her eyes widen. "No! Tell me Tommy's okay."

For a second time, Murray clears his throat. "By chance, would you be related to Robert Foos?"

"I'm Robert's sister, Nicki Foos."

Hidden beneath the chair, Murray's feet tap nervously on the floor below. "I take it your brother is indisposed at the moment?"

Silence.

"Has Robert been taken ill?"

As the commander chuckles, Murray detects an evil twinge in her voice. "As you may soon find out, Captain Murray, things on this outpost have a way of vanishing. My brother, like many things around here, vanished mysteriously a short while ago." Commander Foos' eyes squint at the desktop console. "Did you know the frigid methane lakes below are so vast, they could swallow an entire armada of starships such as yours and no one would be the wiser?"

Murray's eyes home in on the photos of the commander's brother and Captain Thom on the wall behind her. He stares at the name of "Nicki" overlying "Robert" on her desk plate. He begins to stutter. "W—well, I hate to break this to you but ..."

The commander leans into the desktop camera as if scrutinizing Murray's wrinkling face. She then breaks into one of her well-documented rants. "That's just like Thom, pulling a fast one. If you say he's dead, I'll never believe you. Ha. Such a joker Tommy is."

"I guess you never got the memo," Murray mumbles, staring directly into the screen. "You see, we had an unfortunate mishap a while back. I was on the bridge with Captain Thom when the frontal viewports cracked. He shoved the bridge crew out the airlock just seconds before the door slammed shut, sealing his fate inside the doomed bridge. Video clips show the captain in his spacesuit struggling to attach a lifeline when the viewports shattered. Being sucked into space, Thom Mallory became our first casualty of that day."

The commander's face sharpens. Wiping at damp eyes, she turns away for a moment before facing the camera with narrowing eyes. "I take it your armada is in dire need of the outpost's methane reserves, Captain Murray?"

Murray nods. "Your brother and the good captain had previously made a deal. Can I expect you to honor those arrangements?"

The commander reviews a few papers in an opened folder on her credenza before closing the folder. "I see my brother was to supply methane fuel to three starships. Funny how there are many more than three."

"Yes, it's a funny thing." Murray grits his teeth, doing his best to remain cordial. "We have no intention of inconveniencing you, Commander. After a few dozen low-pass fueling orbits, we shall be on our way."

The Commander grins wide, stretching her aging cheeks like old rubber bands. Murray gulps at the signs of the rough life which Brutus had implied, right in front of him accentuated on the high-def screen. Nicki Foos opening her mouth wide reveals her sharpened incisors. "I shall expect a complete passenger roster and manifest uploaded to my outpost within the hour. Am I making this clear, Captain Murray?"

"Perfectly." Murray scans his timepiece. "But that's eight minutes from now."

"Then you'd better act like a rabbit. Hop. Hop. Hop," she says, whisking him away with her hand.

"Now if we can—"

The commander's scarred hand reaches for the viewer. "Foos, out."

*

Binky's log – 769-003017:

So wicked Nicki Foos did away with her brother and is now running Titan Outpost. This certainly throws a monkey wrench in the negotiations.

CHAPTER 47
The Huddle

Day 770: 1600 Titan Outpost Orbit: 24 hours

Second Tenulian word of the day is 'snarble' - roughly interpreted as embellishing facts with half-truths.

Third Tenulian word of the day is 'argshnod' – the middle of nowhere.

Standing tall in his private quarters, Captain Murray addresses his fellow negotiators. "First, an update on the *Phoenix's* missing captain. Argent's ID badge was discovered beneath a spare bed in his suite. None of his clothes or personal items seem to be missing. Investigators are scanning the captain's suite for DNA."

Brutus grins widely, as though knowing he has already placed his wager. "4,000:1 odds say it's the handiwork of that petite ex-councilwoman."

"You are making harsh assumptions, Brutus. It could be anyone." Andorf winces. "It is well known the *Phoenix's* captain was widely hated."

Murray grins. "What was her name again?"

"Rita Ambrosia," Andorf snaps.

"Now, putting that aside, we have more pressing matters." Murray displays open palms at his fellow negotiators. "You are both not going to like what I'm about to say. Andorf ... Brutus ... I think you had better sit down."

Unlike Brutus, Andorf complies. "Have you connected with Commander Foos? Has he scheduled a time for the negotiations?"

After scanning furniture designed for someone much thinner, Brutus remains standing. "How'd Robert look? I've heard he's developed a limp over the years and is using a cane."

Murray shakes his head. "I don't know how to say this so let me put it this way. Concerning the pending refueling on Titan, what could possibly be our worst-case scenario?"

"Well, Robert could have reneged on the original agreement with Captain Thom." Brutus smirks. "But that would never happen."

"Think, worse," Murray says.

Andorf smirks as well. "Titan's methane lakes could have evaporated, leaving no fuel for our thirsty starships."

Brutus chuckles. "It's highly unlikely every lake has gone dry. After all, the lakes are what power the orbiting outpost."

"Think worse," Murray says. "Much worse."

Brutus chuckles louder. "The only thing worse would be if Nicki Foos were in charge of Titan Outpost. But that could never happen … not while her brother was alive. No. Robert would have no part of his kid sister assuming command of his outpost."

Murray raising a brow sends Brutus staggering about the room. "What if there was no Robert Foos, Brutus? According to Ms. Foos, her brother mysteriously vanished. In his absence, your old girlfriend assumed control. She is now the outpost's commander."

"But … but" Head in hand Brutus continues to stumble about the captain's quarters.

Andorf gulps. "Are you implying Nicki Foos did away with her own brother?"

"She wasn't the least choked up about her brother's disappearance," Murray winces. "In fact, she was gloating. The woman's pure evil … evil I tell you."

Brutus stares out Murray's private viewport. For a long moment he appears to be lost in space. "I wouldn't put anything past Nicki. The gal had a wicked temper. Let's be glad she doesn't have a clue I'm stationed aboard the *Atlantis*."

Murray raises his other brow. "The armada's passenger roster was uploaded to the outpost ten minutes ago. It was one of the commander's demands. There was little time to purge names."

"For crying out loud, Captain," Andorf yells. "What are we going to do now? The armada is relying on the outpost's methane fuel to continue our mission to planet Nero. Without refueling we are stranded in Argshnod."

Brutus turns his head. "Argshnod?"

"It's the latest Tenulian word," Murray adds. "It means 'the middle of nowhere.'"

Red-faced, Brutus approaches the captain. "You don't know Nicki. There's no telling what she'll do if … when she discovers I'm aboard the *Atlantis*. I'm sorry, Captain, now there's no way I'll be able to attend the negotiations."

Murray wipes sweat dripping off his forehead. "There's a half million names on that roster. There's a good chance the commander will somehow overlook your name, Brutus."

Andorf places a hand on Brutus' shoulder. "It is finally time you made amends with this Nicki Foos, big guy."

"Come on, Brutus. Take one for the team. Kick whatever bad blood remains between the two of you to the proverbial curb."

Brutus begins to hyperventilate. He extracts a crinkled, fiber bag from a rear pocket. He takes several shallow breaths. Brutus appears calmer. "Perhaps you've got things jumbled up, Captain. Things could not have gotten so terribly bad."

Murray shakes his head. "I'm telling you the truth, Brutus. In no way have I snarbled anything of this."

"Snarbled?"

Murray halfway grins. "Another new Tenulian word."

Brutus turns. He slams a fist down hard onto the captain's fancy desk. "Dammit! It's not my fault. How would I know Nicki would be stationed at Titan Outpost, let alone end up running the damn place? Look guys, I'm as shocked as you. Hell, if I'd known earlier, I would've changed my name … used an alias such as uhh … uhh … Harry Georgison."

Andorf winces. "The plumber?"

Murray's eyes narrow upon the Goshi. "Calling a pipefitter a plumber is a good way to …"

"I know. I know," Andorf peers down at his crotch. "To get my pipe bent."

Murray smirks. "So, has anyone identified our hacker?"

Andorf and Brutus shake their heads.

"Perhaps good fortune will reign," Murray says. "Stranger things have been known to happen out here in space."

Brutus' face contorts. "You'll need to find a replacement. Has anyone shown the slightest inkling of interest?"

Andorf rubs his chin. "Gregory exhibited a passing interest in visiting the outpost. Being technically savvy, he may be a viable alternative."

"Gregory Gray?" Brutus says, choking out the words. "What a terrible idea. One look at Metal Man with all his appendages and the commander will send us everyone packing."

Grinning at the chief engineer, Murray takes a deep breath. "Well, Turk *has* volunteered. I've heard he can be one hell of a tough negotiator."

"But it comes with a steep price," Andorf adds, stretching his words.

"Like that'd really work." Brutus chuckles. "I can see Turk pulling off his shoe in the middle of negotiations and pounding it on the table. I'm sure that'd go over well."

"But Turk's a pirate. You know this. I know this. He's used to getting his way."

Andorf nods. "Turk will slice right through Commander Nicki's hard-nosed tactics."

Murray grins mischievously at the chief engineer. "Perhaps Turk would be more flexible if we gave him the recipe for Booger Stew."

Brutus begins to sweat. His jaw drops. He goes cross-eyed. "How could you even consider such a thing, Captain? Turk and his warriors would round up every last gypsy and go on a killing spree. We would all be rounded up, thrown into airlocks, and cast us into space."

"What if we provide an alternate secret ingredient?" Andorf says. "Perhaps a flavor neither Turk nor anyone this side of Madagascar has ever heard of ... something like cream of caspin. The commander can blame me if he discovers otherwise."

Brutus rubs his chin. "Nah, it'll never pass his spectrometer tests."

Murray rubs his chin. "I know of a chemist aboard the *Mayflower* ... an old friend who made a good living off concocting flavors for a popular soft drink outfit back in Atlanta. Perhaps he could conjure up an ingredient chemically similar ... one that tastes like ..." The captain sniffs. "You know."

*

Binky's log – 770-163019:

Yikes! The captain uploaded the complete passenger list. This is not the time to throw away your paddle.

CHAPTER 48
Meltdown

Day 770: 1800 Titan Outpost Orbit: 22 hours

What?" Turk yells. "The crazy kid sister is running the outpost?"

"The captain uploaded our complete passenger list." Burak gulps. "He had no time for redaction, sir. Foos demanded it within the hour."

"Dammit Murray!"

"Not only will she discover her old boyfriend on the list but that he's a wanted man."

Turk's eyes widen. "Every last one of our starship captains is considered renegades by their respective empires."

"Indeed." Burak raises a brow. "But unlike the chief engineer, none of the captains are wanted for murder."

Turk grins. "Are you trying to cheer me up, Burak? Nothing you say will ever make me like that stinking gypsy."

*

Binky's log – 770-181046:

Turk has every right to be pissed. I'm no too happy with Murray either.

196

CHAPTER 49
Anxiety

Day 770: 2200 - Titan Outpost orbit: 18 hours

Chomping a blackberry groat, Brutus lingers in the A-deck grand suite's reception area, mumbling to himself. "What's taking her so long? Why can't Nicki decide one way or the other?"

He quenches his parched mouth with a swallow of pino juice. Shaking off the tartness, he pulls up the lengthy passenger roster on the wall-mounted display and easily finds his name. "It's right there near the top of the list," he mumbles. "Even searching my first name pulls it near the top of the list. I knew I should have changed it when I had the chance."

"Perhaps I was wrong about Nicki. After all, it's been well over twenty years. Surely, she has long forgotten me."

He takes another swig of the tart juice. "The commander has barely had time to review the long passenger list. Perhaps she'll overlook my name."

*

Binky's log – 770-220805:

As Murray said, stranger things have happened out here in space. But having an evil bitch in charge puts everyone's future at risk.

197

CHAPTER 50

A Second Encounter

Day 770: 2300 - Titan Outpost orbit: 17 hours

Fourth Tenulian word of the day is 'fiasmo' – meaning a near miss.

A nagging red light bathes the captain's darkened quarters in throbbing red flashes. Towel drying his hair, he reluctantly accepts the incoming message. To his dismay, the comm-link goes live as he drapes the towel over the chair back. Murray takes a seat.

A lieutenant donning a neatly-pressed uniform flashes credentials at the viewer. "Your passenger roster has been reviewed, Captain. The commander demands answers."

Watching the officer turns to saluting his superior, Murray leans back in the leather chair. The viewer morphs to an image of Commander Foos surrounded by wall-to-wall plaques and trophies as before. He notes how the name "Nicki" masks a much longer first name on all awards.

The commander smirks at the camera. "What's this I see about your starship captains? My latest intergalactic report lists bounties on each of their heads. There are huge rewards for the return of forty-six apprehended starships. Hmm, funny how I count forty-six starships in your armada. A coincidence, wouldn't you say, Captain Murray?"

"A coincidence indeed" Murray maintains his best poker face while gritting his teeth. Despite years of card playing, he finds Nicki Foos a most formidable opponent. He must be careful not to display his hand too early in the game.

Appearing to be reviewing a list of scrolling names on a second screen, the commander looks away for a moment. The scrolling list suddenly stops. "I see one of your chief engineers bears a death sentence on his head."

"Busted," Murray mumbles, beneath his breath.

"I take it the Canine Empire is not keen on someone slicing off the head of a high-roller on loan from the Hotot Empire, let alone being robbed of their premier deep-space starships. A Maximillian Harigados, this report says. What an odd name."

"Not for an alien beast," Murray again mumbles. Twitching in flashback of the final confrontation back on Earth, he recalls Serin releasing hundreds of loyal revolutionaries from political confinement. Leading the group, Serin confronted the almighty Max and bravely stood her ground.

The commander cocks her head to one side, as if expecting an immediate response. Clearing her throat loudly, Murray awakens from his thoughts. He opens his eyes to see the commander on the mini-viewer appearing to be losing patience. He stutters at the sight of her narrowing eyes.

"I—I witnessed the momentous event in person, Commander. The man in question watched the high, holy-roller as you call him, swat Serin into the crowd. He simply took matters into his own hands." Murray displays his palms. "You can't blame a man for defending his own wife, can you?"

"What?" Foo yells. "Serin Gray, leader of your little revolution was married to this chief engineer?" The commander glances back at her list. "I see Serin carries a high price on her head as well. It appears she is responsible for the death of three guards at some sanitarium call the Cos."

The mere reference to the political prison sends chills running the length of Murray's spine. Feeling like a trapped rat, he fixates on his view-screen.

"If only I didn't despise the Canine Empire … and those other empires for that matter. They stranded me in this desolate place," the commander says, beneath her breath. "On the other hand, I could make a small fortune off their capture. For returning say forty starships, I'd be handsomely rewarded."

Hearing the commander's faint words, he is troubled but somewhat relieved by the woman not mentioning the chief engineer by name. Murray sighs. *Perhaps we can get through the negotiations after all. We could refuel and be well on our way before the commander realizes her oversight.*

Ignoring Murray, the commander continues to speak to herself beneath her breath.

Clearing his throat, Murray regains the commander's focus. "I believe the original agreement with your brother must be honored. Titan Outpost is to supply our starships with liquid methane from multiple lakes spanning the moon's surface. In turn, we shall restock your consumables until the next starship can service your needs."

The commander grins widely. "As written in fine print of every contract, plans are always subject to change, as I'm sure you are well aware, Captain."

Murray gulps at sight of the commander's eyes returning to scan the long list of names on the journal. "Do we have a problem, Commander? Terms can always be revised."

"If anyone back home caught wind of me even speaking with you, I'd be forever branded a global conspirator. Word would eventually funnel back to the Outpost. My world would be thrown into total chaos. There'd be mutinies and countless numbers of assassination attempts."

"Not necessarily so, Commander. Now if we—"

Commander Foos reaches for her terminate button. "I'm sorry, Captain, I cannot help you."

"Wait! I'm sure we can work around these minor—"

Murray's view screen darkens. Gazing at his own reflection scowling back on the blank screen, he ponders what he more he should have said.

It's a good thing Commander Foos doesn't know the man of concern is her estranged boyfriend, my chief engineer, Brutus Bittner.

Murray sets about pacing the private quarters, mumbling to himself. "Perhaps bringing Turk into the negotiations team *is* the more viable solution. He'd have to wear sandals of course but Turk is definitely the better choice."

*

Binky's log – 770-231705:

Holy sh..! That was a close one. Still, what are we to do now?

CHAPTER 51
Nightmares

Day 771: 0300 -
Titan Outpost rendezvous: 13 hours

Andorf knocks on the A-deck's master suite's door until it opens. A groggy, half-dressed chief engineer steps into the hallway. He rubs his half-opened eyes. "Jeez, Andorf, it's 3am. Don't you Goshis ever sleep?"

"You of all people should know better."

Brutus' cupped hand covers a demanding yawn. "What's it now? Are you hearing voices again?"

Andorf's eyes narrow. "Now it is different. Each time I begin to doze, I see black, six-sided things, swarming around me like mosquitos. There are thousands of them ... sweeping down on the armada from everywhere. They were slamming into starship hulls and clinging to them like barnacles. Many would overshoot, circle back, and then latch onto the others."

"Stop it, Poo!" Brutus shivers. "Your crazy visions will be giving me nightmares. Thinking about them will keep me up. I'll never get back to sleep."

As Brutus turns toward his cabin, Andorf grabs hold of the chief engineer's

201

bulk arms. "Wait! There is more. I believe we have serious problems with our captain."

Shaking loose, Brutus yawns again. "Captain Murray? What the hell are you talking about?"

"I sense there is more going on than the captain admits. He is not being totally honest with us about your ex-girlfriend." Andorf winces. "Nicki Foos already knows your presence aboard the *Atlantis*."

"Is this another one of your random deja-vu moments or are you just being paranoid? What would Murray gain by deceiving his own teammates?"

"What if Murray believes he can pre-negotiate the refueling on his own terms without pressure of an in-person meeting? He would come across as a hero by handling the commander by himself and keeping you out of the equation."

Brutus brushes Andorf away with the back of his hand. "Look, it's late. I can't deal with this right now. I've been pulling double-shifts and need sleep. Refueling negotiations are hours away. I've got to be on top of my game."

"But—but you need to take this seriously."

Brutus steps inside his cabin and then slams the door. Hearing the grand suite's door latch, Andorf stands in the hallway scratching his chin in wonder. *If Brutus will not take me seriously, perhaps there is someone who will.*

*

Binky's log – 771-031913:

I believe those flying hexoids Andorf and I have been visualizing and people chanting numbers may be terribly bad signs. And it's serious when you cannot trust a teammate. A second opinion always helps.

202

CHAPTER 52
A Friendly Chat

Day 771: 0330 -
Titan Outpost orbit: 12.5 hours

Andorf's reaches for Gregory's cabin door and it opens on its own. Hearing someone shuffling about, he steps inside. There Gregory stands, arms folded and grinning.

"You're late. I expected you well over an hour ago." To Andorf's amazement, Gregory waves his hand and the cabin door shuts. Andorf gazes in awe back at his friend.

"What? How?"

"Think you're the only Goshi aboard the *Atlantis*?"

"Well—uh."

"Serin had these abilities as you must know. I believe it's hereditary. So, by the look on your face, I take your little impromptu meeting with Brutus didn't go so well."

"It appears the chief engineer values rest over reason." Andorf gazes at Gregory. "At least *you* are always awake. Sleeping disorders is another trait we share."

"So, what's this I hear about Murray yanking the rug out from under the chief engineer? Next thing, he'll be asking Turk to replace him."

"Nothing is certain." Andorf smirks. "Did you know Turk's crew has resorted to calling him an admiral? You know, with Nicki Foos calling herself a commander and such. A case of one-upmanship, I would say."

Gregory smirks. "Go ahead. Grant the pirate his title. The last thing we need is for him to be pounding on the negotiating table like a spoiled child."

Andorf raises a brow. "There is a certain matter concerning the Admiral."

"I'll bet he insists on bringing his trusty saber … 1-8-2 I believe he calls it."

Andorf grins awkwardly. "The admiral refuses to wear sandals."

"It figures. Have you heard the latest? Odds against the ex-councilwoman are running six thousand to one."

"As I have heard," Andorf mumbles, staring hypnotized at Gregory's collection of animated windup tic-toc clocks lining the entryway. Each brightly-colored clock bears a slightly different time but all of their kitty eyes sweep back and forth in perfect sync. Andorf's head sweeps back and forth, following the animated eyes.

"Andorf! Andorf," Gregory fumes. "Are you even listening to me?"

"Huh? What? Oh yeah, Turk." He turns and stares at his friend. "What concerns me and everyone else is Brutus' romantic past finally catching up with him. Jeez, Gregory. He is placing the entire armada at risk. I also suspect Murray is not admitting Foos already knows about his chief engineer."

"We absolutely can't pull Brutus off the negotiation team. The chief engineer knows shuttles inside and out plus a great deal about the armada's starships. So, what if he had a sordid past?" Gregory grins at Andorf. "We've all had our fair share of childhood indiscretions, haven't we?"

Andorf reluctantly nods.

"If the captain insists on Brutus' replacement then perhaps *he* is the one not to be trusted."

"On this point, Gregory, I totally agree."

"And didn't Turk once suggest raiding the outpost with a few thousand of his warriors? That alone proves the pirate is out of control. But I'm curious. Whatever you do to appease him, never ever reveal the secret ingredient in Booger Stew. I can tell this hasn't occurred as no gypsies have yet been cast out of the airlocks."

Andorf winces. "I offered him the next best thing."

Reading his best friend's readily available thoughts, Gregory's eyes cross. "You wouldn't! Tell me you didn't!"

Andorf half-way grins.

"What's to stop him from attacking the outpost anyway?"

"You do not understand. Turk and I have somewhat become friends over the past few months. He gave me his word."

"What?" Gregory yells. "You accept the word of a crazed madman? Are you forgetting about the bastard stabbing his own brother for merely snoring? What's to stop him from using our own weapons against us? Now with the pirates having phasor pistols plans, there'll be nothing to prevent him from ravaging our starships and leaving us stranded."

Andorf smiles. "Are you forgetting? The admiral wants our Galactic Drive technology. Only a select group of our gypsies have technical drive knowledge. Besides, from what I've learned about Nicki Foos, I prefer the crazed pirate over Brutus' erratic ex-girlfriend."

Gregory rolls his eyes.

"So, what if Turk sends warriors down to the outpost? How much damage can they do with a few hand-held phasor pistols? They would eliminate Commander Foos and her subordinates and then remain to run the outpost."

Gregory's eyes widen. "Think bigger ... much bigger. Some things are much worse than pistols.

Reading his best friend's thoughts, Andorf's eyes also widen.

"That's right. Turk's implemented photon cannons on four of his starships. He's now contemplating using the outpost for target practice." Gregory paces about the living area in silence. He pauses to glare at his best friend. "As little as I care about Brutus, this only proves the chief engineer is the least of our problems. If Murray is holding back information about Foos as you suspect, I'd say ..." Gregory's eyes suddenly narrow as if trying to read his best friend's thoughts. "Wait! Why are you looking at me like that?"

"I was hoping you could—"

Gregory's eyes suddenly widen. "Attend the negotiations in the captain's place? Andorf! Surely you jest." Gregory throws both arms out. "Look at these. First sight of my metal appendages will immediately throw Foos on the offense. She'd totally flip out."

"Well ... I—"

"Uh huh, that's right. I've seen all the scared faces ... especially out there in the *Atlantis'* hallways. Don't you think I hear people calling me names such as 'The Metal Man'? You've seen it yourself." Gregory clears his throat. "I believe there's more going on with these negotiations than anyone suspects. I feel it in my gut."

Andorf winces. "I tried to reach out to the commander Foos but I could not get through."

"It is impossible when someone lack conscience."

The Goshi gazes into Gregory's dark browns. His face sours at Gregory's thoughts again becoming his own. Andorf swallows hard. "What do you mean not everyone survives?"

"Open your eyes, Andorf. Look way deep inside. You also know this to be true." He raises a brow. "I'm not the only one who sees this."

Andorf takes a moment to evaluate Gregory's thoughts. He swallows hard. "Wait! You mean Binky knows? I must warn the—"

As Andorf turns to leave, Gregory grabs his best friend's arm. "You cannot warn anyone. It is absolutely crucial everyone enters the refueling negotiations in clear mind. Under no condition can Brutus and Captain Murray be made aware of the danger that awaits them."

*

Binky's log – 771-034402:

Hmm. Why does the idea of Turk raiding Titan Outpost sound more promising?

CHAPTER 53
Turk's Knee-Jerk

Day 771: 0700 - Titan Outpost orbit: 9 hours

In the middle of a long-winded rant, Turk slams a fist onto the counter and stares down his crew. "Commander Foos cannot treat us this way. How dare this bitch stand between us and the methane fuel my thirsty armada desperately needs? Isn't she aware who she is dealing with? Why, my warriors have conquered vast armies ... confiscated complete lines of deep-space starships, overcame the Oryx Empire ..."

The admiral rambles on as the *Aegean's* helmsman, comm-spec, and navigator cower behind their consoles. Unlike the crew, Burak boldly approaches the armada's admiral. "The female commander is highly irrational. She's impossible to deal with. Perhaps we should activate your plan of sending brigades of armed warriors down to the outpost."

"How are our photon cannons progressing? Shouldn't the weapons be online?"

"The weapons are operational by they require alignment." Burak grins wide. "And here we have a fine target right in front of our eyes."

The admiral grins slyly at his next in command. "I suppose you're right, Burak. Perhaps a small display of force would loosen Foo's tight grip of the badly-needed fuel."

The comm-spec's head surfaces from behind his radios. "I—I don't think that would be such a good idea, Admiral. Are you forgetting the verbal agreement with your little Goshi friend?"

Turk grumbles, beneath his breath. "I've promised no such thing,"

"You promised him you wouldn't attack the outpost unless provoked."

"A test firing of the cannons is all I'm suggesting." Turk throws open palms upwards. "Who's to blame if crosshairs were misaligned and a portion of the outpost accidentally becomes damaged?"

"Making enemies out here is the last thing we want," the navigator says. "What if our descendants—?"

"And it's mankind's greatest engineering endeavor," the helmsman adds.

Turk growls. "What's the latest on the missing starship captain, Burak?"

"You mean Argent of the *S.S. Phoenix*? He's still missing and Rita Ambrosia is nowhere to be found." Burak grins. "Odds are running ten-thousand to one against the ex-councilwoman."

"Sick!" Turk yells, suspiciously eyeing Burak and his crew. He grabs trusty 1-8-2 saber and flails it high in the air before pointing it threateningly at each of his crewmembers. "And best none of you be getting any ideas."

*

Binky's log – 771-070825:

The admiral is on the verge of a full-blown assault. I would advise the outpost commander to become more hospitable.

CHAPTER 54
Sandals

Day 771: 1100 - Titan Outpost orbit: 5 hours

Five new symbols scroll across the armada's message boards, increasing the Tenulian alphabet to forty-seven. The admiral winces at Andorf and the *Atlantis'* Captain Murray as they are let inside the *S.S. Aegean's* bridge. "The first words were Turkish-based, much easier on one's ear," Turk says. "But these new ones sound like rubbish. They are too alien to utter, let alone remember. Everywhere I go, I see children laughing at their elders' twisted tongues and wide-opened mouths as they attempt to mimic the latest enunciations."

Murray grins at Andorf. "I believe it was *your* declaration for everyone to speak this strange concoction you call Tenulian.

Andorf nods. "We must share a common language. It is necessary to unite everyone on the forty-six starships."

Turk grumbles. "I suspect you're both here to announce I'm replacing the thieving gypsy." Turk projects open palms toward his visitors. "Everyone knows I'm the better negotiation candidate."

"The Captain and I couldn't agree more." Brutus' sordid past demands his replacement."

Murray takes a deep breath. "I must warn, thus far Commander Foos has been unreasonable."

Turk reaches beneath his garb and extracts his trusty sword. He raises the piece engraved with numbers '1-8-2' high and swings it wildly in the air. "That bitch won't know what hit her when I'm done with her."

Andorf's eyes widen at the size of ole 1-8-2. "Put that away, Turk. We are no longer dealing with duopolistic empires."

Murray nods. "You can't be slicing someone's head off merely because they disagree with you."

Turk grumbles. "It's always worked in the past. Perhaps what this Nicki Foos needs is—"

"Lower the sword," Murray says. "We don't need to start an interstellar incident way out here in Argshnod."

"Argshnod?"

Andorf raises a brow. "In the middle of nowhere."

"Now about your mannerism, Admiral." Murray clears his throat. "It has been suggested by many that you should attend the negotiations wearing sandals."

Turk's mouth curls. He spits on Murray's well-polished shoes. Extracting his sword out of its scabbard, he again holds ole '1-8-2' high in the air. "Sandals? Sandals? Do I look like a bloody tourist vacationing on the French Riviera?"

"Well, we thought—" Andorf and Murray both stutter.

"Starship admirals don't wear stinkin' sandals."

*

Binky's log - 771-111643:

As much as I disdain Turk, I believed the pirate would make a satisfactory replacement.

CHAPTER 55
A Switch Hitter

Day 771: 1200 - Titan Outpost orbit: 4 hours

Upon entering the captain's private quarters, Brutus takes a moment to look around. A collection of miniature uniformed players with hand painted numbered uniforms on the credenza capture his attention. Twenty-one characters have been setup on a baseball field as though they were playing a world-series game.

"Don't," Murray yells, watching the chief engineer reach for the miniature third base umpire.

Brutus winces at the captain. "How can Turk refuse to wear sandals? Doesn't the insolent bastard know he's putting our refueling operation at risk?"

Murray raises a brow as he strolls about the quarters without words. Each time he begins to speak, he pauses.

Brutus' thoughts run wild as his eyes follow the captain. *What if Andorf's suspicions about Murray are correct? Perhaps the captain is not being totally honest.* As if to gain the captain's attention, he reaches for the shortstop. His hand is blocked by Murray's quick reflexes. Brutus retracts his hand and then reviews his timepiece. He grins back at the captain. "You sent the outpost commander our passenger list two days ago. She must suspect I'm aboard *one* of the armada's starships."

The captain clears his throat loudly. "I'm thinking if only ..."

"If only what?"

"What if Turk was to attend negotiations in your place wearing socks?"

Brutus chuckles. "It would be beneath the pirate's dignity. He'd never go for it."

The captain scratches his head. "Well, we certainly can't have him pounding on the negotiating table with his boots, can we?"

Head tilted, eyes widening, and gazing at the captain, Brutus takes multiple deep breaths.

"I mean, so what if we grant the pirate his boots? His abrasive nature may be just what is required to deal with Nicki Foos. After all, she certainly doesn't seem to want to hear anything I have to say. Perhaps the commander would buckle under at the admiral's brashness."

"Wait! Wait! Wait!" Brutus casts both hands outward. "You don't understand. If memory serves me, such tactics won't work with Nicki—I mean Commander Foos. She won't buckle under such pressure."

Murray grunts. "You're not leaving me without alternatives, Brutus. We're back to banking on Foos overlooking your name on the long passenger roster. By now, she's had plenty of time to parse through it."

"You've confirmed the commander knows of many incidents back on Earth … how one of your chief engineers wears a bounty on his head for murder. It's only a matter of time before she ties me to that event. If Nicki knows about Serin, she certainly knows about me."

Murray suddenly appears to be on the verge of hyperventilating, Brutus offers him a wadded-up fiber bag from his back pocket. Murray pushes the chief engineer's hand aside. "Damn, Brutus! Why'd you have to go and have a fling with Nicki Foos? No one has volunteered to be on the negotiating team. With Gregory Gray being too scary looking and Turk complaining about sandals, there's no one to replace you."

*

Binky's log – 771-120954:

It appears we are back to the original three team members. Now, what will make the outpost commander more reasonable?

CHAPTER 56
Deceit

Day 771: 1230 - Titan Outpost orbit: 3.5 hours

After all these years he has the audacity to come here to haunt me." Nicki Foos snarls. "The bastard won't be as welcomed this time."

The lieutenant tilts his head. "Commander?"

The commander's eyes narrow. "I suspect an old boyfriend to be aboard their lead starship. I cannot verify until I check back with Captain ... uh ... what's his name?"

"Murray."

"That's right, Captain Murray of the *S.S. Atlantis.*"

"What do you propose, Commander?"

Nicki Foos snickers. "With the armada desperate for my methane fuel, I seem to be holding all the cards. If I play them right, not only will we reap in a huge bounty but end up with a few starships of our own."

*

Binky's log – 771-123943:

Oh, why must we deal with this narcissistic bitch? Surely there must be someone else.

CHAPTER 57

A Change Of Heart

Day 771: 1300 - Titan Outpost orbit: 3 hours

Tenulian word of the day is 'magatagren' — deceit for the purpose of personal gain and/or advancing popularity.

Unable to sleep after his late-night rounds, Murray takes a seat at his credenza. Replaying the commander's queued messages, he analyzes them for loopholes. Surely there is some hidden clue to persuade the unyielding Nicki Foos to negotiate.

The red light on his viewer flashes. Against better judgement, Murray presses the accept button. Pixilated squares on the display solidify into an image of Commander Foos, smugly poised in a well-oiled executive chair. This time, she appears unnervingly calm.

"I apologize for my rash behavior during the last encounter, Captain Murray. Perhaps there *are* terms we can find mutually acceptable."

Murray wonders if the commander is setting a trap after discovering Brutus' name in the long passenger roster. Leaning back into the leather chair, he focuses on Nicki's face. Her eyes appear painted on like stickers. Her swelling lips seem slightly out of sync with her voice.

"It is quite understandable, Commander. I apologize as well for the abrupt change of plans. What began as a small fleet of three starships soon became an armada of forty-six. I can see how this could possibly have been a bit overwhelming."

The Commander nods. "Indeed it was. Now, upon closer inspection of your passenger roster, one passenger in particular was noted … a man named Bittner, stationed aboard the *S.S. Atlantis*. By chance would this happen to be a Brutus Bittner from the Canine Empire?"

Murray swallows hard. Staring directly at the viewer camera, he grins, sheepishly. "Oh, you know him?"

The commander's image fades. Murray catches himself cursing and about to throw something at the viewer. He mutes the microphone and then walks laps around his private quarters, mumbling to himself.

"So, Foos knows about Brutus. With her putting me on hold, things are not looking good. I would not be surprised if she terminates the fueling negotiations even before they begin."

Hearing shuffling papers, Murray hurries back to his leather seat and unmutes the viewer. Wiping beads of sweat off his brow, he awaits the commander's reply.

Flanked on either side by faithful lieutenants, Commander Foos reappears. All appear to be sporting shit-eating grins. "An amiable solution may be within our grasp, Captain. You and Bittner are to accompany me in the outpost's PL-259 conference room—1900 sharp. I shall present my terms at such time. Coordinates and link codes for docking bridle SO-239 have been downloaded to the *Atlantis'* database. Don't be late."

Murray nods. "Please if you will, make arrangements for one other. Andorf Johnson shall be accompanying us."

Commander Foos snickers. "A threesome, hmm. This should prove interesting. Foos, out."

*

Binky's log – 771-131829:

It has been confirmed. Nicki Foos knows about our chief engineer. Still, she agrees to meet. I feel a trap being set for our negotiators. Wait! My human Andorf is on that team. I cannot let anything happen to him. I must take things into my own paws.

PART 5
TITAN OUTPOST

CHAPTER 58
The Approach

Day 771: 1600 - Titan Outpost orbit

The armada's forty-six starships slow for low orbit of Saturn's largest moon. Cameras home in on the eleven-thousand-mile ring of modular sections, seemingly stacked end-to-end like children's dominoes. Closer examination reveals fine scratches along the ring's once shiny surface. Port numbers on a cluster of docking pods zip past too quickly to catch anyone's eye.

Lacking windows, Titan Outpost reminds Murray of his incarceration in the Cos back on Earth. He shivers at the sounds of case stampings in the next-door power-cell factory ... the wretched smells of human parts being injected with GMOs. They still haunt him.

Murray dims the viewing portal in his private quarters. Returning to the credenza, he updates Andorf via inter-ship messaging. A messenger is sent down to the bowels of the starship to locate and retrieve the third team member. The captain mulls over in his mind just what he expects of the meeting. From opening salutations through to the grind of negotiations, he walks about with animated hands and vocalizing, playing out the scenarios.

Worst case: Being in the same room with Brutus, Foos will be steaming mad. She'll volley barrages of vulgar words, perhaps going as far as to threaten to rob the chief engineer of his life. Brutus will attempt to soften her rage by mentioning passionate moments they once shared. After an hour of arguing, both will lick their wounds and allow the negotiations to proceed.

Best case: The commander has overcome her bitter past. She consents to modify previous arrangements between her brother and Captain Thom. Goshi Andorf will be there to keep the commander's mood swings in check. Of course, she'll demand compensation for the additional starships but will allow all forty-six to be refueled. With Goshi Andorf present, what could possibly go wrong?

Scratching his chin, Murray rolls one of many prized baseballs signed by major league all-star players over the past seven seasons across his desk. It comes to rest against his collection of miniature Louisville slugger bats, engraved with player's numbers. His thoughts drift back to simpler times on the mother world.

Oh, if only I were back home right now. I'd be warming my butt in a box seat above home plate, sipping a cold one, and watching the world-series play out.

*

Binky's log – 771-160754:

Captain Murray is planning out the negotiation. With him being such an avid baseball fan, I bet he expects to hit one out of the park.

CHAPTER 59

The Last Meal

Hoofing it down the G-deck hallway, Brutus' taste buds perk at the aroma of a fancy four-course meal. He spots a courier just steps ahead opening a dumbwaiter access door. He pauses to help but his offer is rejected. And so, stomach growling, he trails behind the rolling cart.

Brutus follows the courier and cart inside Captain Murray's private quarters. He salivates watching the presentation of the four-course meal, wondering which dish he would sample first. Would it be a sporkful of mango-ginger soup ... or perhaps a scoop of yam risotto in miso butter sauce ... or maybe a taste of the Tofu Wellington? With the captain peering out his viewport, he reaches to snag one of the caramel napoleon mini-bites. The courier slaps his hand before making a hasty exit.

With Murray clearing his throat loudly, Brutus grins awkwardly at the *Atlantis'* captain. "You wanted to see me, sir?"

Murray's eyes return to the viewport, appearing to take note of the starship's dwindling orbit. He lowers the shade and then smirks at the chief engineer's drooling lips. "I normally begin with the soup, but go ahead, Brutus. Take a few mini-bites."

After wiping his mouth on one of the fiber napkins, Brutus fills the napkin with dessert bites. At the captain's discerning stare, he returns all be a few of the tasty treats.

In spite of an apparent dwindling appetite, the captain steps closer to the cart and then lifts his spork. "I wasn't sure if you received the latest news. Negotiations with Commander Foos are on. Our meeting on the outpost is set for 1900."

Brutus chokes down the mini-bites and then looks for something to wash them down. Without signs of resistance, he dips a straw and then sips Murray's cannabis tea. "1900? That's two and a half hours from now. I've been pulling double shifts, Captain. I'm running on little sleep."

Murray's eyes narrow at numbers projected on the ceiling and back at the chief engineer. "You will have ninety minutes to rest up, Brutus. I shall meet you and our Goshi in the shuttle bay at 1800 sharp."

Brutus grins sheepishly. "It's a good thing Foos is still unaware of my presence."

"The commander was very particular in her demands." Murray clears his throat loudly. "She requested you by name and wants you to be present during the negotiations."

"Wait! Nicki Foos knows?"

Murray nods.

At the thought of seeing his first love after so many years, Brutus' heart begins to race. He clamors for words. "D—did Nicki refer to me by name? W—was she ...?"

Murray begins to pace about his private quarters, shoveling a sporkful of Tofu Wellington into his mouth on each pass around the serving cart. After the third pass, he pauses to glare at Brutus, speaking while trying to swallow the steaming main course.

"I've said it before, I don't trust this woman. You should have seen the way she interrogated me with those beady hazel eyes and whiny voice. It was like bracing for an impact, knowing there was nothing else you could do. Not only do I feel a stiff wind blowing but the three of us are facing it head on."

Awestruck, Brutus takes multiple shallow breaths. His twitching hands reach deep inside his rear pants pocket. He looks away as he takes breaths into the wrinkled fiber bag. It takes a long moment for him to regain composure. "If it's any consolation, I know the commander despises all Earth's empires. After all, they stranded her out here, two years from home. I know the outpost relies on starships such as ours to replenish their consumables. Perhaps we should emphasize these details and use them to our advantage."

Murray loads a sporkful of yam risotto, but after inspecting the embedded orange speckles, returns it to the plate. "I've worked the resupply issue from different angles," he says, stirring the mango-ginger soup. Whatever I conjure up, nothing seems to equate. I suspect the commander wants more than just supplies. At this point, I wouldn't take revenge off the table."

Brutus crosses hidden fingers. "No worries, Captain. Everything will be fine. I suspect, once the commander overcomes her animosity towards me, negotiations will be smooth sailing."

"Then explain why I have a gut-wrenching feeling that I'm enjoying my last meal."

"Of—of course the commander is bitter. Can you really blame her after being dumped in Argshnod for who knows how long? The only friends she must have are those serving beneath her and even they may one day stab her in the back and take control of the outpost."

"Sheez, Brutus. You sound like one of those denying E-Cons back on Earth. Open your eyes! Can't you see what's going on?"

Watching Murray pace around the four-course meal while occasionally taking bites, Brutus' again salivates. His drooling lips dry up at the thought of Nicki Foos. "Once you get past her outer cast-iron shell, Nicki's actually a warm person. You must understand, Captain. Nicki's lived beneath her brother's shadow all her life. Now in command, she's flexing a little muscle, that's all."

"Warm you say?" Murray expels food bits into a fiber napkin. His eyes narrow upon the chief engineer. "Nicki Foos did away with her brother. You were once Robert's friend. Aren't you the least bit concerned what she may have done with him?"

"Well—I—"

"I can say with assurance, the commander has no intention of honoring her brother's arrangements let alone revising them to accommodate forty-six-starships. You should've heard her warning of our starships facing chilling graves in the methane lakes below. For all we know, the outpost is packed to the gills with armaments, poised and ready to attack the armada on our low orbit."

Brutus half-way smiles. He looks about the captain's private quarters before speaking. "Turk's crew scanned every square inch of Titan and Saturn's nearby moons. They found absolutely no weapons signatures of any sort."

The captain winces. "Running low-level FT-8 decryption sweeps, my comm-spec detected trace magnetic signatures across areas of the ring. As an engineer, you must agree numbers never lie."

Brutus raises a brow. "FT-8? You mean the ancient modulation explored by radio hams of distant past? I suspect Pol was merely picking up spurious noise off the outpost's docking bridles."

"Then tell me this, Brutus. How could anyone being two years from her home world have no way of defending herself? Mark my words. She's got weapons. This I am sure. That woman is not to be trusted. Here, have a listen to her messages."

Murray sequences through a series of buttons to play the queued messages. From her rant about Captain Thom, digressing to her concerns about the forty-six wanted starship captains, Murray cringes at the commander's irritatingly whiny voice. The message queue terminates with the commander's near-jealous rant about Serin.

Brutus winces. "I must admit, Nicki sounds steaming mad but …"

Holding a loaded spork inches from his expectant mouth, the captain freezes. He returns the barely touched Tofu Wellington to the plate, grumbling even louder than his belly. Pushing the dinner cart aside, far from the chief engineer's grabbing hands, he stares Brutus down with narrowing eyes. "Can I be honest with you?"

"Of course, Captain."

"I have grave feelings about attending these negotiations. Bargaining with this old girlfriend of yours will be nothing but trouble. If she hadn't insisted on your attendance, you would have been replaced."

Brutus smirks. "By who? Turk?"

Murray nods.

"Oh, I'm sure that'd go over well. The guy cannot even keep his shoes on. Why, I wouldn't put it past the pirate to raise his saber and do away with the commander for merely sneering at him. You've heard what he did to an older sibling."

"Well, there's always Andorf's friend, Gregory."

Brutus snorts. "You mean Metal Man? We've been through all that. The commander would take one look at him and send us all packing."

The captain shrugs his shoulders. "Who else is there? Huh? Who would you suggest?"

Brutus wipes sweat off his brow. Glancing briefly at the captain's heaping plate of barely touched food on the cart just feet off, Brutus wipes drool off his lips, this time with the back of his hand. He takes a deep breath before staring back at the captain. "People change, don't they, Murray? You said it yourself. Surely Nicki has moved on after so many years."

Without hesitation, Murray plays the final excerpt where the commander agrees to meeting contingent upon Brutus' attendance. It wraps up with 'Don't be late.'

"The commander was flanked by highly-decorated lieutenants." Murray's mouth contorts. "All were sporting shit-eating grins. And you heard what she said about an amiable solution being within our grasp ... how she'll present her terms. Coordinates and link codes for the docking bridle have been downloaded to our database. What the hell are we to do?"

Hearing the commander's shrieking voice after so many years, Brutus' face sours. He takes multiple deep breaths trying to find air. He pulls a wadded-up fiber bag from a rear pocket, holds it over his face, and takes multiple breaths. Returning the bag to his rear pocket, he winces at the captain.

"So—so I take it Turk is out of the question?"

"Sandals! The pirate refuses to wear sandals. And I wonder why I am feeling sharp knives stabbing my back?"

Brutus smirks. "We've broken free from an oppressive empire, overcame the crisis of the starship losing life support, and even merged our tiny fleet into a huge armada commandeered by a crazed pirate. Now we're dealing with a single belligerent woman. Really, how bad can things really be?"

"If you need a reminder of what can occur, take a look at my burned off finger," Murray yells, throwing his abbreviated digit in the chief engineer's face. "Here's what the malicious Canine Empire did to me. And look what happened to my predecessor, the late Captain Thom. There are reasons why I'm the second starship captain in just twenty-two months. The *Atlantis'* captain's is a dead end position, a final destination for whoever occupies the chair. And now with Commander Nicki Foos in charge of the Titan Outpost, space has become even more dangerous."

Smirking, Brutus turns away. "A dangerous place indeed."

*

Binky's log – 771-164601:

Binky shivers. *What if we allow the admiral to go barefoot? He could then attend the negotiations in Andorf's place.*

CHAPTER 60

Dilemma

Day 771: 1700 –
Refueling Negotiations: 2 hours

B inky hops about Andorf's cabin, pausing frequently to gather thoughts. *Surely, I cannot allow my human counterpart to participate in the upcoming negotiations. Something terrible is about to happen on Titan Outpost. I can feel it in my lagomorph bones.*

Binky leaps into his favorite litter box which is topped off daily with premium Timothy hay from the *S.S. Inca*. He nestles inside the litter box, creating a hole in the matted hay.

In the past, Andorf has walked blindly into dangerous situations. He always somehow whittled his way out of trouble, tumbling out unscathed. I've kept my wiggly nose out of his business up until now. But this time it's different. The junior Goshi is not ready. He's only recently discovered the enlightened path. A confrontation with evil Nicki Foos is well-beyond his skill set. It would set him back a lifetime. If human Andorf leaves on this mission, he may not survive.

Unable to relax, Binky leaps out of the litterbox. He hops into the bedroom chinning each pair of Andorf's shoes.

Of course, the fueling negotiations are necessary … in fact critical for the armada to continue on its energy quest. But why must my Andorf attend? Humans Brutus and Murray can handle this one on their own. Let them deal with Commander Foos by themselves.

*

Binky's log – 771-170739:

There must be something a seven-pound rabbit can do other than claiming ownership of his human's shoes. My stomach aches. It's in knots worrying about human Andorf. Oh, I am not well. I feel a sick coming on.

CHAPTER 61
Slip Slidin' Away

Day 771: 1750 –
Refueling Negotiations: 70 minutes

Second Tenulian word of the day is 'stasis' – a severe loss of appetite.

Just as Murray had earlier complained, Brutus feels those very same knives stabbing his back. Grinding his teeth to bear the pain, he escorts the captain toward shuttle #2.

"Where the hell is our third team-member?" Murray yells. "Doesn't your friend respect tight schedules?"

Nearing the shuttle's rear hatch door, Andorf greets the pair with a shaking head. "I'm worried about Binky. He has been moping around and will not eat any of his treats. I suspect the furry guy has developed stasis."

Murray's face contorts as if swallowing something terribly bitter. "Stasis? What the hell is stasis?"

Andorf winces. "Gastrointestinal stoppage is the leading cause of rabbit deaths, you know. When rabbits quit eating, things quickly escalate into a full-blown crisis. So, needless to say, guys ... I will not be attending today's negotiations."

Jaw dropped, Murray stares bewildered at Andorf. "What? Wait! You can't be doing this at the last minute. Why can't Binky just man-up. He could puke like everyone else?"

Brutus raises a brow. "Rabbits can't vomit. Isn't that right, Andorf?"

Andorf nods. "I can and I must. And yes, Brutus. That is true."

"We'll be back before you know it," Murray yells. "I order you to come with us,"

Recalling Brutus' words, Andorf repeats them. "I am not one of your lackey crew, Captain. You cannot order me around."

Murray shakes a fist. "But Foos knows about Brutus. We're counting on having a Goshi to deal with the bitch. Take a look at Brutus. He's been working double shifts, running on zero sleep. You don't see *him* backing out at the last moment."

Brutus covers a wide yawn with his hand.

"You don't understand, Captain. Binky is not a young bunny. He never ever refuses treats. This could be his demise. I must be with him when he transitions to the Rainbow Bridge."

Murray waves his abbreviated hand at the Goshi as if wishing he still had his middle finger. "And so just like that, you're blowing us off. All because a ...?"

"Oh, yes, I almost forgot." Andorf hands Brutus a small black box. "Here's something Gregory cooked up."

"What's this, another one of mechanical man's crazy gizmos?" Brutus inspects the sealed black box. It has no lights, switches, only tiny vent holes on all six sides.

Andorf shrugs his shoulders. "It is some kind of pressure sensor. Gregory believes it is critical for your survival."

Brutus sets the box down and begins to walk towards the shuttle.

After picking up the black box up, Andorf hands it back to the chief engineer. "Gregory insists you keep it on your person at all times. It has something activating the shuttle's emergency homing beacon." After watching the chief engineer drop the gizmo into one of his deep pockets, he turns away. "Just be aware of anything not quite right and most important ... keep your wits. I wish the both of you good luck."

Before the captain can refute him, Andorf is gone.

*

Binky's log – 771-180503:

Binky runs across the living area and chomps on the first of many treats his human left behind. *Whew! I didn't know if that would actually work. Life can now resume.*

CHAPTER 62
Negotiations

Day 771: 1800 –
Refueling Negotiations: 60 minutes
Third Tenulian word of the day is 'Kahu' – a protector.

B rutus leads the captain into shuttle #2. Murray turns and snarls. "Sheez! That guy is way nuts about that damn rabbit." He leans into the chief engineer. "I heard he actually believes his pet is telepathic."

"Binky is more of a kahu than a pet," Brutus says, pushing Gregory's gizmo further inside his deep pocket. He leads the captain into the shuttle and then secures the rear hatch door behind them. "I will say this. Andorf's rabbit has saved the guy's life on more than one occasion. I bear witness to the fact."

"Kahu. Kahu. Oh yeah, a protector of sorts. It's just not right. No man should be enslaved by another, let alone by a four-legged fur-ball. The way Andorf acts, you'd think Binky was his—" Murray pauses to stare at the chief engineer's troubled face. "Wait! What's wrong, Brutus?"

The chief engineer scratches at his head. "Did you notice anything strange about Andorf? Goshi or no Goshi, the guy's usually not as abrupt. His face was pale. His hands were shaking and he was stuttering. There is more going on with Andorf than just his sick rabbit."

"Come to think about it, Andorf *did* appear afraid."

Brutus raises a brow. "Afraid he'd never see us again."

"No! Wait! Are you telling me Andorf knows what'll transpire on Titan Outpost? He couldn't possibly know. Not unless the rumors of him reliving past lives is true."

Brutus shrugs his shoulders. "Even I suspect trouble from the moment we dock." He pulls Gregory's small, black box from his deep pocket and examines the device in his huge hands before dropping it back inside the pocket. "Why else would techno-nerd Gregory piece together a doomsday box?"

The moment Murray assumes helm position, coins spill from his pocket. Many coins clank on the floor and pool around their shoes. Brutus scoops up a handful and flashes them at the captain.

"What are you doing with these now-worthless slugs?" Shaking his head, Brutus returns the loose change.

"I'm hoping to trade with the natives." Murray listens to the coins clinking dropping into his pocket. He and Brutus then strap in as the shuttle verbally sequences through pre-flight checks. At all green lights, Murray eases the shuttle out of the *Atlantis'* underbelly. Piloting the craft toward the man-made ring around Titan, he wrinkles his nose at Brutus. "There's one thing really bugging me about Commander Foos."

"And what's that, Murray?"

"The commander is in her what ... forties? As you say, she's been stranded here in Argshnod for years with no apparent love for anyone back on Earth."

"That's correct. State your point."

"Besides doing her brother in and assuming outpost operations, what in holy hell does the woman do out here in her spare time?"

"How would I know?" Brutus says, shrugging his shoulders. "It's been twenty-five plus years since I last saw Nicki. I really don't know much about her."

"You know her better than anyone in the armada. Haven't you even the slightest idea? I mean, you'd think she'd have a past-time other than claiming other people's trophies. Something like puzzles or macramé or ..." Murray winces. "Compiling a weapons arsenal."

"We've been through this before. Her outpost is totally defenseless. Turk's crew scanned every inch of Titan and other nearby moons. They found no weapon signatures of any sort."

"That woman is seriously deranged I tell you. I wouldn't put anything past her. We are staking our lives on Turk's readings."

Visualizing a military-style space battle taking place in the commander's domain, Brutus swallows hard. He begins to speak but freezes.

"Did you have a good look at the outpost, Brutus? It lacks viewing portals. Yep, not one single window. The last thing I'd want is to spend the rest of my days in another forced confinement without windows."

Turning to peer outside, Brutus spots a pair of footlockers secured behind the rear seats. His eyes widen at sight of the bright red hazard stickers plastered about them. "Damn! I forgot about those suckers," he mumbles." He turns about face. "Is it too late to turn the shuttle about?"

"No! Not you too," Murray yells.

"But ... but ..."

The captain eyes Brutus suspiciously. "Nearing our programmed descent is no time to be getting cold feet. First Andorf and now—"

"It's nothing of the sort, Captain. Did you know we're carrying biohazards aboard this shuttle?"

Murray spins a full one-eighty in his seat. His eyes immediately draw toward the pair of footlockers, plastered with red hazard stickers and East-African transit stamps. He gulps. "Are those what I think they are?"

Brutus nods. "Indeed. Eight-hundred pounds of rare Carnga nuts, imported from the Isle of Madagascar."

"What the hell, Brutus? We're carrying aphrodisiacs? Are you planning a peace offering with your old girlfriend? There's no mention of orgies anywhere in the Art of Negotiation Playbook. Believe me, I've read the book from cover to cover."

"I honestly forgot they were there, Murray. I'll have my techs move them into the cargo hold upon our return."

Murray peers at his unstained hands, cringing as if imagining what could happen if the footlocker seals were breached. "I've heard carnga nuts are nasty little suckers. They can permanently stain your hands a pale olive-green color. I would've expected you to have destroyed the whole lot."

"I'm surprised you know as much about the sinful treats."

"Growing up, my family frequently vacationed on the Quirimbas Islands of Mozambique. The waters there are every shade of blue from turquoise to cobalt …"

Brutus quiets, listening to the captain ramble on about his privileged childhood. He peers out a small portal at the shuttle's forward lights reflecting off the frigid lakes down below. The shimmering surfaces fade as their shuttle passes over the dark side of the moon. Moments later, docking portal SO-239 appears on the console screen, dead on a collision course.

Auto-firing thrusters dampen the craft's approach to a more manageable docking speed. A slight bump confirms alignment with the docking pod. A second bump ensures the outpost's magnetic clamps have snugly secured the shuttle's nosepiece inside the mating bridle. When the outpost's air supply engages, a sweet taste of intoxicating air oddly tickles Brutus' nostrils.

Moments later, Brutus twitches at the slight pressure on his temples. He watches the shuttle seats swivel in ninety-degree complements. He sees the craft split apart and retract beneath his feet, leaving him and Murray standing on a pristine terrazzo floor with geometric patterns extending in every direction.

With overhead instructions barking at them from hidden speakers, the negotiators mindlessly follow sequenced sub-floor chase lighting. Brutus' skin itches at the feel of hidden eyes scrutinizing their every move. In passing, he takes note of docking portals crammed together more tightly than physically possible. The chase lighting terminates abruptly at conference room PL-259, not a footstep too soon.

A door swooshes open, revealing an oblong table and polished chrome chairs in an otherwise empty room. The room appears sterile with its brushed-titanium walls and absence of color. Brutus takes a seat on the far side of the table, facing Murray. A seven-foot android lacking personality appears out of nowhere. Its humanoid-hands place opaque glasses on the table before him and Murray. Brutus pulls a hand-scanner from his pocket. Reviewing the device, he finds the bubbling blue beverage to be safe but slightly intoxicating. Reaching for his glass, he freezes at the clog of approaching footsteps.

The conference door swooshes open. Brutus swallows hard at the tap of shoes stepping inside. His heart throbs. Though he has not laid eyes upon his lost love in nearly three decades, he trances at the first sight of Nicki Foos' with her short-cropped dirty-blonde hair. She appears not a day older than when she was in her mid-teens.

Ignoring the chief engineers' possessive gaze, the commander casts a manila folder. Forms spilling out of the folder fan out across the oblong table.

Murray swivels nervously in his polished-chrome chair, eyes darting between the middle-aged commander and papers spread out on the table before him. He reaches for the papers but freezes at the commander's irritatingly whiny voice.

"I have reviewed the armada's manifests and ..."

Brutus and Murray exchange glances. Gulping, both stare at the commander.

"Your armada has nothing to offer. Our pantries are well-stocked for the next three years. Nothing on the outpost is in dire need of repair. So gentlemen, you appear to be wasting my time." The commander's eyes narrow. Her mouth curls into a smirk. "My liquid methane shall remain on Titan's surface."

Brutus grips the seat tightly as if only to restrain himself. He snarls at the commander's gloating smile. He opens his mouth but Murray beats him to the punch.

"You can't do this, Commander. Our starships have slowed to orbit. We have barely enough fuel to maintain orbit a few more hours."

The Commander's widening grin nearly devours her face. "You heard me, Captain. I cannot help you."

Brutus' mouth sours. His vision darkens. He attempts to stand but instead collapses into his seat, staring at the bubbling blue drink on the table before him. He reaches for the drink but finds his arm frozen.

At the Commander's nod, the seven-foot android releases Brutus' arm before exiting the room. She sneers at Brutus struggling to leave his chair and then laughs at the emergency mask falling out of his pocket. "Still wrestling with claustrophobia, are we, big guy?"

Brutus finds it difficult to maintain his focus on the Commander as he struggles to reach for the mask on the floor. He recalls Andorf's departing words warning him of things not being quite right. *The room with its brushed-titanium walls ... the oblong table ... the slightly intoxicating bubbling blue drink. It all feels odd. With the exception of Nicki's wicked laughter, seems out of place. Even the commander's whiny voice sounds off. Why has she not aged since I last saw her? And how could she know about my claustrophobia? I hadn't developed until after we split up.*

As though the commander were merely a holograph, her face flickers for a sixth of a moment. Brutus blinks hard and finds himself strapped down, being worked over by the seven-foot android's stronger-than-human hands. Struggling to breathe, events flash before him as though he were living segments of another's life on rewind. After a second hard blink, he has returned to his chair at the oblong conference table, again staring at the bubbling blue drink. As before, the commander casts a folder on the table. Its contents fan out, but this time forms spilling out float inches above the table.

A faint voice echoes in the back of his head ... a voice he has not heard in many years. The scruffy voice pounds louder and louder as if battling his foggy thoughts. *"Wake up! Wake up, Master Brutus! You are in deep trouble. You must get the hell out of there.'*

"Binky?" Brutus mumbles, stumbling to his feet. Bracing against a missing table, he catches himself from falling. His hand passes right through the table's holographic image. He grabs his emergency oxygen mask off the floor and slaps it over his face, knocking the temporal probes off his head. He takes multiple deep breaths.

Awakening a minute later, Brutus finds himself strapped inside shuttle #2 sitting opposite to the captain. After looking about the shuttle and spotting temporal probes at his feet, he slowly pieces together what had occurred.

After securing the mask on his face, he yanks the temporal probes off Murray's head. He then releases the emergency mask from beneath his seat and slaps it over Murray's face. Stumbling about the shuttle, he manages to seal the rear hatch and detach from the station's air supply. The shuttle's air scrubbers instantly engage.

After a good minute, Murray begins to stir. Awakening to see a bulky man hovering above, he claws the mask off his face. "What happened? Where is everyone?" At Brutus' insistent hands, he returns the mask to his face.

When the shuttle's air exchanger dings, Brutus' rips the air mask off his own face. "Didn't you find it odd how the shuttle came apart and dissolved into the floor? What about those docking portals? They were crammed together impossibly close. No one in their right mind would build anything so impossible."

Murray yanks off his mask. "The shuttle coming apart? Portals crammed together? What the hell are you talking about?"

"Think, Murray. Try to remember what just happened?"

"Well, I recall Commander Foos screaming something about you having had your chance and her huge Goober-droid beating you with its large, human-oid hands."

"Oh, yeah," Brutus says, rubbing his aching jaw. His eyes suddenly widen. "We never left the shuttle. We were drugged, brainwashed by the commander's temporal probes."

Murray reaches inside both pants pockets and turns them inside out. "And robbed! That bitch stole my coins ... every last one of them."

Brutus gazes at the vacant area behind their seats. "The footlockers full of Carnga nuts ... they're gone as well! I've got to warn Nicki. She can't possibly know of their catastrophic effects." Brutus begins to staggers toward the rear hatch. "She's in terrible danger."

Latching onto Brutus' belt loops, the captain is dragged through the shuttle's cabin. Kicking and screaming, he applies shoe brakes to no avail. "Are you kidding me? After what your ex-girlfriend just put us through? Who cares if the bitch is left with permanently-stained olive-green hands? She lured us here with no intent of releasing a single drop of her liquid methane."

Mumbling to himself, Brutus turns away. "Not to mention the nut's near-lethal side effects."

"Snap out of it, Brutus. The woman drugged us, robbed us, and will most likely kill us ... like what she did to her own brother. How can any woman become so bitter? What the hell'd you do to her?"

"Well—I ..."

"You had us walking into a hornet's nest back there. Hadn't you considered that?"

Brutus pulls free of Murray's weak grip but freezes at the commander's irritatingly whiny voice screeching at them through the shuttle's speakers.

"After thirty years, Bittner, you have the audacity to return for seconds? You should have moved on me when you had your chance. I can tell you this ... you won't get away so easily this time, you bloody bastard."

The commander's screechy voice suddenly ceases as do the shuttle's radios and navigational devices. Many dashboard indicators flash red error messages. Brutus surfaces from beneath the access panel grasping a fistful of frayed wires in his hand and sporting a wide grin.

"Tell me you didn't do what I think you just did."

The chief engineer shrugs his shoulders. "Oops."

"Damn, Brutus! Without radios, we've got no auto-guidance. I'll have to manually pilot the shuttle, blindly guessing the armada's location. And how will we ever contact the armada?"

Binky's raspy voice again interrupts Brutus' thoughts, this time loud and in dead center of his brain. *Fly out away before it's too late. Fly! Fly like you've never flown before.*

Murray's eyes widen. "Did you hear that—that strange voice telling me to fly like I've never flown before?"

Brutus chuckles. "That was Binky, Andorf's rabbit. Now do you believe he's telepathic?"

Manning the helm controls, Murray glares back at Brutus. "I've been drugged, robbed, and my head's still spinning. Right now, I don't know what I believe. All I know is I've to get us the hell out of here ... before anything else goes wrong."

*

Binky's log – 771-195112:

Didn't I tell you the commander was not to be trusted? Now with negotiations flushed down the crapper, what happens next is anyone's guess.

CHAPTER 63
A Discovery

Day 771:2100 –
Refueling Commencement: 60 minutes

Sitting in his cabin living area, Andorf winces at his best friend. "That is correct, Gregory. By some miracle, Binky has fully recovered from stasis. Just look at him over there munching on his hay."

"As I've said before, Binky knew you were heading for disaster." Gregory stares at Andorf's bunny. "You knew didn't you, Binky?"

Binky quits eating hay only long enough to blink his eyes at Gregory.

"Did you see that? He winked at me."

Andorf nods. "He does that a lot. I suspect Binky faked his illness to prevent me from attending the negotiations?"

Gregory nods. "What about our negotiators? We haven't heard from them in over an hour."

Binky hops out of the litterbox and tears across the room. He leaps into Andorf's lap and then nudges his human's belly, begging for pets. At his cheeks and forehead being rubbed, the furry guy clicks his teeth loudly.

Andorf stops petting Binky. He lowers his head, peers deep into the Binky's eyes. After merging thoughts with the seven-pound lagomorph,

Andorf's jaw drops. "Brutus is in deep trouble. Binky has already warned him."

Binky hops off Andorf's lap and scampers off.

Andorf clamors to his feet. "I must notify the admiral, inform him about the negotiators."

Gregory grabs his friend's arm and prevents him from walking out. "We can't leave."

"What do you mean we cannot leave?"

"Just what I said, Andorf. Everything's been locked down."

"What?" Andorf yells. "Are you telling me I cannot even exit my own cabin?"

"Turk's placed the armada in battle-ready mode. The floating steps have shut down. Shuttle bays are all sealed. Every starship bridge has been secured. The only communication permitted is between starship bridges."

Andorf reaches for his door but it refuses to open. He turns the knob but finds it is frozen. Gregory discovers the same. With both now grasping the knob the door belligerently opens. Andorf dashes into the hallway. Gregory follows. Binky hop after them.

*

Binky's log – 771-213708:

Now I'm worried about the captain and chief engineer. With all the confusion taking place aboard the shuttle, I cannot get into either of their heads.

CHAPTER 64

No Word

Day 771: 2140 –
Refueling Commencement: 20 minutes

Turk paces about the *Aegean's* bridge, growling at one crewmember and then the next. He pauses to stare down his next-in-command, growling even louder. "Are you positively sure the outpost is unarmed? Even bearing photon cannons, my armada's taking awful big risks."

Overviewing telemetry controls, Burak points out the interferometer's flat-lined display. "Look for yourself, Admiral. Scans over the past weeks of Titan and the adjacent moons reveal absolutely nothing. There are absolutely no weaponry signatures of any sort."

"What about my negotiators? It's been over two hours. Shouldn't they have checked in by now?"

The comm-spec gulps. "Not a word, sir. I'm no longer picking up the shuttle's telemetry. It's as though their radio devices have been disabled."

"What about a debris field?"

Burak shakes his head. "I've located nothing near the docking portals."

Turk growls louder. "I don't like any of this. With the missing Goshi and no communications, we've been left totally in the dark. Anything could have happened down there on the outpost. If it weren't for Andorf's rabbit getting sick, I'd have the Goshi thrown in the brig." Turk strokes his greying beard. "Oh, I never should've trusted that Brutus gypsy with his ex-girlfriend."

"Who knows what the two lovers are doing?" Burak mumbles.

"I knew I should have gone in his place … been there alongside Murray in case things turned ugly." Turk removes his trusty sword from its scabbard and holds it high in the air. "My trusty 1-8-2 would have convinced the commander to negotiate on *our* terms. If only the others hadn't insisted I wear sandals."

"Sandals?" Staring up at ole 1-8-2, Burak gulps. Using hand gestures, he prompts the admiral to lower the large sword. "If I didn't know better, Admiral, I'd say you've developed a genuine liking for the gypsy bum."

Turk presses the tip of 1-8-2 into Burak's cheek. At the sight of blood dripping onto his bridge floor, he returns it to the scabbard. "Bah, nothing of the sort! Looking after my armada is what I'm doing. You think its easy being an admiral? Perhaps you'd like to—"

"I—I was only saying …"

"Well, don't just stand there, Burak. Help the comm-spec discover what happened to our negotiator's shuttle. Find out why their comm devices suddenly went silent." Turk scans his timepiece. "How long are these negotiations supposed to last? Here we are orbiting Titan on vapors while those clowns are on the outpost socializing with the commander. How much longer can the armada able to maintain orbit, Burak?"

"The *S.S. Inca* is the largest vessel in the armada. I suspect she has less than an hour."

"Order the starships to line up in fueling positions."

The next-in-command winces. "I wouldn't do that, Admiral. Without the commander's consent, assuming positions could be interpreted as an aggressive act on our part."

Turk snickers. "You've told me yourself, Burak, Foos' outpost is defense-less. We have yet to align and test fire our photon cannons. Remote sections of the outpost would certainly make appropriate targets … perhaps a few of their least-used docking portals."

"What about the agreement with your little Goshi friend?"

"Bah! Agreements are made to be broken. Other than sacrificing one shuttle and a couple crew-members—"

Burak's jaw drops. "Turk! You can't be considering abandoning two highly-valued crew members. Crews of the original three starships wouldn't stand for it. They'd break from the armada rather than abandon one of their captains and engineers."

Turk's eyes narrow at his next in command. "Think I haven't thought this over? Nothing comes without risk, Burak. If the crews resist, we'll tow their starships with ropes if we must. As for Andorf, he has been displaying little love for the gypsy. He'll eventually get over it."

The navigator's head surfaces above the navigational console. "We've already been branded as fugitives by Earth's seven empires. Do we really need another enemy this far in space?"

Turk shakes his head. "Foos despises the empires. After being stranded out here in Argshnod, I have no doubt she hates Earth's empires even more than we do. Thus, we have mutual enemies. Inform the armada. Whether we hear from the negotiators or not, operations are to commence at 2200 sharp. The *S.S. Inca* and the *S.S. Atlantis* will lead the refueling pairs."

Burak glares at his superior. "Aye, sir. I'll place the armada on high alert."

"At the first sign of trouble, all ships are to break formation and rendezvous above the moon's northern polar cap."

*

Binky's log – 771-214733:

With opposing hot-heads running the show, I feel a space battle on the horizon.

CHAPTER 65
Waiting It Out

Day 771: 2150 –
Refueling Commencement: 10 minutes

The forty-six-starship armada circling above Titan's frosty methane lakes line up in pairs. With engines running on fumes, each captain anxiously awaits commencement orders, with or without Commander Foos' blessing.

Pairs of photon cannons have been mounted on four select starships. Tapping energy directly off starship power grids, the upgraded weaponry is capable of sending continuous photon sprays with no need of recharge. Although cannon calibrations are assumed to be within design parameters, there have been no test firings thus far.

For the largest and least maneuverable ship, the *Inca* with her seventeen majestic decks, added weaponry appears misplaced. Though brave in battle, her captain struggles with technology and has second thoughts of using untested weaponry.

In contrast, the *Calypso's* captain favors gadgetry and has retrofitted the bridge with the latest navigation gear. Never having experienced live battle situation, she aims to be prepared with the cannons whenever confrontation rears its ugly head.

The *S.S. Conquest* and *S.S. Aquila* have likewise been fitted with aft and rear cannons.

Acting Captain Jobriah Cates fills in during for the *Atlantis'* Captain Murray during his absence. The expatriated copter pilot has ample offensive maneuver action under his belt. Jobi, as he prefers to be called, has no reservations of initiating risky refueling procedures in the midst of Commander Foos' unwelcoming domain. Jobi almost welcomes the commander's aggression as he jockeys the *Atlantis* into the premier spot in the fueling lineup alongside the much grander *S.S. Inca*.

*

Binky's log – 771-215214:

The stage is set for space battle. I wonder who attacks first and what weaponry Nicki Foos actually has in her arsenal.

CHAPTER 66
Stuck

Day 771: 2153 –
Refueling Commencement: 7 minutes

Captain Murray fires shuttle #2's reverse thrusters. The small craft lists to one side and then the other. At the chief engineer's direction, he fires thrusters only in short pulses. Still, the outpost's docking bridles maintain a firm grip.

"The controls aren't working, Brutus. We lack power to break free. What'd your ex-girlfriend do to my shuttle?"

"I suspect the bridle clamps are still engaged." Brutus gazes out the frontal viewports. He then dives beneath the console.

The captain holds cupped hands at his lips. He calls out to the chief engineer. "Don't go ripping anything else loose down there. You've done enough damage by disabling our comm and navigational devices."

"Oh no. I was afraid of this." Brutus resurfaces. His face is dripping in sweat. "To conserve fuel, shuttle thrusters have been hard-wired for short bursts. It'd take me hours to bypass the circuitry and even then, I doubt we'd have enough power to break free of the bridle clamps. Get suited up, Murray. You're going on a space-walk."

245

While racing Murray toward a utility pantry near the shuttle's rear hatch, the chief engineer details intricate procedures of disabling the bridle's maglock from opening access panels to separating the electrical connectors.

"The release procedure on each bridle half is identical. And don't forget, you must stay clear of the lethal high-voltages."

Murray nods as he opens the pantry door.

"And watch out for deadly eddy currents flowing between the bridle and the shuttle's hull. The strong magnetic fields will latch onto your space-suit. You'll be glued down, unable to move. It'd take a fiberglass crowbar to break you free, but doing so would rip your suit wide open."

"Not a good thing." Murray cringes as he pillages through the cabinet. He extracts a space-suit and looks it over. "Sheez, Brutus. The procedure seems awfully complicated and takes a long time. Are you sure we'll have enough air?"

"Forty-minutes should be plenty. Now, limit your contact with anything metal. Use only one hand or knee … never more. Always keep one hand behind your back. Last thing you want is for those eddy currents grabbing hold of you."

Murray offers Brutus an extra-large suit and then watches it fall to the floor. "What the hell, Brutus?"

Brutus wipes sweat off his reddened face. "It—it's really not that difficult, Murray. Take both air packs and—"

"You must be kidding me! I can't perform such complex tasks by myself. What happens if I'm alone out there and one of those eddy thingies grabs hold and glues me to the shuttle? I'll be stuck out there by myself."

He tosses a second extra-large spacesuit at Brutus. It too falls to the floor.

"I—uh—said nothing about *the both* of us going out there."

Murray winces. "Look, I don't like this any more than you. Being cramped in this shuttle reminds me of incarceration at the Cos. I'm not staying in this tin can any longer than necessary. So, suit up. Let's get this done and get the hell out of here."

Brutus stares at the extra-large suits at his feet. He pulls a fiber bag from his pocket, places it over his mouth, and takes several shallow breaths.

With the suit's bladder tightening around his torso like a blood pressure cuff, Murray struggles with the self-tightening boots. He grabs a helmet but pauses at sight of the chief engineer's sweat-drenched face. "I hate to pull rank on you but—"

"As I've said before, Captain, you can't order me around."

"I know. I know. You're not one of my lackey crew. Dammit, Brutus! Everyone in the armada is relying on us. The *Atlantis* needs a captain and certainly their chief engineer. Think what happens if we don't return. Starship crews would arm themselves. They'd go after Foos and her compatriots."

"Well … I … uh."

Murray's eyes soften. He grins at Brutus coyly. "What about number six?" he says, stretching the words. "I'm sure she'd be mighty lonely without the gentle caress of those over-sized hands."

Brutus begrudgingly steps into the extra-large spacesuit. He cringes at his toes cramping inside the undersized boots. He wipes his face and reaches for the largest of the helmets. Taking a moment, Brutus leers back at the captain, wanting nothing more than to toss the helmet aside and scream at the top of his lungs. Instead, he takes a deep breath and seals the helmet fittings, uttering words beneath his breath.

"I'm doing this for you, number six."

*

Binky's log – 771-220802:

It appears the vengeful commander disabled the negotiator's shuttle. With the negotiator's lives in jeopardy, I'm glad human Andorf is here, safe in our cabin. Binky hops around the entire cabin. *Andorf? Andorf? Where'd you go?*

CHAPTER 67

Quenching A Thirst

Day 771: 2200 – Refueling Procedures Begin

Filling fuel tanks to capacity grants the armada a fifteen percent margin as it continues onward toward a sling around Neptune, Eris, and then a string of asteroids bearing lithium-iodide signatures beyond. Engineers will then have a decade to work through details of carving up massive crystalline structures required to supply fuel for the newly-designed Galactic Drives.

At the admiral's nod, *Aegean's* comm-spec broadcasts the long awaited 'all clear' message. First to break orbit, the *S.S. Atlantis* descends through the dense nitrogen clouds and then lowers long fiber-meshed drag hoses to sip at the first of many dark, murky lakes. The *S.S. Inca* partners alongside. Using a series of short intervals, both starships slurp frosty liquid methane before proceeding onto the next lake.

In orchestrated maneuvers, starships dip below the clouds in pairs and begin to replenish their near-empty fuel tanks. With other starships trailing behind, the *S.S. Phoenix* and its fuel mate, the *S.S. Nigiri* take long slurps from Lake Rogers. After three lake passes, the fueling routine becomes a mundane series of synchronized tasks.

Ship radios awaken to the *Atlantis'* urgent warning. "Be aware! We nearly clipped the outpost's feeder lines on our pass over Salisbury Lake. All ships must avoid Salisbury Lake."

The *Aegean's* comm-spec monitoring the situation winces at the admiral. "It's a good thing the *Atlantis* hadn't sliced that fuel line. The outpost's commander would've noticed our refueling run and declare war with us."

Turk's eyes narrow upon his naïve comm-spec. He takes long, deep breaths. "Foos is holding our negotiators as hostages. She already knows, radioman."

Burak appears from around the corner. He scowls at the admiral's silent gaze. "No! I hope you're really not sacrificing the *Atlantis'* captain and chief engineer are—?"

Turk nods. "Expendable pawns. It's been haunting my thoughts since we first slowed for orbit."

"But the *Atlantis*, *Mayflower*, and *Phoenix* ...," Burak says. "They'll gather an army and go after the commander bearing only hand-held phasor pistols."

Turk growls. "If the *Atlantis* remains behind, they won't need their Galactic Drive, will they? Make plans to raid the starship. Confiscate whatever pieces they've completed and store them in *Aegean's* shuttle bay."

Burak winces. "That won't fly, Admiral. We lack the required engineering skills to complete the design. The Galactic Drive technology remains but in the heads of a few select gypsy engineers."

"Then we shall apprehend their engineers. We'll work them day and night."

Burak shakes his head. "The council will never go for that."

"More sanctions?" Turk laughs. "A lot of good sanctions do. I'll label the Second Council as incompetent ... install a Third Council in their place."

"The last thing anyone wants is another empire-like dictator and his puppet council."

Turk slams a fist down. "Dammit, Burak, nothing comes without risk. The negotiators knew what they were getting into when they signed on, especially Brutus with his questionable past. As for the *Atlantis* ..." Turk spits on the floor. "Andorf and those no-good gypsies will take whatever scraps I toss them. Now, radioman, have you located the negotiator's shuttle?"

Turning his attention back to the radios, the Aegean's comm-spec swallows hard. "Not a peep, Admiral."

*

Binky's log – 771-224056:

The armada began refueling without Commander Foo's blessing. My gut feelings are that Turk won't be too keen on her response.

CHAPTER 68
Spacewalk

Day 771: 2245

Donning bulky spacesuits, the negotiators squeeze into the shuttle's small airlock. Murray struggles to reach around Brutus to shut the inner door. They attach the first tether lines to hooks on alternate sides of the outer door. Waiting on the tight chamber to depressurize, each checks the other's air supply and helmet seals. Both rummage through tool pouches, taking inventory of non-metallic tools.

Brutus speaks into his helmet's mic. "We have forty minutes of air, Murray ... more than enough time to release those electrical connections and return safely to the shuttle."

At the green 'GO' light, the negotiators set countdown timers and activate their air valves. When the rear hatch opens, both step outside the shuttle and attach secondary tethers before detaching from primary hooks. With the outer hatch closing behind, Murray turns left. Brutus turns right.

Implementing a tedious 'clip/release/clip' technique, Brutus and Murray crawl along opposite sides of the shuttle. After a series of strenuous strides, they reach opposing halves of the shuttle's nose bridle.

Brutus grabs hold of his bridle half with one hand and extracts hardened aluminum power tools from his suit's pouch with the other. Releasing hold of the bridle, he methodically works his way around the access panel, removing fasteners. The cover with its captive screws pulls loose and floats off, only to return and stick hard to the bridle cover.

"Ah. Witness eddy currents at work, Murray."

Brutus oversees the captain mimicking his own hand-motions as previously directed, effective but not as expedient. Wedging a gloved hand beneath layers of cellular-vibrafoam insulation, Brutus feels for the well-buried equaphase wiring harness and its terminating electrical connector.

Murray's knee slips off the bridle. Drifting away, he fights a tangled tether line. An over-compensating tug sends him heading on a collision course with the bridle. Despite turning about, his shoulder slams hard into the bridle. Murray tries to pull free using the line, but finds himself not only tangled in the line but glued to the bridle by those very same currents his chief engineer had earlier warned. He struggles to work free to no avail.

"Help me, Brutus! I'm nailed to the bridle. For the life of me, I can't get loose."

Watching Murray struggle, Brutus takes a moment to evaluate his best approach. "Quit squirming!" he yells. "You'll rip your spacesuit wide open."

Waiting helplessly, Murray calls out the time. "Thirty-one minutes of air remains."

Brutus works feverishly on his bridle half. The electrical connector snaps apart, releasing him and the access cover to float above from the bridle. A firm tug on the tether cable sends him sailing in Murray's direction. He flips over the other bridle half in an Olympic-worthy triple backflip and then magically appears hovering above the captain's partially-removed access cover.

The extractor tool slips from his hand and floats away. Murray bats the tool with a flailing hand and sends it floating toward Brutus. "Heads up, Brutus, low curve ball heading your way."

Brutus catches the power tool. Staring at tool in hand, he chuckles. "You sure know your baseball."

Murray nods." You can say I've attended my fair share of games. It's what I miss most about Earth. Et tu, Brutus?"

"Huh?"

"And you? What do you miss most from back home?"

"Sleep," Brutus says, as he systematically unscrews the last of Murray's fasteners. With the second panel floating past, he keeps safe a distance from Murray, knowing if he too were to be captured by eddy currents, there will be no hope for either of them. They would be glued against the docking bridle for all eternity.

Brutus' gloved hand reaches through thick layers of vibrafoam insulation, feels for the electrical connector. Deliberately using a single hand, he pulls and pulls on the connector. The connector wiggles but refuses to detach. Brutus gives it his all. After a few tries, the complete connector housing breaks free of the chassis and dangles by its heavy-gauge cables. "Uh oh!"

"What's the matter now?"

"The complete assembly broke free of the chassis. Now I'll never get ample leverage to separate the connectors using one hand."

"Then use both … oh yeah."

Brutus reaches deep inside his tool pouch and removes an old, reliable tool. He grins at the channel-lock-cutter handles expanding to a full sixteen-inches and at their sharp cutting blades gleaming against the shuttle's starboard lights.

Murray gags into the helmet mic. "Wait a minute, Brutus. Didn't you warn me about using anything metal around these eddy currents?"

"Sue me." Brutus clamps both feet firmly against the bridle housing and feels them captured by the eddy currents. Battling the magnetic forces pulling the tool off to one side and then the other, he struggles to push the cutters deep within the vibrafoam insulation.

Brutus bends his back more and more, until it refuses to bend any further. He then feels a pop and with it an excruciating pain running the length of his spine. Reeling in pain, his movement becomes less restrictive. Gritting teeth, Brutus forces the cutter deeper. As the tool bumps one of the connector wires, he opens the jaw and clamps it firmly over its insulation. A hard squeeze and … SNAP! The cutters cut clean through the wire.

He and Murray remain glued to the bridle. "Damn!"

"What's the problem, Brutus? Why aren't we floating free of the bridle?"

"I cut what must have been a redundant ground wire." He opens the cutter's jaw and plunges it deep through the insulation until it bumps against a second wire. Toes crossed for good luck, he again squeezes the cutter's jaw shut. His arm muscles tire as he feels the teeth bite through the wire's insulation and …

A bright flash blinds him as he and Murray float away, free of the bridle.

"What's happened to my eyesight?" Murray yells.

Brutus grabs blindly at his and Murray's tether lines. "I assure you, Murray, your vision will soon return. Now hurry. Feel your way along the shuttle."

Blindly clipping and unclipping his tether in orderly fashion, Brutus follows behind the captain. As sight returns, the helmet's air-gauge display comes into focus. "We've still got eighteen minutes of air, Murray. That's plenty enough to …" He pauses, suddenly chilled as he gazes at the outlines of dark objects approaching in the near-distance.

Murray pauses as well. "What the hell are those hexagonal things, Brutus? I see hundreds of them and they're—"

One hexoid buzzes past Murray's shoulder. A second one zips past, ripping his tool pouch wide open. Tools spill out and float away. A handful of hexoids zip between him and Brutus before circling back and slamming into the shuttle's hull.

With eyes barely able to focus, Brutus stares at the next wave of clusters of hard-to-see, black hexoid drones whizzing past. As with the others, the hexoids arc in semi-circles before returning to slam into and accumulate along the shuttle's body. The chief engineer gulps. "I was afraid of this, Murray. We're in deep trouble."

"Wha—what do you mean by deep trouble?"

"You recall asking what a forty-year-old woman stuck way out here does in her spare time?"

Murray nods.

"She assembles an arsenal of magnetic crusher drones is what she does. Hurry! Get your butt inside the shuttle. Pilot us out of here, while the shuttle's still capable."

*

Binky's log – 771-225917

My question about the commander's response has been answered. I only hope the negotiators can make it back inside the shuttle while it's still in one piece.

CHAPTER 69
Mayday

Day 771: 2300

The armada is well into the refueling process when clusters of hexoids appear from high above. Like the winds of darkness, masked by blackness of space, swarms of magnetic crusher drones swoop down, tearing through the *Mayflower's* long drag hoses. Liquid methane spews into space as the starship takes multiple hits on her upper hull.

The *Mayflower's* captain's eyes widen at camera images of liquid methane spewing into space. "Shut down the pumps!" he yells. "Jettison the hoses! Pull up! Pull up! Radio the armada! We are under attack!"

The comm-spec throws his hands up. "It's no use, Captain. I'm getting impossibly high standing wave readings on the radio. It's as though our antenna array has been—"

The captain's jaw drops as he stares at the exterior camera's hull images. "Encapsulated. Switch to the emergency antenna. We must warn the armada."

"But the receive-only antenna is a painted-film membrane. It cannot handle the power."

"Reduce output to a quarter watt. We must get the word out."

Swarms of drones slam into and attach themselves to the *Mayflower's* hull. The starship manages to outmaneuver a majority of the circling drones but still takes hit after hit. While swarms veer sharply to pursue in her wake, the *Mayflower* manages to broadcast a weak warning before the thin membrane antenna vaporizes.

"Mayday! Mayday! This is the *S.S. Mayflower*. Magnetic drones have attached to our hull by the hundreds. Many more are closing in on our stern. Avoid these leaches at all—"

Like fawns sipping innocently at lakes, the remaining starships begin to take drone hits. Heeding the *Mayflower's* feeble warning, they retract fueling lines and attempt to out-navigate the drone's haphazard paths. Avoiding the infestation becomes nearly impossible as drone numbers quadruple. No starship escapes the major onslaught.

The majestic *S.S. Inca* spins about to face the oncoming storm. With her stem-mounted cannons unleashing a photon fury at the seemingly impenetrable drone wall, the starship stands her ground. Hexoids glow deep red before breaking off, leaving a donut-shape hole in the central core. Replacement hexoids move to quickly fill the gaps.

Venturing a risky maneuver, the *Inca* lists to one side before flying through the narrowing gap. The drone wall splinters into individual hexoids. All give chase before merging with hexoids already in hot pursuit.

"Narrow the photon spread," the captain yells at the young gunner. "Modulate aft cannons in a microwave sweep. Fry those suckers like week-old hot dogs."

"Hot dogs?"

"Just do it, gunner!"

The *Inca* fires tight-focused photon beams at small bands of drones. The hexoids glow red hot. Seconds later all shatter into fragments. The fragments merge, forming fewer but larger hexoid magnets. Drones break pursuit of the other starships to join those attacking the *Inca*.

"There's too many of them," the helmsman yells. "I can no longer navigate clear of the mess."

The *Inca* takes hits on all sides. Drones accumulate heavily along the ship's outer hull and lock together to create one huge magnet. Support beams creak as her outer hull deforms. Hull breaches are reported on multiple decks. Navigational controls go dark. The crew struggles to level off but the *Inca* begins to descend uncontrollably. The comm-spec lifts the mic and broadcast a desperate plea.

"Mayday! Mayday! This is the *S.S. Inca*. We are unable to maintain stable course." He turns to the captain. "It's no use. Our radio's dead."

The captain wrestles the mic from the comm-specs hands. He switches to ship's intercom. "Abandon ship! This is not a drill! All hands, abandon ship!"

Escape pods stream out of the *Inca's* underbelly, climbing up and away from the doomed starship and its destined grave in the Lake Delanie. Rescue ships swoop below the cloud cover. Doing their best to circumnavigate the swarming drones, they gather escape pods using large drag nets. Pods are still pouring out of the *Inca* when she plunges stem-first into the frigid methane lake. Moments later, a frothy spray of crystallized bubbles is all that remains of the once majestic seventeen-deck *Inca*.

*

Binky's log – 771-232901:

Yikes! The whole armada is under attack.

CHAPTER 70

A Dire Situation

Day 772: 2340

Circling the designated rendezvous spot, high above Titan's northern polar cap, the *S.S. Aegean* monitors a dire situation. Amidst radiograms pouring in, Turk and his crew are doing their best to coordinate rescue operations. Burak has been chicken-scratching numbers on multiple notepads. Frantically running a tally, he informs the admiral of their lost starship.

"Turk slams a fist hard onto the counter. "No! Not our majestic *Inca!*"

Rescue ships close nets as they escape drone swarms by rising through the thick nitrogen cloud ceiling. As before, one courageous starship remains behind. The *Aegean's* comm-spec's voice revs with excitement.

"The *S.S. Calypso* has taken up the fight, Admiral. Firing frontal photon cannons, she's providing cover for drifting escape pod rescues."

Clusters of magnetic drones appear off the *Calypso's* port bow. She continues to fire. Many drones break from the pack only to circle back and attack the *Calypso* on its bows. With so many hexoids accumulating on the ship's outer hull, navigational controls soon fail. Pods eject out the *Calypso's* underbelly as its crew struggles to maintain control. Within minutes, the *Calypso* plunges downward, toward a frigid grave.

Turk's comm-spec relays the news.

"No! Not the *Calypso!*" Turk yells, again slamming his fist down. "Order a second rescue. Not a single pod is to be sacrificed."

With aft and bow photon cannons blazing, the *S.S. Conquest* and *S.S. Aguila* race down through the thick cloud cover. Their modulated photons create huge gaps in the hexoid swarms. Drones glow red hot before shattering into dust.

Rescue ships fly through gaping holes. Taking random drone strikes, they fan nets and snag escape pods before bolting upwards, away from the massive drone swarm.

Turk listens to rescue reports pouring in on radio speakers, pacing the *Aegean's* bridge while assessing escalating losses. Burak feels the Admiral's heated breath on the back of his neck as he feverishly chicken-scratches numbers.

"Six-hundred more pods collected, Admiral. The *Aguila* reports an additional four hundred. The *Sabrina* scooped another three-fifty."

Turk looks over his next in command's stalled scribe, rubbing his head as if trying to decipher chicken-scratches on the notepad and determine why Burak quit writing. "Is that it? Surely—"

The radio breaks with a report of fifty-seven pods additionally rescued by the *S.S. Sagittarius*.

Scratching a new tally, Burak presents it to Turk. "Last of the rescue ships are heading back to the rendezvous point, Admiral. Final pod tally is seventy-three hundred and twenty-four."

Turk drives his fist hard onto the counter. "That leaves three-hundred and twenty-five unaccounted from the *Inca* ... another fourteen-hundred and ten with the *Calypso*. Double-check your scratch, Burak. Certainly, you've miscounted."

Eyes widening at hearing Turk's numbers, Burak walks off, keeping well outside the swath of the angry admiral's saber. "That's the final count, Admiral. Seventy-three hundred and twenty-four pods have been rescued."

"What about our negotiators, radioman?" Turk yells. "Has anyone located their shuttle?"

Gazing at one another, Burak and the comm-spec shake their heads in silence.

*

Binky's log – 771-235308:

Commander Foos has put the armada on the defense. How long will it be before Turk goes after the outpost?

CHAPTER 71

A Moment Of Glory

Day 772: 0012

Nestled in a cozy office deep inside the outpost, the commander Foos sits, face swelling in pride. "That makes two of their bloody starships. Ha. Next time they'll think twice before messing with Commander Nicki Foos."

"What about the forty-four starships circling above our northern polar cap?" the Lieutenant says. "Two of them are armed with aft and bow photon cannons. If we don't take care of them now, the armada will regroup and come after the outpost. Orbiting above, they're easy targets."

"I doubt that, Lieutenant. No one would dare attack the empires' greatest collaborate engineering feat. Besides, if their armada ever makes it to planet Nero, their descendants will need to stop at the outpost on their return home."

The lieutenant's mouth contorts. "But their armada is run by a crazed Turkish pirate. With your gypsy boyfriend out of the picture, there'll be no one to temper the hot-headed admiral."

Commander Foos turns and slaps the lieutenant's face. "Boyfriend?" she snarls. "Next time you say that, you'll be taking a swim in one of the methane lakes below. Now, prepare a second drone battalion. Adjust targeting sites for the northern polar cap. I look forward to destroying this Turk and the rest of his bloody armada. But only disable two of the starships. We shall have them for our own services."

"Which ones are you suggesting?"

Nicki Foos scratches at her head. "Hmm. I'll take their lead ship, the *Atlantis*. Make the other one Turk's ship."

"The *Aegean*. Aye, Commander."

*

Binky's log – 772-001922:

Hurry, Turk! Hurry! Get the armada out of harm's way.

CHAPTER 72

The Crush

Day 772: 0020

Appearing like disjointed spiders, Brutus and Murray crawl on their arms and legs along the shuttle's hull toward the rear hatch. Every stretch is a painful effort for Brutus as he bends one way or the other to dodge errant hexoids zipping past. His eyes widen at the sight of the captain attempting to peel one of the magnetic drones off the shuttle body.

"Leave that sucker alone, Murray. It's a molecular magnetoid. There's no chance in hell of removing it."

"How can that be? The shuttle's titanium skin is barely magnetic. The viewports are transparent aluminum."

"Molecular magnets act like sponges," Brutus says. "They adhere to whatever they contact. Nothing short of an impact or a thermal blast can break their bonds."

"What about a sledge hammer? I've heard smashing magnets will break their bonds."

"And you happen to have such a hammer?"

Murray shakes his head.

"Alas the futility."

The negotiators continue their slow crawl. Nearing the shuttle's rear hatch, they duck, narrowly dodging fresh waves of hexoid drones buzzing overhead. The drones circle back to strike around the perimeter of the hatch door, accumulating atop one another around the door frame.

Brutus cringes at sight of the deforming frame. He tugs on the outer hatch door, but it refuses to open. Leveraging his trusty sixteen-inch cutters, he pops door trim off and then pauses to watch the pieces float away. "Those cheap bastards," he yells. "They've left out half of the Calico fasteners."

"Damn beanos!"

Using the cutters, Brutus works along the doorframe, snapping off protective covers. Breaking off a frame section, he wedges it between the door and shuttle body. To his chagrin, the piece bends like plastic. He inserts the cutters beneath the door and pries but even the large-handle tool lacks enough leverage.

"Hurry, Brutus. We've but twelve minutes of air."

Brutus breaks off a second frame piece and crams it in the gap to brace the other piece along with the cutter handle. Murray jams remaining pieces on the opposite side of the door and hammers them with his gloved hand. He and Murray pry hard but the door moves barely an inch.

"Move you piece of …," Brutus yells out, kicking the door while Murray pulls on the handle. The outer hatch door finally separates. A second kick widens the gap barely enough for Murray in his bulky spacesuit to slip through.

A sharp frame piece snags Murray's suit, ripping a two-inch gash in one of its sleeves. The suit begins to vent precious breathable air. Insulating plasma gel embedded within the fabric oozes out. Within seconds, the congealing goop seals the tear.

"Damn, Brutus! I've lost two minutes of air," Murray wedges inside the airlock. Careful not to rip his spacesuit again on the many sharp edges, he kicks on the outer door. He then jams a fire extinguisher in the gap, allowing enough space for Brutus to slip through. The inner door flies open to Brutus' firm kick.

Both safely inside, Murray attempts to fit the inner door back into what remains of the distorted frame. Brutus sprays thick foam lines around the door's perimeter and then tosses last of the cans aside. Hearing the shuttle's cross-members flexing in duress of external crushing, he and Murray know hull integrity failure is imminent.

In zero gravity, the captain swims toward the instrument pane. He promptly engages the air exchanger. He peers back at the chief engineer. "We're in serious trouble, Brutus. The cabin won't pressurize. I've got seconds of air left."

At the sound of dashboard alarms wailing, Brutus hurriedly swaps Murray's dual suit tanks with fresh units. Murray returns the favor. "Another forty minutes of air won't get us far. Let's dial back our tank air pressures, stretch our air supply to eighty minutes."

Seemingly in agreement, the shuttle's hull lets out a series of loudening groans. Brutus' eyes widen at sight of bowing cross-members, and distinct pops of rivets snapping as the hull begins to buckle. His suit struggles to compensate for his increased perspiration. He swallows hard.

"We haven't much time, Murray. Get us the hell out of here."

Murray fires reverse thrusters in short bursts. The contorted shuttle nudges away from the docking portal. Alternate thruster firings turn the shuttle toward the moon's northern polar cap. With pounding on the outer hull becoming painfully deafening, Murray looks about the shuttle. "Why are there so many of those damn things?" he yells. "Why do they keep attacking us?"

"Magneto-compressors act together as one huge magnet. Their attraction is so strong they'll crush anything having the misfortune of coming between them."

Over-stressed cross-support members groan louder. With shuttle's sides flexing inward, Brutus dives for the floor. Wedging himself between the seats, he encourages the captain to do the same. Murray locks thruster controls and then squeezes on the floor beside Brutus.

Drones encapsulate the twin thruster exhaust ports, crushing them like tin foil. Overheating thrusters sputter and shut down, leaving the shuttle drifting powerless. Dashboard alarms wail louder and faster. Suddenly, every panel indicator quits. The shuttle goes dark as it begins to lose forward momentum and arc in a slow decay.

"Things are looking really bad, Captain."

"Really bad, like seventy-five minutes of air remaining and peeing in my spacesuit kind of bad?"

Brutus shakes his head. "Bad like running out of air and you taking a dump in *my* spacesuit kinda bad."

The captain gulps. "There's one thing I must know before we die, Brutus."

"And what's that?"

"What in the world could you have possibly done to piss off that whiny Nicki bitch? What event made her so bitter?"

"I don't want to talk about it. Can't we just—?"

"Look, Brutus. We're running out of air and being crushed to death. It's our last moments for crying out loud. Just who the hell am I going to tell in the next …" The captain checks his air supply. "Seventy-three minutes if we live so long?"

"Well … me and Nicki were in our early teens. I was readying myself to kiss her goodnight … our very first kiss." Brutus perspires so heavily his spacesuit's environmental controls cannot keep up. He ignores the suit alarms. "A hairy hand grabbed my collar from behind and dragged me through a wooded backyard full of thickets. I was tossed into a dark, spider-infested tool shed."

Brutus begins to hyperventilate. He takes a moment to catch his breath with Murray egging him on with his gloved hands.

"There I was—backed into a corner—staring at a fuming preacher. The beastly-huge man was holding a large, red axe high above his head. What the hell was I supposed to do? I was barely sixteen with nowhere to run and this man was about to end my life with a single swing of his big, red axe." Brutus takes a deep breath. "Somehow, I managed to scramble past the burly man and ran out the shed door, never once looking back."

"Sheez, Brutus. It's no wonder you have claustrophobia and a fear of red axes." Murray shivers. He draws a cross over his chest and begins to chant. "Cross my heart and hope not to die. May I awaken, eating momma's sweet apple pie."

Brutus smirks at the captain's pseudo-prayer. Hearing overhead cross-members giving up, he fiddles with his spacesuit's environmental settings. "Drop your suit temperature to ten degrees, Murray. Reduce your air supply to five percent."

"But we'll be frozen. We'll pass out. What if we never awaken? We'll never get to see ourselves die."

"Dammit, Murray, do as I say. If by some miracle we *do* get rescued in time, we'll be found barely conscious, but still alive. Now do what I said. Reduce your suit's temperature and flatten on the floor like me. We're about to be crushed big time."

The shuttle's orbit degrades, sending it heading for a wet grave on Saturn's largest moon. It shudders beneath the thickening layer of noxious clouds. The black box in the chief engineer's pocket beeps as it triggers the shuttle's distress beacon. A weak, desperate plea for help is broadcasted through the shuttle's warped titanium hull.

Cracking viewports spray shards of transparent aluminum onto the negotiators as the shuttle flattens like a pancake. Slipping in and out of consciousness, Brutus feels Gregory's black box buried deep within his pocket flattening. He hears the eerie creaking, the shuttle's hull buckling, and both frontal viewing ports snapping off like a popped can lids. The spacesuits sound alarm warnings but no one hears. Our brave negotiators are down for the count.

*

Binky's log – 772-032812:

There's still no word from the negotiators. I only hope Commander Nicki has not destroyed their shuttle.

CHAPTER 73

Just Ask Binky

Day 772: 0030

After hiking the *Atlantis'* main stairwell, Andorf and Gregory arrive out of breath at the G-deck bridge. They tug on the bridge door but it refuses to open. Binky presses front paws the door and the door slides open. Gregory leads the charge toward the communication console.

"Hey, you can't be in here," Pol yells, jerking headphones off his head. "The armada's in battle- mode. The outpost commander attacked us and it won't be long before—"

Andorf slaps an open hand over the comm-spec's mouth. "It is urgent. We must send a message to the Admiral. Commander Foos is readying an attack with a second drone battalion."

Pol peels away Andorf's hand. His eyes narrow on the threesome. "How could you possibly know this? I've not intercepted any outpost transmissions."

Gregory's eyes narrow as well. "Are you questioning a Goshi? Even I can feel this for myself. Ask Binky, He also knows. Go ahead, ask him."

"What?" Pol yells. "You're getting this information from Andorf's rabbit?"

Peter and Acting Captain Job appear from behind. Within seconds, Andorf, Gregory and Binky find themselves outside the bridge.

Gregory shrugs his shoulders. "What do we do now?"

"We have another chance." Eyes narrow, Andorf focuses all thought on the Admiral located on the *S.S. Aegean*'s bridge.

*

Binky's log – 772-003634:

I knew the guys couldn't force their way into the main bridge by themselves. Binky breathes deep. *It was my idea to contact the admiral. They can thank me later.*

CHAPTER 74

A Glimmer Of Hope

Day 772: 0039

Helmsman," Turk barks. "Run another scan over the outpost. This time focus on the docking bridle SO-239 where shuttle #2 was docked."

The helmsman complies. With cameras homing in on the outpost's twelve docking portals, he spots one portal with missing bridle covers. "You are not going to like this, Admiral. There's no sign of the negotiator's shuttle and …"

"And what?"

The helmsman's eyes widen. "The portal where our negotiator's shuttle was docked appears damaged. I see a debris field. Many pieces have signatures of a shuttle's rear doors. It appears Foos destroyed our negotiator's shuttle."

"Are there any human remains, helmsman? Surely, if our negotiators were in the shuttle when it was destroyed there would be bone fragments … traces of human DNA."

The helmsman shakes his head.

Face reddening, Turk paces about the bridge, growling. "The *S.S. Conquest* and *S.S. Aquila* are to converge on the outpost."

Burak's face squinches. "What about the promise with you made with your little Goshi friend?"

Turk slams his fist down. "Dammit, Burak! Are you questioning me?" He turns back to the comm-spec. "Oh, I should have never made that agreement with Andorf." He turns back around to face the comm-spec. "Get the word out."

A single red light flashing brightly on the console grabs the comm-spec's attention. His hands suddenly become busy. "Admiral! I've detected a faint signal. It appears to be a homing beacon of sorts."

Turk's jogs over to review the radio console. Delay that attack order, comm-spec.

"Yes, Admiral," the comm-spec replies, as he fiddles with the radios. "I've pinpointed the signal's origin just seconds before the signal abruptly ceased." The comm-spec grins. "It was nearing the moon's surface."

Suddenly, the distant twinge of a Goshi's voice echoes throughout the admiral's head. He turns suddenly and yells at the helmsman. "Drop us down below the cloud ceiling. Let's have a closer look."

Burak scowls. "But we'll be an easy mark for Foo's drones. We'll be crushed like the *Calypso* and the *Inca*."

Turk slams a fist down hard, this time driving it through the counter. His eyes suddenly widen as a scruffy voice echoes in his head. "Foos is launching a second drone battalion. Have the *Conquest* neutralize the outpost."

"Aye," the comm-spec says.

"The *Aquila* shall lead the way and provide us cover. Take the *Aegean* in NOW, helmsman!

The helmsman gulps. "Aye, Admiral."

*

Binky's log – 772-005105

Aha! There's a beacon of hope. It appears Gregory's little black box got the homing beacon out. Thank you, Gregory. Thank you, Goshi Andorf.

CHAPTER 75
More Than A Wanting

Day 825: 1420

Tenulian word of the day is 'cintaroja' – wrapped in red tape.

Though months have passed, the attack at Titan Outpost weighs heavily upon everyone's thoughts. In respect to lost friends and family members of the *S.S. Inca* and *S.S. Calypso*, Tenulians refer to Commander Foos' aggressive act only as 'The Incident.' Nothing else remains to be said.

Listening to monotonous machinery clicks and mechanical pumping noises, Brutus discovers his body movements are severely restricted as he thrashes about on an undersized sickbay cot. The large man groans in discomfort.

"Ah, you are awake," a friendly voice says.

Squeezing his good eye open wide enough to squint, Brutus spots Andorf and others poking their heads between the makeshift room dividers. He again tugs on the restraints. "Where am I? Why am I bound like this?"

Andorf halfway grins. "It required three of your gypsy friends to secure you down."

With all the innocence of a seven-year-old, Mila dances closer. "It's for your safety, Papa."

"And for safety of the medical staff," the nurse adds, patting Mila's head. "High dosages of strong meds were administered. Only now are you coming off months of heavy sedation."

"Papa. Papa. Papa," two-year-old Sarak says, waddling past Andorf with both hands out. He attempts to climb up one of the bed legs until Andorf picks the toddler up and sets him loose on the floor. He then joins twin sister, Ayla, already playing with a handful of toys.

Brutus does his best to identify the many voices inside the room and beyond. "Such terrible dreams I've had," he says, gurgling out the words. "First, I was digitized … left with but two choices. There were replicas of myself … dozens of them, walking about the …"

Scanning the room's strange décor, Brutus struggles to cock his head to one side. As before, he troubles to speak. "Where am I? This isn't the *Atlantis*. What is this strange—?" Lying flat on his back, the chief engineer suddenly gasps for air. He begins to hyperventilate.

The nurse reaches across Brutus and straps a respirator mask over her patient's face. Moments later, she removes the mask to vacuum out his airways. Checking his pulse, she smirks. "Digitized? I haven't heard that political expression since my training days back on Earth."

All but the nurse appears to be listening intensely, straining as to not misconstrue his sloppy words.

"What's wrong with my voice? Is it difficult to understand me?"

The nurse cringes. "We spent all last month reconstructing your large frame and the better part of this month reshaping your twisted vertebrae. It was snapped in three places but seems to be healing well. Your jaw on the other hand is a work in progress."

Mila stares wide-eyed at her Papa's full body cast. Her eyes home in on his exposed cherry-red face as she creeps closer. Without hesitation, she reaches for his swollen nose. "I've never touched a real live mummy before. Can I touch, Papa? Can I?"

Examining Brutus' upper body wrap and discolored face, Andorf grabs the seven-year-old's out-stretched hand. "You look terrible, Brutus. Commander Foos did a real number on you."

The nurse cringes. "How could any woman be so hateful?"

Closing his eyes, Brutus swallows in great pain. He struggles to tip his head to one side and speak out the side of his mouth. "I don't understand. Nicki used to be so …"

Andorf steps around Mila to appear at Brutus' bedside. The under-sized cot flexes as he sits. "I take it Commander Nicki was that first girlfriend you had spoken about … the one whose father cornered you in a wood-shed with that big red axe?"

Brutus' face squinches. "How do you know this? I've never mentioned her father to anyone … certainly nothing about the axe." Sucking air between his gritted teeth, he squints. "Murray! Murray told you, didn't he? Wait until I—"

The room quiets. Only clicks, mechanical pumping sounds, and the twins playing on the floor are heard. The nurse takes her time speaking. "For weeks, you've been mumbling in your sleep. It's been only these past few days could we halfway understand you were referring to a backyard shed, a preacher, and his big red axe."

Andorf snickers. "By the looks of you, Brutus, I'd be more afraid of Commander Foos than her father."

Lips curling to prevent angry words from spilling out, Brutus gazes at his old friend. He begins to sneer but instead wails out in pain. After a long moment of catching breath, he changes the subject. "How's Binky? Did he survive the stasis crisis?"

"Binky's my house rabbit." Andorf grins at the nurse, then back at Brutus. "He began eating shortly after your shuttle departed the *Atlantis'* underbelly." Andorf snarfs. "It appears Binkers faked his illness to prevent me from attending the fueling negotiations."

The nurse grins at Andorf. "It appears that furry little guy saved your life. Had you been in that shuttle, you too would have been crushed … most likely be in a coma like—" She hushes at the light touch of Andorf's hand.

"Murray," Brutus gurgles out. "What about Murray? Why isn't anyone talking about Murray? He's in the next room, isn't he? I must have words with him."

Again, everyone goes silent. Even the twin toddlers on the floor quit playing with toys and gaze up at their Papa in silence. After a long uncomfortable moment, Andorf taps Brutus' shoulder. "I hate to say this but ..." He eyes the nurse before returning to face his old friend. "Murray was not as fortunate as you."

Brutus squirms on the undersized cot, moving arms and legs as far as the body cast and hemp-rope restraints allow. "Fortunate? You call this fortunate?" His good eye widens. "Wait! What do you mean? Murray and I were in the shuttle together. Why isn't he in the next bed?"

Andorf winces. "Well, that's just it. Shuttle #2 was crushed flatter than a run-over tin can."

"And you were severely deflated," the nurse adds. "It took our medical staff weeks of slowly expanding your rib cage. Only then could we begin to repair broken ribs and reshape your head. We haven't completed the work refusing your fractured spinal cord."

"Murray," Brutus growls. "I want to see Murray!"

Peering at Andorf and then back at her patient, the nurse wrinkles her nose. "The captain's chance of survival is currently in the single digits. We—"

"This cannot be," Brutus says, gurgling out his swollen mouth. "We were just—"

"Captain Murray is in another starship's sickbay," the nurse says, clearing her throat. "You've both been under *my* medical care for several months."

Brutus squirms in his bed. "What about these restraints? Why I am I still secured down like this?"

At the twins encouraging laughter, Mila twirls across the floor, spinning about as though she were a ballerina. "You were twisting like those dancers in that sixties movie, Papa—" She makes faces at Andorf. "—I'm sorry, Daddy. I've been visiting Papa Brutus every day."

The nurse nods as she checks the heavy ropes securing Brutus to the small cot. "Your little girl has been here most every day since you arrived in sickbay. As she implied, you were indeed swinging your arms about and kicking your legs about wildly. We couldn't have you injuring yourself further, let alone hurting any of the staff." The nurse turns and winks. "It indeed did take a handful of your gypsies friends to secure you down. They used the armada's strongest hemp rope."

Brutus takes shallow breaths as to not choke on his words. Gazing up at Andorf, he speaks slow and deliberate. "I'm begging you, Poo. Have Ms. Warden here release me."

"Sometimes it takes more than a wanting," Andorf says, eyes narrowing on the hemp. After a few seconds, the rope's strands begin to untwine … ten … fifteen … twenty strands at a time.

The nurse gasps at the rope ends appearing to separate by themselves. At the knotted ends releasing, she abruptly exits the room.

Turning his head as best he can, Brutus peers around at the strange room decor. "You never answered me, Andorf. Where am I? This is definitely not the *Atlantis*."

"You are currently a guest aboard the *S.S. Aegean*. It's a mighty fine starship if I might say so."

"What?" Brutus growls. "The *Aegean*? Turk's starship?"

Andorf nods.

Mila struggles to pull the heavy rope aside. After tugging at the rope's frayed ends, she drags it across the room before running back to Brutus' undersized cot. "You haven't told Papa, have you, Daddy? Can I tell him? Can I? Can I?"

"Tell me what?" Brutus says, gurgling bubbles out his mouth.

Andorf wets his lips. "Ever since 'The Incident,' I have been seeing things … things well beyond my own lifetime."

"The Incident?"

"When we were attacked at Titan Outpost," Mila yells out.

Raising his head above the engulfing pillows, Brutus breathes in snorts. "Even knowing your sordid past, Andorf, I find this unbelievable. Perhaps you're merely …"

"Listen, Papa!" Mila says. "Listen to Daddy."

"Analyzing sequences of near-life events, I have stepped through each scene, painstakingly mapping highlights of what shall play out over the next thirty years."

"That puts you at what, age sixty-five?" Brutus says. "That's hardly the wretched, old man who dies at the Cos as you had once mentioned."

Andorf nods. "That occurs sometime in my late-nineties. And so, there is a matter of a thirty-one-year gap I cannot figure out. Sarak eventually reveals time gap to his son, Gorin, but for now, the missing three decades remain a mystery."

Brutus turns his head enough to see the twins playing on the floor. "Sarak?" he says, snarling the best he can. "Our toddler, Sarak?"

"I have also witnessed the forbidding gales of planet Nero, where twenty-foot pterodactyls circle overhead, occasionally swooping down to—"

"Eat the miners!" Mila blurts out, making chopping motions with her hands.

"And I've seen dripping stalactites and water pooling on the darkest cave floors of Eden where the last vestiges of mankind will be scavenging for food and picking lichen off damp walls. Is this the world our descendants inherit upon their return to Earth?"

Careful not to trip over her younger siblings, Mila again dances about the floor. "Tell Papa about the jelly creatures … the ones who call us hairy sacks of water."

Squirming on the undersized cot, Brutus struggles to cover his ears between the pillow and one of his swollen hands. "Stop it! Stop it! You're both making my stitches ache. Tell me something useful … like repairing my shuttle."

"No chance of that." Andorf winces. "The shuttle still had magnetic drones attached. Turk's crew could not risk dragging the crushed inside their own ship. You and Murray had to be extracted while in space. The crushed shuttle with all the crusher-drones attached was jettisoned into space."

Brutus growls the best he can muster. "Turk!"

"It was actually Binky who informed the admiral of Foos' intent to launch a second drone battalion at the armada." Andorf winces. "Against my earlier pleas, Turk had the *S.S. Conquest* fire round after round of photo cannons until the outpost exploded."

"Now the remains of mankind's greatest engineering endeavor lie strewn across the moon's surface," the nurse says, returning to Brutus' bedside. "I say good riddance to that evil bitch."

"As for Turk," Andorf continues. "To everyone's surprise, the admiral insisted on being your rescuer. His crew encapsulated the shuttle inside a tent and pumped air inside. Many of Turk's men worked tireless hours cutting you out of that mangled mess. Reviewing the images, I never would have believed anyone could have survived if I had not seen it myself."

"I watched the video too, Papa. They blew you and the captain up like big balloons," Mila says, expanding her arms.

"And it's a good thing you're aboard Turk's starship," the nurse says. "*Aegaen's* sick bay is equipped with all the latest medical equipment."

"Turk only wants the Booger Stew recipe. My fellow gypsies and I have sworn an oath of secrecy. No one will divulge the special ingredient. We'll all take it to our graves … every last one of us."

The nurse steps back from the unbound patient, grimacing at the missing restraints. "I'd say you owe the Admiral more than some stinking recipe."

Andorf grins. "The matter has already been settled. The Admiral's wife is expecting."

The nurse smiles and turns back to her patient. "If you hadn't put yourself into hibernation, you wouldn't be lying on this bed. With the *Atlantis'* captain's vital signs at rock bottom of the chart, we eased him into an induced coma."

"Murray?" Brutus gasps. "Not my bloody Mary."

"Bloody Mary?"

"He means his buddy Murray."

The nurse grimaces. "As I had previously mentioned, things are not looking good for the captain." She gazes at Andorf. "Has anyone found his replacement?"

Andorf winces. "Jobi Cates is currently the acting captain. I heard he performed quite well during The Incident."

Brutus leans his head to one side to review the roomful of tricorders, automated genome mappers, and subdermal pico-sensor embedders. Peering back at the others, he raises a brow. "Vital signs? Induced coma? Aren't we suddenly professional?"

The nurse winces. "Serin's death was certainly a wake-up call. We've made significant medical advances these past couple years."

Andorf smiles. "But you would not know this, hiding out all day in the greasy bowels of the *Atlantis*."

Brutus lifts his head slightly. He takes a hard listen to the humming floor which everyone else has learned to ignore. "I hear the starship moving. I take it we've successfully fueled up?"

"Only eighty-percent." Andorf smirks at Brutus. "Hearing nothing from the negotiating team, Turk ordered the fueling operation to begin without the commander's blessing. In the middle of it all, Foos attacked us with thousands of magnetic crusher-drones. Our forty-four ships rendezvoused at Titan's northern pole and before orbiting Saturn."

"Wait! Forty-four starships?" Brutus grumbles. "Don't you mean forty-six starships?"

The nurse's face saddens. "We lost the *Inca* ... nearly three hundred passengers and crew."

"And another fourteen hundred with the *Calypso*," Andorf adds.

Brutus feels his face reddening, his blood pressure rising. "What?" he yells, choking on phlegm and convulsing as if losing his mind.

The nurse rushes to Brutus' bedside to help Andorf hold Brutus down as he twists about on the undersized cot.

"The outpost was supposed to be defenseless!" Brutus says, slurring his words. "There were no weaponry signatures. Turk's crew told us so."

"We had no clue your girlfriend was packing," Andorf says, in a calming voice. "The magnetic drones were well hidden. They went totally undetected."

Brutus squinches his face. "I'll get even with her if I have to—"

"Settle down," Andorf says. "Or else we will call your gypsy friends and have tied you down again."

"I've always believed, the best revenge is to live well," the nurse says, grinning at the others. "Say, did you hear the latest on Captain Argent? The killers turned out to be Argent's own bodyguards. And to think, the winner of the bet turned out to be someone aboard your very own *Atlantis*."

Andorf grins. "The final odds were over a hundred-thousand to one against the ex-councilwoman, all rewarded to a single player."

The nurse also grins. "The guy won his own suite, a slew of girlfriends, and will have catered meals delivered to him for the rest of his life. Guess I gambled on the wrong side of *that* one."

Brutus balls an unwrapped hand into a fist. He does his best to shake it at Andorf and the nurse. "Enough of the lost bets. I can't be stuck here. It takes work to keep these collection of welds rolling, much more than you can imagine."

"Collection of welds?"

Brutus wails out in pain. His eyes roll about. "If not for the thousands of resourceful gypsies who designed and constructed the original three starships, the heavily-loaded *Atlantis* would have never escaped Earth's gravity. Now help me up. I've got starships to—"

The nurse puts her full weight behind Brutus, forcing him to lie still.

Andorf lends a hand. "Take it easy, Brutus. Your gypsy friends have been handling things back on the *Atlantis* expertly these past months."

"Months? Gypsies have been handling my mechanical equipment for months?"

"Yep. It seems those same gypsies are quite inept at maintaining starships." Andorf scratches his chin. "For reasons unknown, they were most eager to abandon their kitchen duties in favor of working in a grungy mechanical room in the bowels of the *Atlantis*."

The nurse prompts Mila closer. She helps the twins up onto the undersized cot. The cot flexes. "During the scheduled intense rehab, you'll have plenty of time to reacquaint yourself with your family."

Brutus grins at the little ones and then points fingers at the adults. "In space you must wear fear in your heart. You can never be complacent with Lady Space. The moment you turn your back, she'll rear her Medusa-like head and bite you in the—"

The floor shudders. Everything within the room vibrates violently. Andorf finds himself and the nurse sitting on the cold vinyl floor, steadying themselves against the bed while staring up bewildered at Brutus.

"What the hell just happened?" the nurse yells above the twin toddler's giggles. Adjusting her white smock and cummerbund, she rises to her feet.

"Some visionary you are, Andorf," Brutus mutters out a corner of his contorted mouth. "I thought you said you had everything mapped out. How could you miss something this big?"

"Obviously, there are minor variations," Andorf mumbles, rising as well.

Nurses stream into the room. Shuffling about, they clean whatever they dare pick up off the floor with sanitary wipes. Many items reappear in another place than before. Only one thing appears to be missing.

Andorf scans the room in a full three-sixty. He begins to panic. "Mila! Where's Mila?"

Glossary of
Common Tenulian Terms

Argshnod (191) – the middle of nowhere.

Braunswag (144) – a misdirected concern.

Briar (173) - someone of authority who rules without conscience.

Bugafied (180) - having high anxiety.

Capado (133) – an imposter, someone masquerading as someone else.

Chisanakoto (169) – doing small things.

Chocto (157) – unwanted recognition.

Cintaroja (270) – wrapped in red tape.

Conta Kuuntan (141) – a swear word too graphic to explain.

Contra con (146) – expecting the impossible.

Fiasmo (198) – a near miss.

Froglump (186) – having a mighty bad feeling.

Gaucho (161) – something more than expected.

Jinkojo (149) – over-crowding.

Juliano (173) - saddled with an impossible task.

Koshhald (188) - loosely interpreted as 'expecting one thing but settling for something quite different.

Klaw (155) – acting out of fear.

Kurmanji (171) – beyond despair, to languish in despair.

Magatagren (214) – deceit for the purpose of personal gain and/or perpetuating popularity.

Kahu (230) – a protector.

Mesolvatis (151) – a mediator.

Naybudah mi fond (52) – it is nothing, my friend.

Pisane (178) – nagging sensation, like walking barefoot on sandpaper.

Sham (165) - to fix simple problems by going to extremes.

Snarble (191) - roughly interpreted as stating half-truths as facts.

Stasis (228) – a severe loss of appetite.

Wackamots (162) - an overwhelming collection of unexplainables.

Look for

WINDS OF
THE GOSHI

Gary McConville

Lagomorph Publishing LLC

http://www.lagopub.com

The author may be contacted at: garymcconville.com

Gary lives with his wife, cats, and house rabbits. Each estranged rescued pet carries unspoken tales of past lives. His hobbies include amateur (ham) radio and working on electronic projects.

Book 1– A Stiff Wind Blows
Book 3 – Winds Of The Goshi
Book 4 – The Howling Winds Of Yestermore

Destined to become reality in a not-too-distant future. Binky